I0664424

Regicide

The Richard Jackson Saga, Volume 13

Ed Nelson

Published by Ed Nelson, 2024.

Table of Contents

Other books by Ed Nelson

The Richard Jackson Saga

In the Richard Jackson World

Stand-Alone Story

Cast in Time Series

Dedication

This is dedicated to my wife Carol for her support and help as my first reader and editor.

Thanks to my Editors, Ernest Bywater, Lonelydad57, Old Rotorhead, Lon, and Antti.

Also, the Bellefontaine High School Class of 1962, just because.

Professionally edited by Janet E. Rupert

Quotation

That's the way it happened, give or take a lie or two.

James Garner as Wyatt Earp describing the gunfight at the OK Corral in the movie *Sunset*.

Copyright © 2021

Chapter 1

On the first Wednesday of the new year, 1963, I had a call from the White House. The president would like to speak with me. Would I please take the call?

I had received a lot of calls from the White House, and rarely was the word "please" used. They wanted to know if I would take the call. It was usually, "Stand by for the president."

"Most certainly."

While I said this, I was puckering up. The Kennedys and my family and I were not on the best of terms. It would be more accurate to say we were on the outs.

"Rick, this is John. I need a favor."

Before, I was tightening up waiting for a punch; now I was getting ready for a car crash.

"What sort of favor?"

"We need your influence in South Vietnam."

"What for?"

"A warlord in the Golden Triangle is getting out of hand. He is close to unifying the whole area. As you may know, this area is where most of the world's heroin comes from. The only thing that has limited their production has been the infighting there. If this guy controls the entire area, the cost of heroin will go down, and our problems will multiply.

"We need to get a SEAL element of four men there quietly and quickly. That is where you come in. If you could have them flown in and get them upcountry, it would be a tremendous help."

"I'll do it. Who is my contact? The CIA?"

"Yes, the CIA for now, but I can see a time when they will be part of a special warfare command. I don't like the idea of the CIA having their own army; they cause enough problems as it is. At this time, I retain approval on all missions. You will be contacted by a SEAL commander from Team 2 in Little River, VA. In the meantime, could you set things up with the South Vietnamese?"

"I can, Mr. President."

"Rick, I have told my father and Bobby to lay off. This feud between our families is getting us nowhere."

"That is good to hear."

"Knowing that, will you put new products in the US?"

"No promises; let's see how things go for a while."

"I will keep a tight rein on them."

"Time will tell."

"You have gotten cynical since I first met you."

"Thank you for the education, Mr. President. I will be waiting for a call from the SEALs."

At that, I hung up. Wow, I just hung up on the president of the United States. How many nineteen-year-olds can say that?

I placed a call to South Vietnam. It only took the long-distance operator two hours to make the connection. I got through to the president's chief of staff.

I told him that I would be flying to South Vietnam shortly and would like to arrange the rental of an aircraft to fly up the country. A DC3 would be perfect.

He told me he could arrange the aircraft and asked if I could share why I was doing this. I told him I would update him and the president when I got there. This was an open line.

Even saying that may be giving information away.

An hour later, I had a call from Commander Steve Wallace from SEAL Team 2.

"I was told to give you a call about our trip upcountry."

"Yeah, a guy who lives in a vanilla house asked me to give some of your guys a lift."

"When can you do it?"

"As soon as you want to. My plane is staged at Ontario Airport, so it could be there in six or seven hours; make that ten as I have to round the crew up."

"So late afternoon tomorrow?"

"Yeah, we can take off at o'dark thirty and be there."

"Can you fly into Norfolk?"

"Can it take a 707?"

"No, we better meet at Pax River."

"Okay, we can do that, but we will need advance landing permission."

"I'll arrange it. Use the call sign Hollywood."

"That works. We will land around two p.m."

"See you then."

I went in search of my parents. Dad was at work, with Mum at some charity planning meeting, so I had to wait until they got home.

I told them that JFK had called and asked a favor while declaring his family would back off. Mum was cynical about the whole thing but decided that wait and see was the best choice.

As far as the favor, they saw no problems with flying a team of SEALs into South Vietnam and providing them a DC3 to get upcountry to carry out their mission.

While it hadn't been discussed, all three of us thought it would be best if I waited around to give them a ride out.

I called my chief pilot in the afternoon, and he assured me the plane would be ready. Its engines had just had a three thousand flight hour rebuild and were good to go. In this case, the engines had been pulled and rebuilt engines hung. That lessened the aircraft downtime. At the same time, the airframe was inspected.

It was nice to know the plane would probably stay in the air.

This flight had a full service on board. That meant two flight crews to relieve each other in the air and extra stewardesses for the same purpose. Food was on board for ten passengers. I requested that enough food for the trip out and back be on board.

I didn't want to depend on some catering service in South Vietnam. I had done that once, and that would be the only time.

It was a good thing we weren't like the commercial airlines. We had both refrigerators and freezers on board.

The flight east didn't seem to last long, at least to me. I went right back to bed as soon as we took off. Another four hours of sleep did wonders. Also, a shower and shave didn't hurt.

I debated on what to wear. The ever-present Harold had me in what I called California casual: slacks, polo shirt, and sports coat. No bright colors.

Landing at Patuxent River along Chesapeake Bay was beautiful. Even though it was the middle of the winter with ice on the river and shore of the bay, it was still a striking view.

During the landing, I sat up front with the cockpit crew. There were no hassles with our landing call sign. As we were landing, two Phantom F4s were taking off, side by side.

Our copilot had gone through the test pilot school there and had been stationed there for a while until he got the urge to make more money. Dusty told us the F4s would make a racetrack circle around the bay for six hours and land. New pilots would take over and keep flying the planes.

Each change to a Navy aircraft had to have fifteen hundred hours of flight time before they could be introduced to the fleet. This included everything from a change in the seat upholstery to new weapons systems.

To keep costs down, they would test many proposed changes at the same time. The test pilots would make notes during their circles.

That sounded boring to me. Dusty agreed. He said it had been known for a pilot to swing wide and leave a sonic boom across the Eastern Shore that woke all the chickens. That was when I found out that was a major industry there. Talk about things you don't need to know.

After landing, we followed a Jeep to a pad outside of a hangar. The hangar was out of sight of anyone driving the perimeter road. As soon as the engines were shut down, armed Marines surrounded the aircraft.

Stairs were wheeled out, and four men came up the steps, each lugging a seabag full of gear. As soon as they crossed the threshold, the door was closed, and we taxied out for a quick turnaround.

Since the trip was about nine thousand miles, we couldn't do it non-stop by taking the great polar route. The flight plan called for us to refuel in Alaska, then Japan, before going to Saigon City.

This would make the trip around twenty-four hours with refueling stops.

Chapter 2

During the flight, I got to know a little about the SEAL team members and what was required to be a SEAL. It was simple: be able to jump out of airplanes, swim forever, and be a ghost on land. Those abilities got you a ticket to play the game. Once in, you had to show that you hadn't "any give up in you."

I thought I was in good shape. When they described their initial BUD/S requirements, I knew I was a wimp. They had to explain that BUD/S stood for Basic Underwater Demolition/ SEAL training and what took place.

One of the guys was a little fellow; he stood five feet in his stocking feet. I towered over him. He described having his hands and feet tied together, being thrown into fifteen feet of water, and then having to retrieve a facemask. He used his teeth to bring it up.

They did have the grace to ask me about my escape from Siberia, and I appeared to meet their requirements for being a ghost on land. They approved of my hang glider tactics to get away from the tracking dogs.

Mostly, they slept on the flight, as they explained that once they hit the ground, they might not get any sleep for days. That, and they went over their equipment.

I knew enough about classified operations not to ask for any details. My job was to get them into South Vietnam and arrange for the government to allow them to transit to the north so they could get into the Shan State of Burma. They intended to go through Laos to get there.

I did ask if they were going by air or walking in. They told me it would be good if I could arrange a ride by air to the Laos border, and they would walk from there.

That did sound like a time-sensitive journey to me. I asked if they could parachute in. They could but would need the proper aircraft and someone crazy enough to fly into the area.

When we landed in Saigon, I was whisked away in a new limo, which was bought with my money, to see the president.

He wanted to know what was so sensitive that I couldn't talk on the phone. I explained the outline of the mission. He thought the goal was good but agreed with me that they could never hike that far in the country without getting caught.

He then shared with me that South Vietnam had several agents living in a village near where the SEALs needed to go. They could establish a drop zone for the SEALs if they could get flown in.

I asked if the DC3 that I had requested was available. He told me that one leftover from World War II had just been reconditioned, and they would be glad to sell it to me.

Bless their little capitalist hearts.

The price was reasonable. Now, all I needed was a flight crew. My next stop was the US Embassy to ask for the local CIA contact. Of course, no such person existed. I was allowed to talk to an agricultural attaché, as he might know someone who could help me.

I didn't know his name, but he was one of the guys I had seen being outed by the Russians in LA. He recognized me and chose not to play any games, which I appreciated.

I told him I needed a pilot, a copilot, and a jumpmaster. He knew of a pilot and even a jumpmaster in the area who could be hired quickly, but not a second person qualified on the DC3.

Making an executive decision, I decided I could go as the copilot since I was qualified on twin engines. The pilot could teach me what the differences were while we were in the air.

Okay, I'm not always the sharpest tool in the shed.

The SEAL team had been waiting in my 707 while I was in my meetings. When I returned, a South Vietnamese Air Force major was waiting with the keys and logbook to my newly purchased DC3.

It took another day to find the pilot and jumpmaster, both retired from the French Air Force. I thought all the French had been kicked out of the South, but many who lived with native wives were still there.

After a long walk around and discussing the aircraft, I decided I could fly safely with them. My chief pilot on the 707 told me I was crazy, and none of the 707 crew would go with me.

The little guy, Harry Beal, almost had one of the stewardesses talked into it, but she backed down at the last minute. Harry told Marge that he forgave her and would see her when he returned.

While we were waiting on our French crew members, I got a message that two nights from now, at a given set of coordinates, gasoline drums would be lit to outline a drop zone. The SEALs would have to jump in.

It would be a long walk out. Still, that was better than having to walk both ways.

I made some phone calls and got permission to refuel in Hanoi, so we would be in good shape fuel-wise.

The SEALs had several radio sets with them. They decided to leave one and take two with them as the chance of failure while walking in had dropped. They left it with me with a list of frequencies they could use. We didn't see where it would be needed, but they believed in over-preparation.

For parachutes, they had the newest type that acted as an airfoil instead of the type used by army paratroopers. With those, they could land within feet of their target zone.

I didn't know it was possible to carry as many weapons as they unloaded from their duffle bags. After cleaning and checking each weapon and making sure that it had a magazine in the well and the safety was on, they were ready to jump.

Their gear in the duffle bags would be pushed out the door first with a line attached to their waist so they wouldn't get crushed by their gear when hitting the ground.

They had a simple plan: jump into the area and then do what they called snoop and poop around until they found the warlord. Kill him with a sniper shot and walk back home.

They had maps of the area which showed where the warlord stayed. They planned on hitting him when he came out of his mansion. They even had pictures of his house and him.

It was a mansion. I suspect a Frenchman built it. He looked Chinese to me, and when I asked if he was, they shrugged.

On the flight to Hanoi, I made a pest of myself asking the pilot questions about the aircraft. He got a little surly the third hour into the flight, so I laid off for a while.

One thing I found interesting was that the plane required 232 quarts of oil, more than the fuel load of a single-engine plane.

Taking off was supposed to be strange. You had to bring the tail up so the aircraft was flying level. This was to bring the tail seven feet off the ground.

When landing, he did share that enriching the mixture before landing was backward to most planes. Pushing them forward makes for a very underpowered plane.

I took the controls for a while and found it was heavy on the controls. One could get a real workout flying the plane. I found that the trim tabs were a pilot's best friend.

I figured that I could be checked out on this plane with another ten or twenty hours.

We took off from Hanoi just at dusk and made our flight to the Golden Triangle. When we reached the designated coordinates, lights flared below. They had heard our aircraft, which was circling at ten thousand feet.

The jumpmaster had the SEALs ready to go. The aircraft door had been removed for this flight, so it was easy for them to go out.

After Harry Beal, the last man, left the plane, we turned for Hanoi. They were walking out, but I wanted to stay in the area if we were needed.

I had the radio they left with me and tuned it to the correct channel. About half an hour after the drop, the radio squelched twice. They were down in the landing zone with no injuries.

We returned to Hanoi, where my pilot and jumpmaster left for a night on the town. I just hoped they didn't get arrested. It turned out to be a vain hope as the police let me know they were in custody and not to expect them back soon.

It was a good thing I had brought a sleeping bag and extra food. I would spend the next two days listening for signals from the SEALs. I did wonder how I had gone from providing transportation to South Vietnam to listening for mission signals in North Vietnam. I suspected I shouldn't tell Mum.

Chapter 3

My pilot was in jail, along with the jumpmaster. I made phone calls to the government, but suddenly, no one wanted to talk to me.

It was a case of me having to offer bribes, or they were in bed with the drug lords. Probably both. No one was touching me, but they certainly weren't helping.

Having nothing else to do until I could free my flight crew, I waited by the radio to see if the SEAL team came on the air. If they did, they had dire problems.

The team was supposed to walk out, so I could have flown home as soon as they were dropped. That was all well and good, but I remembered that in war, the enemy had a vote. This was war.

Two days later, my flight crew was still in jail. I did manage to find out that they had gotten into a fight in a brothel and that someone had been stabbed to death.

They were both being held on murder charges and wouldn't be getting out shortly. The only reason the aircraft wasn't seized was that I was on board. If I left, it would be impounded as a flight risk.

One thing they had right; it was a risk to fly this plane.

Late afternoon, the third day, the radio came alive. The SEAL team had accomplished their mission, but one man had been severely wounded, and they could never carry him out. He would die before they could get him to safety.

When I answered, it took a few minutes for us to gain trust in our communications. When a guy said he was looking forward to seeing Marge again, I knew it was Harry Beal at the other end.

Now the question was, "Was he under duress?"

No matter the answer, I couldn't be certain. That is until I thought to ask him if he was still thinking of joining the Wallendas.

"That ship has sailed."

That told me he was not held captive. I had allowed him to lie, and he hadn't. It was not the best way to handle it, but it was all I could think of at the time.

"How close are you to the drop zone?"

"Our friends are hiding us very close to it."

"Is there anywhere near there that the plane can land?"

"Yes, there is an open field that is long enough to land and take off from. It looked clear of obstructions, but you never know about potholes."

"Can they light the place up like they did the drop zone?"

It took a couple of minutes for the reply to come back, but the answer was "yes."

"Okay, the plane is good to go, and it is two hours flying time, so when they hear the engines, have them light the zone up. If possible, make a visible arrow showing the wind direction."

"Will do. Hurry if you can. Steve is in a bad way."

I knew it was terrible radio procedure on a covert op, but you do what you have to do.

"On my way."

The DC3 hadn't been tied down, but I had to remove sandbags from in front of the tires. I did a perfunctory walk around.

The obvious problem here was that I wasn't checked out on this aircraft, and it normally took two people.

One person could fly it, but the controls were so heavy that a person would tire out.

As Mum would say, "Needs must when the devil drives."

She talked about the devil a lot.

I fired up the first engine and counted twelve prop blades passing by before trying the other. The second one had the same procedure.

At least the Hanoi air control tower wasn't manned at night. It also meant there were no runway lights. Fortunately, for being a tail dragger, you could see out the front fairly well.

To this day, I'm not certain how I did it, but I got the bird up in the air. Now the problem was to find the small village. I had no navigator and no idea what the winds aloft were doing to my flight path.

I was able to follow a road west out of Hanoi into Laos, so my first hundred miles or so were on track.

The plane had a rudimentary autopilot, so I could set it and look at the maps we brought for the first flight in.

There were enough villages with lights along the way that I was able to feel confident that I was on track. Also, as the lights of the next town came upon the horizon, I could tell I had little wind drift that night.

Thank the lord for small or not-so-small favors.

The last twenty or so miles were the tensest. I flew by compass heading towards where I thought the small village was.

The radio came alive with, "We hear you. We are lighting up."

At first, I couldn't see the lights of the burning fifty-five-gallon drums. But all of a sudden, I saw one of them, then others.

I circled the area until I was pretty sure of the runway layout. Well, the open direction of the field. I was going to put to the test the DC3's ability to land on rough ground.

The next problem I faced was getting this plane on the ground. How do you tell where the ground is at night? I had no reliable landmarks.

All I could do was turn on the landing lights and go in low and slow. I hoped the lights would show me the ground before I crashed into it.

As I passed the first set of drums, I saw land below. I was too high but had enough open area to bring it down. The plane was a beast fighting me all the way. I was too hyped up to notice it now, but I would pay a price later.

I had to stand on the brakes while idling the engines. At least there were no large ruts to cause a ground loop.

As the plane rolled to a stop, a car came up alongside the rear door. Three men jumped out of the door. One of them was using a fireman's carry to handle a fourth.

No sooner were they out of the car than machine-gun fire ripped into it. The car was shredded and in flames. If anyone was in it, they were gone.

The guys helped each other to the plane. I had to turn the plane around so we could take off. I had idled the engines but hadn't shut them off. I had planned on a quick turnaround, just not this quick.

I could hear bullets tearing into the plane's fuselage, but nothing vital had been hit, to my knowledge, at least not yet.

As I completed turning the plane around, I heard yelling from the back.

"We're in!"

I started my forward roll. The DC3, at least the one I had, featured a mirror outside the pilot's window, just like a car.

It was dark out, but by the light of the flames of the burning car, I could see one last man running, hanging from the doorway. He hadn't got on board before I started rolling.

That was when I saw Harry Beal catch the door frame and lift himself one-handed. In his other hand, he had some sort of light machine gun, and he was firing it at some unseen target.

I could still hear bullets hitting the aircraft, so I started zigzagging down the field as we picked up speed. I heard the door in the back thud closed, whether Harry was on board or not. I couldn't check at that moment.

He was because he came up to the cockpit as I rotated the nose. He sat in the co-pilot's seat and put on the co-pilot's communication gear.

"Where's your pilot?"

"In jail in Hanoi. He and the jumpmaster got in a fight in a brothel and killed a guy."

"Are we going back for them?"

"No way, I have broken so many rules tonight that they would keep me forever."

"Well, we appreciate it."

"How's Steve?"

Steve wasn't his real name; it was the one he was using on this mission.

"He'll make it now; we didn't have enough antibiotics with us. When we got to the village, there was a kid in dire need, so we used them on her."

"So where are we going?"

"We have enough fuel to make Saigon."

"Good."

"Did you get your guy?"

"Oh yeah."

That was the last I heard of that. Harry went to the back to check on the other guys. They were chowing down on some K-rations, probably old when Custer was making his stand.

While I flew, Harry worked the radio. He reached a contact in Saigon who arranged for a doctor with the antibiotics to meet us. I had him contact my real flight crew to have the 707 ready to go.

At least they had lights at the Saigon airport and a manned control tower. I landed the plane and taxied over to the 707.

I turned off the engines of the DC3, and we left it. A doctor was on board the 707. He was being paid to accompany our wounded guy to the States.

Only when we were on board my jet did I realize how tired I was. That had been a wild ride.

I slept most of the flight home. We refueled in transit at Tokyo and landed at some airbase in Alaska. There, the SEAL team disappeared. At least they got off the plane.

We flew on down to Ontario airport in California. The flight was treated as though we had just returned from Washington, D.C.

I wondered what happened to that DC3 I left in Saigon. I suppose it is still flying somewhere in the world.

Chapter 4

It was the middle of the day when I got home. Both my parents were waiting for me. I knew I would have to face the music sometime, just not now.

Dad asked, "Rick, what did you do in South Vietnam? We thought you were just ferrying a SEAL team into place."

"Things got out of hand."

"How?" Mum asked.

"When we got there, we couldn't round up a full crew to fly the team to Laos."

"Round up a team; I thought you were just allowing them to fly on your plane. Once you got there, they were on their own."

"The CIA was going to have them hike up there. They would have never made it, much less got back. At that point, I went to the South Vietnamese government for help. They sold me a DC3 and gave me leads on a flight crew."

"So, you were done?"

"Well, no, we had a pilot and jumpmaster but no co-pilot."

"So, the mission was aborted?"

"I decided that since I'm checked out on twin engines, I could act as the copilot."

"So, you flew into Laos and helped drop the SEAL team."

"Yes, sir."

"Idiot."

"Yes, sir."

"Then what?"

"After the SEALs jumped in the designated drop zone, we flew on to Hanoi."

"Why there? Why not back to Saigon?"

"The SEALs had left a radio with me. I figured that I had better keep the plane close if the pilot had to go back in."

"Did he?"

"No, he and the jumpmaster got in a fight in a brothel and killed a guy. They are still in jail."

"How did you get back to Saigon?"

This was worse than being grilled about my schoolwork.

"I flew."

"Flew what?"

"The DC3."

At that point, my dad lost it. "Damn it, Rick, spit it out; tell us all that happened."

"On my second day there with the flight crew in jail, I got a radio message that the SEAL team had accomplished its mission but were in trouble."

"You slept with the radio?"

"I slept on the plane with it. One of the team members was wounded and would not survive being carried out. He had an infection."

"So, you flew a DC3 by yourself, found them, landed, picked them up, and flew onto Saigon."

"That is about it."

I hoped they wouldn't ask if there was any trouble with the pickup.

"Was there any trouble with the pickup?"

"The warlord's men chased them down. While I turned the plane, their car got shot up, but they got out okay. Two of them managed to get the wounded man on board."

"What about the fourth man?"

"The fourth SEAL, Harry Beal, was firing at the warlord's men while lifting himself onto the aircraft, which I had just started to taxi."

"It's a wonder they didn't hit the DC3."

"They did, luckily nothing critical. I zig-zagged enough that they couldn't get a good shot."

"Anything else?"

"No. I flew us back to Saigon. There was a medical team waiting. We all transferred to the 707 and got out of Dodge."

"What about the DC3?"

"I left it there with the keys in it, so it is probably gone."

"The South Vietnamese government called; they want to know what you want to do with the airplane that has over one hundred bullet holes in it."

"Repair it, I guess. I may need it again to fly back upcountry."

Mum looked at me and shook her head.

"Over my dead body."

I took that as a no.

"Your father told them to have it repaired and flown back here to the States. It is a good plane; we shouldn't waste it. Though if I had my way, we would dump it in the Pacific."

Mums get worked up over everything.

"Also, the president would like you to call him when you have the time."

Now seemed like a good time. The president was less likely to give me a hard time than my parents.

The operator managed to place the call in ten minutes. It must have been a record. Half a day would have been fine with me. Being on the phone when my parents were unhappy seemed like a good deal.

"Rick, congratulations on a successful mission."

"Thank you, Mr. President; not what I set out to do."

"But you did it when the chips were down. The country owes you another debt of gratitude, but just like in the past, we can't acknowledge it."

"I didn't do it for any glory."

"That's what makes you a hero. But you do have a job offer."

"What's that?"

"The CIA would like to hire you as a pilot for their Asian airline, Air America."

"No, thank you. On second thought, are they serious?"

"Yes."

"Now that is scary. They are offering me a job like that without doing a background check to see if I could take the job or even needed the money."

"That's what I told them."

We both chuckled at that thought.

"Seriously, Rick, if you ever need anything, call me. Also, there is a SEAL team that would run through brick walls for you."

"I'll keep that in mind; never know when you might have a brick wall that needs running through."

"Smart aleck."

"Part of my job description. I'm still a teenager, you know."

"May I speak to one of your parents, please?"

"Here is my mum. She knows the whole story."

They talked for a while. When she hung up, she had a funny smile.

"That guy is nothing like his dad. It's a shame I hadn't met him first."

I wanted to stick my fingers in my ears and make funny sounds. Some things you didn't want to hear."

"Rick, I do think our problems with the Kennedys are over, at least with JFK. I'm still not sure about Bobby."

After that, I took the afternoon off. I rode George over to the Forestry Service station and hit a few golf balls.

At dinner that night, Dad informed me that since I was here, it would be a good time to have a business meeting. I agreed, so we planned to bring everyone together at the end of next week.

Mum brought up that she had seen a brief article that Nina was dating a young actor from the studio.

That announcement didn't give me any pangs at all. It did make me wonder about all my agony when she cheated on me. Maybe it was my ego about being cheated on rather than a betrayed love for Nina.

Food for thought. As it was, she could date whomever she wanted. It didn't bother me anymore.

Dad also advised me to stop at the Jackson R&D Center to see what all the excitement was about. The chips that they had developed had everyone in an uproar.

I didn't understand this, as other people had made and patented some forms of chips. The only thing we could have done differently was come up with a practical chip. One that worked in the real world and not just in the laboratory. One that could be manufactured.

I told him I would stop by and ask to be updated. He frowned at that statement.

"Maybe I had better call them in the morning and make an appointment so they will be ready for me."

"Good idea."

At dinner, I was waiting for the other shoe to drop. I knew they weren't happy about what I had done in Vietnam. They had grilled me in detail. The one thing I expected was a lecture, at least, if not being grounded, or whatever parents could do with an emancipated kid.

I was about to die with nervous anticipation after dinner, so I asked if we could talk in the library. Mary didn't help when she asked, "What did Ricky do now?"

Mum told her, "Just his normal heroics."

"Oh, okay."

When we got to the library, I asked them what they had to say or do about my actions in Vietnam.

"Why, nothing, Rick, you are an adult now and can make your own choices. We don't agree with this one, but done is done."

"I thought I would be in trouble."

"I guess we could send you to your room with no dinner."

"I just ate."

Dad sighed, "You don't get it. We worry about you but know you will do what you do. Someday, it will catch up with you. It scares us."

"I don't mean to try to be a hero, but when you are there, and only you can do the job, what would you have me do?"

"That's the problem, Rick. We would have you do what you need to do; we don't have to like the situation."

Mum broke in, "It all began when JFK called you to take the SEAL team into Vietnam. There had to be other ways to do that. Once you started down that road, it seemed foreordained that your life would be at risk."

Dad continued, "You do what you have to do when you are on the ground, but you should have never been on the ground in the first place. If you don't learn to say no, events will catch up with you someday."

"I hear you; I have to think about this."

Chapter 5

My first stop of the week was at the R&D lab. I wish I hadn't gone there. I developed a monumental headache trying to follow what they were telling me.

They had come up with a family of integrated circuits that was more efficient than any of its predecessors and more importantly, didn't infringe on any other patents.

Another plus was these could be manufactured with a higher throughput rate. They attributed a lot of that to my suggestion that they use pharmaceutical cleanroom protocols.

Another advancement they made was in the passivation process. This was the stabilization of the silicon surfaces through oxidation. I nodded my head as though I understood what they were talking about.

Also, they were protecting the transistors with a planar process using a thick layer of oxide. At this point, I couldn't even figure out when to nod.

I stopped listening when they started talking about large numbers of p-n junctions for impedance. I never figured out if impedance was a good or bad thing.

In their main conference room, we talked about the best way to proceed. They were upfront that while they had developed the process, they were not the people to implement it.

It would take a manufacturing team to design the equipment to manufacture something new to the world. The cost would be enormous.

We would have to either take in partners or license the right to manufacture the chips. I had excellent luck licensing the shower heads and hairdryers, so my first impulse was to go that way.

After listening to what would be needed regarding personnel and financing, my mind was made up. We would try to license out the new integrated circuit chips. We might even finance a new start-up company if it looked like it could succeed, but we wouldn't take on the project ourselves.

We moved on to what their next projects would be. One director thought they had done as much as they could and that the teams should be reassigned to other projects.

Now, I didn't understand the technology involved, but I did understand that the result was a complete breakthrough in electronics. We could now use these IC Chips for devices with hundreds or even thousands of tubes.

I asked them how long it had taken them to develop what they currently had. It was eighteen months.

Deciding with no actual data, I asked that the team be divided into three groups. The first group would work on optimizing the current production technology.

The second group would spend eighteen months generating second-generation chips, doubling the number of transistors.

The third group would be working on a third generation, which would double the number of transistors once more.

When group two completed their task in the eighteen-month timeline, they moved up to the third step using the data created by group three.

Group three would then move on to another third step or double what they had previously been working on.

If we could keep this pace up, we would always be the leading technical source for IC Chips. Our licensing agreements were to take this into account.

Several people wanted to argue with me because I was just a kid. I stopped all that by reminding them that I owned this company lock, stock, and barrel.

That shut them up. It also reminded me of Mum saying, "Because I said so!"

My next stop was to see Jim Williamson in his office. We had to plan the agenda for the business meeting. Before that, I asked him to look into the appropriate bonuses for the people at the R&D lab.

He thought a one-time cash bonus and a continuing tiny portion of the licensing profits should go into a pool to be shared by the staff who had worked on the project.

I asked him why a tiny portion of the profits.

"Rick, I have talked to them about the applications. We are talking about billions of IC Chips."

"Oh, they still would get rich."

"Right, and it would be over a longer period so that we wouldn't have a lot of immediate retirees."

"This is why I pay you the big bucks."

"Speaking of which."

"You want more!"

"No, I just wanted to get a rise out of you."

We talked about the upcoming business meeting. We both agreed that the format we used in the last meeting worked so we would follow it again.

The following week flew by in a flurry of pre-meeting meetings. I didn't realize so much work went into preparing for a State of the Business meeting.

I had been able to avoid it in the past, but now I knew that I had to be involved if I was to consider this my business.

Since by the time all the meetings were finished, I pretty well knew the status of the business. I asked Jim why we went through this exercise. Why have a meeting?

"This is what a publicly held company has to go through every time they have their annual meeting."

"But we aren't publicly held."

"Not at this time. Someday, it may be in your best interest to go public. This way we will be ready. Also, if the company is ever investigated, we can demonstrate that due diligence was being exercised."

"If you say so; I'm just getting to hate meetings."

"Unfortunately, a necessary evil."

"And all these overheads; after a while, they all run together."

"Until there is a better way of showing charts and graphs, they will have to do."

"Maybe these new chips will help us develop a method of creating them quickly and projecting them without all the heat."

"That would be a powerful tool to make your points."

"That's what we will call it, PowerPoints."

"I think you are getting ahead of yourself, Rick, but keep it in mind.

"I intend to."

On the day of the business meeting, I was up early and got my run and exercise in. After that, a good breakfast, and a shower. I had a new suit, custom-made, from Hart, Shaffner, and Marx. It was dark blue with the finest red line running vertically.

We met in the small conference room for the divisional meetings. The agenda allowed an hour each for Jackson Personal Products, Jackson Home Products, and the Entertainment Division. Jackson Transportation was in the afternoon.

First up was a review of Personal Products. The meeting room was set up with a sideboard with the usual coffee, tea, orange juice, bagels, and donuts.

Even though I had a large breakfast, I had coffee and a crème filled donut.

The new markets we had opened in Brazil, Argentina, Peru, Columbia, and Chile brought in ten million this past year. Way ahead of projections.

It looked solid overall in Africa, but hairdryer sales were still not doing as well as projected in South Africa. Market penetration had started in Egypt and Southern Rhodesia and was moving ahead. We still couldn't get a foothold in Liberia.

Don had talked again to the managing director of the Firestone Plantation. Mr. Dawson was still helpful, but everything was held up by the corruption in the Liberian government.

We continued to refuse to pay the bribes requested. These were for large cash payments. I still supported our position.

Australia and the New Zealand markets were above projections, which had been ambitious in the first place.

Europe was still spotty. The Mediterranean countries were still slow adopters, while the Scandinavians couldn't buy enough dryers and curling irons. We discussed spending more on advertising in the Mediterranean countries but decided not to. A few ads weren't going to change a culture.

The bottom line on the division was that it would earn over twenty million dollars in profit this year, well over the projected sixteen million.

Mark and Sharon Downing flew in for the meeting. It was good to see them. Sharon had had her baby. They had left their new daughter with her mother.

For the newborn's gift, I had fully endowed a college fund.

The purchase of a competitor worked out nicely. The production facility and its infrastructure were filling the need for expansion. The old workforce found that our company was much better to work for. An attempt to unionize their location failed miserably.

The profit pace had been projected at six million. Instead, it would be seven. Mark's sister's wails still could be heard all over the world.

Last, before lunch, we reviewed the numbers of the Jackson Entertainment Division. The accounting group gave us dry numbers from movies and music.

We took a restroom break before the meeting and refreshed our coffee.

Chapter 6

Since I had no new movies out, it was a review of past endeavors. This was from the failed Surfer movie and revenues from *Over the Ohio*. OTO, as we started calling it, had done fantastically well. It had set US box office records and had done the same when released overseas.

The cattle drive movie had been delayed because of some post-production problems.

On the movie front, it now looked like seventy million dollars, which beat last year's projection of sixty million. The music from all songs had been projected at $400,000 but ended up near $300,000. There was hope for American Music, after all.

Susan Wallace was still doing very well. Mr. Spiller had set me up as a silent partner in her talent agency and was kept informed. Even so, I kept my hands off and would continue to do so unless she called for help. By keeping informed, I could step in if her pride stood in the way of asking for help.

It didn't look like she would ever need it. I asked that she be approached to see if she wanted to buy me out. Not that I wanted out, but she might want all the fruits of her labor.

After lunch was Jackson Transportation, as it was usually the longest review. It included the production of shipping containers, the Scottish Line, and Narrow Freight.

Once more, they asked for additional financing, allowing them to grow even larger. I just thought last year's numbers were large.

Freight Forwarding was doing well after being spun off as a new and separate part of Jackson Enterprises. I still liked the FreightEx name for Freight Express but gave it up as a lost cause.

The Scottish Line had added four more ocean-going freighters at sixty million. I asked why it cost sixty million this year for four more ships when we only had to pay fifty million for four ships last year.

It seems some inflation was going on: that or the Buy One Get One Free sale was over.

The book value of the company was now well over one billion dollars. This year's profits had been estimated to be two hundred and seventy-five million dollars, but instead, they were three hundred and ninety million.

Putting it all together, I would make almost four hundred and fifty million dollars this year.

Jim Williamson gave the numbers his overseas accounting teams had recaptured for us. There was still no grand theft in under-reporting of royalties on the beer can pull tabs, but the nickels and dimes added up. The group more than paid for itself. We had wondered if we would need them all the time.

The answer was that we needed the group permanently. This continued attention to the small details would prevent large thefts.

There were two new items on the agenda.

The R&D department's breakthroughs on IC Chips and their products were a major topic. The more we talked about the cost of getting into the manufacturing end, the better licensing sounded to me.

At this point, we had no way of estimating what we might make by licensing, but there would be enough of a tax write-off that there would be no negative consequences from trying my three-step improvement process.

When asked about how I thought of doing it that way, I told them I had learned it in the Gulag logging operations.

The forests were not a monolithic growth. There would be one team out identifying large and useful tree lots, then a team would prepare the logging site by cutting brush and making roads. The third team would do the actual logging.

Dad thought that was a good idea and that maybe I should be sent back to a Gulag every year to learn new processes. I didn't think he was very funny.

The last item on the agenda was my idea of an airfreight line working from a hub concept. Instead of our previous meeting, where I wanted to go worldwide, I suggested a California test case.

When I presented my budget for the operation, all the others were against it. I took what they said in stride. Rather than argue, I would start a separate company without these naysayers. It wasn't as though I didn't have the money.

The only thing left was for the accountants to tell me if I would have anything left after the tax man took his share, not only here in the US but in all the countries we worked in.

Sam Wingate, our corporate attorney, had a tax accountant update me on my earnings and tax position.

I was still in the ninety-one percent marginal tax bracket, and the only way I would ever get out of it was for the government to change the tax rates.

My three-million-dollar salary, oops, five million, so easy to forget what I make, wasn't the real money. It was the company's profits. On those, I would owe over ninety million dollars. Of course, I would keep two hundred and seventy million.

Once more, I made a mental note to consider spreading my money around. The US stock market was great, but there were other markets around the world. I was serious about buying a lot of land in Australia.

At the end of the day, numbers were spinning in my head. It is good that I took many notes and had copies of the presentations.

After the business meeting, which I deemed a success even though they disagreed with my Flying Express idea, we had dinner at the Brown Derby. In the middle of dinner, I realized that we hadn't discussed the Bank of Guangzhou. Probably not, as it was a personal loan, not a JE business.

It was a jovial bunch, which it should have been after the annual bonuses were announced.

Mr. Wingate asked me, "Rick, did you see that looker that just came in?"

I hadn't, but I turned to check her out. She was gorgeous. Blonde, blue eyes, proportional breasts, and legs which went clear to the floor. She must be five foot ten inches—a good height for me.

I asked Mr. Wingate if he knew her. He grinned while he stirred the sugar in his coffee.

"I believe she is Princess Olga Glucksburg from Denmark."

"I wonder what she is doing here, not the restaurant, but the United States."

"I met her father yesterday and had lunch with his family. He is interested in investing in American movies. I tried to discourage him, but I think he is doing it to get his new wife a part in a movie."

He must have seen the confusion on my face as he added, "She is a trophy wife. He has a lot of money. His first wife, Olga's mother, died many years ago, so he recently remarried. I'm not impressed with the new wife. I think she is a gold digger par excellence."

"Is he a prince then?"

"Yes, but he is not in line for the throne. That is a first cousin of his. Olga's children will not continue the title. They will become barons or something like that."

About that time, the parents came in. I saw what Mr. Wingate was talking about. Her father was distinguished-looking. His clothing was discreet but spoke of money. Olga's stepmother was an outstanding representative of her class—a brassy beauty with a tinge of greed.

I bet Olga and her new Mom didn't get along. Mum must have been five years older than Olga if Olga was my age.

I asked Mr. Wingate if he knew Olga's age.

"Nineteen this past month.

Perfect.

Then Mr. Wingate asked me a question that made him a hero in my world.

"Would you like to be introduced to the young lady?"

Would I!

"Yes, I would like to get to know her."

How I said that calmly, I didn't know; my heart was beating like a drum.

My new best friend Sam and I excused ourselves from the table, and he took me over and made the introductions. The parents first, then the daughter.

Dad was nice in a cool way. Her mom was cold. That is until she put it together that I was Rick Jackson, the actor. It did help that Sam mentioned that to her.

Then she couldn't be warm enough, too warm if you asked me. She leaned over in such a way that I got a good look at her stock in trade, an enormous set of breasts.

It was my turn to be a little cool and remote, and I told her it was my pleasure to meet her.

Sam, my best friend in the world, then introduced me to Olga. From how she received me, I think she approved of the slight cut I gave her stepmother.

We talked inanely, at least I did, for a few minutes, then returned to our table. My mind was whirling about how to get to know Olga better.

"Incidentally, Rick, they are staying at the Beverly Hills Hotel if you want to call her."

What a good friend! I could almost forgive him for being a lawyer.

Chapter 7

Later, at home in the library, Mum, Dad, and I talked about an issue that had been bothering me for some time.

"Empress Ping was trying to find which Gulag I was in, and if she had found it, she would have sent forces in to pull me out. I have heard nothing about what you thought or were doing."

Dad got a harsh look on his face.

"Rick, we worked with the US and British governments before that show trial to have you freed. It had become apparent early on who had kidnapped you.

"After the show trial, the whole world was told you were dead. They even showed the firing squad shooting. They didn't show your body.

"To say your mum and I were devastated is putting it mildly. We didn't know what to do. We requested your body and kept getting a runaround.

"The CIA found out that you were still alive, as you were seen being walked out of that courtyard. All that had to be done was to find which train you were being put on. There, it fell apart. The Russians lost you!

"The people who kept the records of who was sent where thought you had been executed. They had no record of you being put on a train. It finally took Popeye working with the Russian mafia to establish that you had been put in a car that sat on a siding for two days.

"There was no record of which train that car was attached to or where it went. It was as though that car didn't exist in the system. Later, we found that was the exact cause. It was a special car that the KGB used, and no records were kept.

"We narrowed it down to seven different possible camps. We had people sent into every one of them. By the time we discovered the one you had been held in, you were gone.

"The camp was in an uproar. You had disappeared, and the dogs couldn't get your scent. It seemed you jumped off a cliff and went away."

"Since that is what I did using a hang glider, I'm not surprised they were confused."

"After that, it was waiting to see if you got out."

I looked at Mum. She appeared uncomfortable.

"Rick, I'm sorry if we appeared unfeeling; we were trying everything. Between MI6 and the CIA, they opened up the entire Soviet prison system. They found agents who they thought had been dead for years."

"Well, that was a good thing."

Dad spoke up, "Your mum made a trip into Russia."

"What for?"

"She questioned the head of the KGB Gulag system as to your whereabouts."

"And he didn't know?"

"No, he wouldn't talk."

"Why is that?"

"Dead men tell no tales."

"Ouch."

"You don't touch my children."

"I like your attitude, Mum, and I apologize for thinking that nothing was being done."

"JFK was afraid we were about to start World War III over it. He pleaded that we didn't do anything that could go public."

"Public?"

"He told us to do whatever we had to but don't get caught."

"Always good advice, and I thought he didn't care."

"Rick, no matter the issues between our families, he is the United States president and cares about all of his citizens."

"All of them?"

"Except for a few major Republican donors, of course."

"Of course."

"To change the subject, I saw a young lady at dinner tonight, and Mr. Wingate introduced us. I'm going to ask her to go on a date tomorrow."

"Ah, the beautiful Princess Olga. We saw you staring at her most of the evening."

"I was that obvious?"

Mum laughed as she poured more tea for herself.

"At least you were able to eat your soup without it dribbling on your shirt."

"You think she noticed I was staring."

"She must have; she had to be careful when she peeked at you. You both were quite funny to watch."

"I hope her father didn't take umbrage."

Dad broke in, "He winked at me when we made eye contact."

"Then he won't be cleaning his weapons when I go to pick Olga up; that is, if she goes out with me."

"Oh no, he has bodyguards. They will be cleaning theirs."

My dad can be mean.

At that, we called it an evening and retired to our respective quarters. It took me a long time to get to sleep, thinking about what my parents must have gone through when I went missing. I also gave some thought to a blue-eyed blonde.

The next day, after my morning rituals, I called the Beverly Hills Hotel and asked for the Glucksburg suite. I was put through to a secretary or bodyguard. I'm not sure which.

"May I speak to Her Highness Princess Olga?"

"May I tell her who is calling?"

"I'm Richard Jackson, the Duke of Hong Kong."

"Hold one moment while I ask her if she is taking calls."

I'm glad I brought out the duke title; it sounded like I needed everything I had to get past the secretary.

"Hello, this is Olga."

"Princess, this is Richard Jackson. We were introduced at dinner last night."

"Yes, I remember you."

"I'm calling to see if you would like to go to dinner with me some night this weekend."

"Only if it is to a real place where American teens go. I'm so tired of formal dinners."

"I know just the place; it is called the Hamburger Hamlet. It is a hangout of Hollywood High students."

"That sounds delightful! Would Friday evening work for you?"

"Yes, it would. The sooner, the better."

Now, why did I say that?

"Okay, now I have to find out what American girls wear, not what is in the movies."

'I'm afraid I can't help you there."

"That is no problem. I will look at the Lady Mary Collection in the latest catalog."

"You know Mary is my sister?"

"No, I didn't. I should call her."

Why can't I learn to keep my mouth shut? Mary and my date, now what could go wrong there?

"Should I tell her to expect your call?"

"No, silly, I know she is your sister. I was just teasing."

"You got me good."

"That is a woman's job—to keep the men guessing."

And I asked her on a date.

"Rick, I have one serious request."

"What is that?"

"My stepmother will ask for your help in getting into the movies. Don't get involved with her in any shape or form. She is bad news, and I fear for father."

"That is an easy promise to make. She rubbed me the wrong way as soon as I met her."

"She is evil and hurts people because she thinks it is fun."

Maybe I should have her call Mary, or better yet, Mum. Well, not Mum; His Highness might not take well to being made a widower twice.

We agreed that I would pick her up Friday evening at six o'clock.

To make the week go faster, I played several rounds of golf, went horseback riding, and even was able to surf on a good day.

Friday, I was in a tizzy about what to wear. At five o'clock, I came downstairs wearing a blue sports coat, chinos, and a blue broadcloth button-down shirt.

Mum sent me back upstairs to put on jeans and a Madras shirt. I tried to object, but she was forceful. No one messes with Mum when she is forceful. I thought of a certain KGB head when I went to change my clothes.

All became clear when I met Olga in the lobby of the hotel. She wore jeans with a Madras shirt, which was untucked and tied at her waist.

Gee, I wonder who had been talking to each other?

I drove us over to the Hamburger Hamlet with the top down on the T-bird and Paul Anka on the radio.

I wish I had given my choice of restaurants more consideration. The first person I saw was Nina, sitting with Tuesday Weld.

I almost backed out, but Olga whispered.

"I know who she is. I read all the papers. Be nice, and let's have dinner."

When we were seated, I managed to sit with my back to Nina. I didn't want to make eye contact. I would have no idea what to say.

I didn't have to say anything because Olga told me.

"They just left."

"Good, that would have been a little awkward. Why, I don't know; she left me."

"Would you want her back?"

"No, twice burnt and all that."

We had an enjoyable dinner of cheeseburgers and fries. We also talked about our respective lives. We knew many of the same people, as we both traveled in some pretty high circles of society.

We took a long way home, and I got a kiss on the cheek when I walked her in.

It might have been more, but I recognized one of the bodyguards waiting for her.

Chapter 8

Olga and I spent Saturday at the beach. The surf was up, and she is an expert surfer. Seeing her in a bikini left me up.

We had a good time. We grabbed lunch at a taco stand. It seemed like we knew a lot of the same crowd. Not that I was friends with many of them. They were what I had been calling Eurotrash.

I would have to change my mind about several of them, but she agreed that many of them were worthless.

They were titled, rich, and bored with no direction. Rather than find something worthwhile to do, they drank, partied, and had a generally good time. They also were rude, obnoxious, and privileged.

If they got into trouble, Mummy or Daddy would bail them out or cover up their wrongdoings.

I began to get uneasy feelings about Olga. Yes, she is beautiful, smart, and used to moving in better circles. She also knew too many in the wrong circles. Was she an observer or a participant?

It didn't take long to sort it out. She had an invitation to a party in Beverly Hills at an actor's house. I knew of him and his ways. I told her I had other plans.

She tried to get me to change my mind by telling me that the actor had the best drugs.

I still begged off, telling her I had a family event. I did; it was called dinner and watching TV with the family. At dinner, I told my parents what I had learned about Olga. They agreed that she wasn't good news.

I didn't understand my little sister. She offered to show Olga one of her necklaces. Mum told her it wasn't necessary yet. It made no sense to me, but whatever.

I did contact my chief pilot and told him I would like to fly to Oxford tomorrow. I was going to visit my grandmum and friends at the school.

The phone rang right after I finished arranging my flight in the morning. It was Olga. She told me she had decided not to go anywhere tonight as it would be no fun without me.

She asked, "Do you have plans for tomorrow?"

"Yes, I have an early flight to England."

"Are you running away from me?"

Coward that I am, I told her no.

"How long will you be gone?"

"About a week. I have to see some people and check in with the Coldstream Guards."

I was making this up as I was talking. I hadn't given any real thought as to what I would do in England. Though what I was telling her actually made sense.

"Can I come along?"

I am a coward.

"Yes, if you want to. I can't guarantee any parties or a good time; this is semi-business."

"Thank you. I have to get away from my stepmother. She is driving me crazy. She is convinced I can talk you into getting a screen test."

"I don't know what gave her that idea."

"She found out you are invested in movies, so you can make things happen."

"Be ready at seven. I will have a car pick you up at your hotel."

"Will we be flying first class?"

"No."

"Oh."

"Please be ready on time. We don't want to miss the flight."

"All right."

I arranged for one of our limos to take us to the airport. She was ready and waiting in the morning. She had two large suitcases packed and ready to go.

When she realized we weren't heading into LA to catch a flight, she asked where we were going. I told her the plane was in Ontario. She didn't know where that was.

We were pulling into the airport through the private aviation gate by this time. We pulled up to the 707, which had the stairs out for us.

She looked confused until she realized that the plane was in my colors with my coat of arms on the tail.

"I thought we weren't flying first class."

"We aren't. This is much better."

We settled in quickly and departed immediately. After that, I gave her a tour of the plane. She couldn't believe I had a duplicate wardrobe in the hold, and Harold traveled with me to care for it.

She became very friendly, and somewhere over the Atlantic, I joined an exclusive club. Events just progressed until it happened. I learned a lot from Olga. She appeared to be a very experienced teacher.

It was not what I had in mind for the first time, but I had no complaints.

I noticed that the stewardesses were very polite to her but also cold and distant. They didn't appear to approve of her.

Not that it was any of their business.

I spent a few hours in the cockpit, adding to my flight hours. When I came back, I got the third degree from Olga. She knew I was the Duke of Hong Kong and a movie actor, but not much else.

I was open with her about my business ventures. She was very interested in what I was worth. Since I was proud of my accomplishments, I told her all. It's not bragging if you have done it. I had done it.

I probably should have been more discreet about my net worth, but she is my love.

Changing my mind, I diverted the flight from Oxford to London. I didn't want to spend the first few days of what I visualized as my honeymoon at my grandmum's. Instead, I planned for us to stay at the hotel on the Strand.

She loved the hotel suite that was ready and waiting. I told her about my different properties around the world. She was impressed and let me know it in some very physical ways.

We didn't leave the suite for two more days. Finally, we decided you could only spend so much time alone. So, we went sightseeing.

The next day, I told her I had to check in with the palace. She pouted that she couldn't go along but soon got over it.

I called Mr. Norman and told him I was in England and would like to see him. He told me he knew I had arrived three days ago. It appears my comings and goings are reported.

When I arrived at his office, we spent several hours reviewing my recent adventures. He told me the queen had followed the attempts to locate me closely. By asking to be updated, it kept the pressure on to keep looking.

Daily reports were given about the trail I was leaving across Siberia. Most of it was by deduction. Who else would steal horses, rob banks, and create general mayhem with a longbow? They could never catch up with me but could follow my trail. It was better than any James Bond movie.

I told him about the movie being made, *Escape from Siberia*, and my cameo appearance. He had a good laugh at that.

MI6 also informed him about my venture into Laos. He told me, "Good show," but there couldn't be official recognition for something that didn't happen.

I replied that I preferred it that way.

He then directed the conversation in a direction I hadn't seen coming.

"I understand that you are seeing Princess Olga Glucksburg.

"Yes, I am."

I didn't tell him she was in my hotel suite. I suspected he knew.

"Rick, for various reasons, she nor her father will ever be received here at the palace."

I wish I handled the next part better. I told him that if she wasn't welcome, then neither was I. He remained calm and said that someday I would understand, and it was for the best if I didn't see the queen today.

I left the palace in a huff. About halfway back to the hotel, I started to wonder why the Glucksburgs weren't welcome.

Later, I even asked Olga about that, and she replied it was some silly financial issue. Before I could ask another question, I became distracted and forgot about it.

We drove up to Oxford the next afternoon and met my friends Tom, Steve, and Bill at our favorite pub. We had a good time telling stories. They were taken with Olga, dressed to the nines, at least for a student pub in Oxford.

They vied with telling her stories about upside-down sailboats and license plates in Monaco. I was amazed that the disgraceful license plate affair had become a grand adventure.

They wanted to know if I was coming back to Oxford. I told them that I had no plans at this time. After a pleasant afternoon, Olga and I moved on to Grandmum's.

While we were riding in the limo over to The Meadows, Olga told me that my friends were nice but a little plebeian for her and that in the future, we would have to travel in better circles.

That set off a second alarm. She didn't care for my friends, and there was a silly financial issue in her background. I was sure it was nothing and my friends would grow on her.

There, Harold was waiting with our luggage. Having a valet was a good deal!

When I introduced Olga to Grandmum, it wasn't the reception I was expecting. Grandmum was polite but reserved. In turn, butter wouldn't have melted in Olga's mouth.

I asked Grandmum if the Queen Mum had visited recently. It turns out she had left this morning. She wouldn't be back until after I was gone, more's the pity.

Not being completely dense, I figured that some investigation was in order.

Chapter 9

The princess and I were shown our rooms. Me to my own, and her to one in another wing of the house. Was Grandmum trying to tell me something?

While Olga was changing clothes and freshening up, I placed a call to the States. I knew who would have all the dirt by now.

"Mum, it's Rick. Have you learned anything about Olga and her family background that I should be aware of?"

She replied, "They have been chased out of Denmark and told never to return. They will be arrested if they step foot in the country.

"By Danish law, they cannot lose their titles or citizenship, but the Danes are so mad they are considering changing the law. It is such an embarrassment that it has been kept out of the news.

"This ban from the country includes the princess. She and her father went through his inheritance, so they got a scheme that defrauded a public pension fund. It was in the millions of dollars.

"They lived high and wild while they could. When they were caught, they were broke again. I hope you enjoyed your flight and hotel stay, but if you are smart, you will run as fast as you can."

That left me in a bit of a quandary. What to do tonight. I knew that Olga would expect me to knock on her door. If I didn't, she would knock on mine.

If I didn't answer her, she would raise a ruckus. I knew her well enough to predict her reaction. I took the easy way out and called her room.

When she answered, I asked her directly if she and her father had been kicked out of Denmark for stealing from a pension fund. She admitted it with no shame.

I told her we were through, even though we had barely started. She didn't take it well. After the shouting, I told her a car would be available to take her to the London airport, and a ticket would be waiting at Icelandic Air.

She wanted to know why that airline and I told her it had good connections. She would end up in LA.

I didn't tell her that it would be a coach ticket. There would be an eight-hour layover in Reykjavik. She would have to change airlines in New York, and there would be another airline in Saint Louis with a four-hour layover. Petty, I know, but it's still fun to think of.

An acquaintance at Oxford had taken the flight from London to Reykjavik to New York with the layovers. His flight to Iceland also had a goat in the passenger cabin. One could only hope.

For myself, I had some bridges to mend. In the morning, after I was certain she had left for the airport, I called Mr. Norman and told him I regretted the unkind words I had spoken.

I had finally smartened up and found out about her and her father. He accepted my apology. I asked him why he didn't tell me himself.

"Richard, one thing I have learned is not to be the one who exposes the feet of clay. Even though you are right, you are never forgiven."

"It was my mum who told me."

"That is different; she has been telling you how wrong you are for your whole life, so you expect it of her."

"You are right about that."

"While you are still in England, the queen wants to see you for lunch tomorrow."

"I'll be there."

I wondered if she would roast me.

Next, I ate crow with Grandmum. She was nice about it, but you could tell she still thought I was a ninny. I knew that because she said so. It didn't bother me; she called Mum that all the time.

I made more phone calls and arranged to meet my friends at the pub this evening. I wanted to tell them that beauty isn't everything and how I dodged a bullet.

I shouldn't have bothered. They thought she would have been worth it until the police hauled her away. Even when I explained she was only after my money, they thought she would be worth a fortune or two.

The next day, I met the queen for lunch at the palace. It wasn't as though she could pop down to Mr. Treacher's place with me and get some fish and chips. I even told her about them. She told me she would try some takeaway.

She didn't mention my Danish princess at all. She wanted to talk about Hong Kong. I gave her an update on the improved quality of their products with the help of Dr. Deming. Also, the marketing plans that are in place to highlight their products.

She thought this was wonderful and that it was a shame that it wouldn't work in England. I asked her why, and she told me that socialism had the country in a state of malaise.

No one seemed interested in getting ahead, just getting by. Those who wanted to get ahead were leaving England. They had what the newspapers called a brain drain going on. Soon, only the mediocre would be left.

She then showed interest in my escape from the Gulag. She assured me that the intelligence services were trying to get me free but were always a step behind me.

I did ask her about my status as an aide. She wanted to continue that but realized I couldn't function as a Queen's Messenger. She still wanted me to keep the credentials for my airplane. It would be convenient for me, and if they ever did need my help urgently, it would be in place.

After lunch, I returned to my hotel suite, where I checked that the rooms had been cleaned and the sheets had been changed.

Now the truth was out about Olga, I got the willies just thinking about her. I hoped I didn't have any diseases. I had the hotel send a doctor to examine me, but it was too early for me to show any symptoms, so he just took blood and urine samples for examination. I later received an "all clear."

The next morning, I boarded my 707 for the flight back to California. Mum had called, and she wanted to borrow the plane to take Mary and her to New York City for an interview on the *Tonight Show*. I wondered how it would go with Mary on national TV. Nothing could go wrong, could it?

When I boarded the aircraft, my first question was about the sheets being changed. My head stewardess sniffed as she told me the ones on the bed had been tossed. I didn't know it was possible to sniff while talking. I thought it was only in stories.

On the flight home, I thought about the last week. I had almost become entangled with a fortune hunter who could have ruined me. At the same time, I learned about some new pleasures in life.

Overall, I would chalk it up as a win.

It would be some time before I would trust any newly met women.

The flight was a good one, and I picked up some more flight time. That part of this trip was a winner.

When not on the flight deck, I seriously thought about what I could do to help develop China and the newly acquired Siberian territories. There was no question that infrastructure had to be put in place—especially roads.

Siberia had no such thing as a through road or train track. That would be the number one priority for that area. The question was how to finance it and set it up to repay loans.

China needed not only roads but also to move beyond subsistence agriculture in the provinces.

Then, there was the setting up of my centralized air freight delivery. I still wanted to have a trial in California. I would need to find someone to set it up.

More likely, several. I was talking about a combination airline and local ground delivery service. I doubted if any single person had that combined knowledge.

I also needed to keep close tabs on the IC Chip development. Multiple fortunes were riding on that business. I didn't want to mess it up.

Halfway across the Atlantic, I started kicking myself. I had been at The Meadows and hadn't checked on how the excavations of the Roman fort were going. Oh well, the next trip.

Somehow, I had to visit Australia and see about purchasing land there. It was about the only civilized country where large swathes of land could be bought at reasonable prices.

With all that weighing on my mind, I took a nap. I had so many loose ends that I couldn't keep track of them. I needed a plan and to stick to it.

Sure, I had plans in place when I went to play golf in Hong Kong. I remember someone made a quote about plans and life happening. That was me, stumbling from one thing to another.

Chapter 10

Upon arriving home, all those thoughts I had were gone out the window. While I was trying to make plans for the future, plans were being made for me.

Crown Prince Chia-Hao of China had been killed in an accident. I had to go to the funeral. His body would lie in state for a week, so I had time to get there.

As soon as we landed in Ontario, they started preparing the plane for a quick round trip to New York City. My sister was going to be interviewed on the Jack Paar show. Mum would be accompanying her as she was only eight years old.

I did send a telegram of condolences to the empress on the death of her son. I also sent separate ones to his wife, Ann, and his children, Chun-Chieh, and May-ling.

Queen Elizabeth sent me a telegram asking that I convey her condolences while her ambassador would give the formal message. That telegram had barely reached me when I received a call from the White House asking for the same assistance.

The one person I didn't send a telegram to was the late crown prince's brother, Prince Haoran. I detested the man and thought he would be the instigator if foul play were involved.

One thing I did accomplish in the next two days was to hire a search firm to find three people: one who knew the airline business, another for local ground freight operations, and a third who could act as the CEO for both operations.

I also asked Jim Williamson to see if we had any contacts in Australia who knew someone in large property real estate. I was interested in anything over five hundred thousand acres.

Between that and catching up with my family, I was busy the next few days. I read a story in the *LA Times* about the Glucksburg family being deported back to Denmark. It appears they were involved in fraudulent activity in Hollywood.

Sometimes, you get lucky.

That weekend, Mum had another one of her many charity fundraisers. I was drafted as an escort for any young lady, as yet to be named, who was brought along by her parents without a dinner date.

This dinner was being held inside instead of being an informal cookout. That meant I had to dress up. I thought about my full uniform rig but decided that was too much. To tell the truth, Harold was the one who convinced me that it was too much.

I was hoping there would be no unescorted females present, but I wasn't that lucky. I had the great honor of escorting Linda Richardson, the daughter of a Los Angeles banker.

Linda proved to be a nice person with what I would call average looks. That meant she looked pretty, as she was all dressed up tonight as though going to prom, but she would be just another girl on the street during the day.

I didn't mean to be harsh in this opinion. The movie industry has given me the habit of thinking about how people would look in various roles. In other words, no ravening beauty, but pretty in a girl-next-door way.

She was a decent conversationalist. She knew of me and had read about many of my business and physical adventures. At the same time, she treated me like a real person. It was a pleasant change after Princess Olga.

To my surprise, the evening flew by. I don't know who was more shocked after dinner when I asked if I could call her for a date.

She gave me a measured look, which told me not to get fresh on our date, as she said she would love to. It left me a little flustered because I had no date plans at the start of the evening and had no idea where to go.

She must have seen the panic in my eyes because she told me there was a movie she would like to see. It was a romantic comedy from England—something about a bookseller and a romance with a high-powered American movie star.

That sounded very familiar to me. Since I had no better idea, I told her that would be fun. I'm sure there is a special circle in Dante's hell reserved for guys who said a romantic comedy would be fun.

I picked her up at her house Saturday evening and had to face her polite parents. At least Dad wasn't cleaning a weapon. You could tell Linda's mother was dying to ask why I was dating her daughter.

I let it be known that it was hard for me to meet ordinary people, especially girls my age. I had to always be on guard against gold diggers.

Linda and I went to the movie, which did have its funny moments. Afterward, we went to a coffee shop where I shared some inside stories about the movie I was almost in.

It was a pleasant evening that didn't even result in a good night kiss. That was okay with me. A night of normalcy was a reward in itself.

Linda told me at the coffee shop that she was getting ready to start college and didn't plan on dating as she settled into school. Since the school term was in the second quarter, I asked her why she was starting now.

She'd had mono last fall and was now pronounced recovered enough to start in the spring quarter. She wanted to concentrate on school, as she would be carrying a heavy load. I could respect that.

It wasn't as though I was desperate for a girlfriend right now. I felt like I had been pushed from pillar to post on the female front recently.

It was finally time for me to fly to China for the funeral. Upon landing, I was taken to the Forbidden City to the suite of rooms I had used previously.

A letter was waiting for me from Ann, the wife of the late crown prince. That puzzled me. She was asking for a private meeting. The letter was hand-delivered, and the messenger immediately escorted me to Ann.

I wasn't sure what her title would be now that her husband was dead. I asked the messenger what I should call her. He told me it still would be "Princess", as she was the mother of the new heir apparent.

I was taken to her presence as soon as we arrived. She was bearing up well, but you could tell she was grief-stricken.

"Duke Richard, thank you for coming."

"I'm sorry to be seeing you in these circumstances."

"They may be worse than you think."

"How could that be?"

"I think my husband was murdered."

That statement took me aback.

"Why do you think that?"

"His death is attributed to a hunting accident. He supposedly tripped, and his shotgun went off, killing him."

"That happens."

"My husband hated hunting and would never have gone."

"Where did this happen?"

"At one of Prince Haoran's estates. That is another thing. He and Haoran didn't get along with each other. He wouldn't have gone there in the first place."

"What does the empress say about this?"

"I tried to talk to her, but they are both her sons. She doesn't want to hear any talk about it."

"What can I do?"

"You are the only court outsider that I know who has the resources to investigate the death without raising suspicion."

"I will have quiet inquiries made about the crown prince's agenda for that time."

"Please do; I fear for my children's lives."

The full import then struck me. Why would Haoran kill the crown prince? The logical answer was to take the throne.

"I will start the investigation at once."

I couldn't bear the thought of something happening to the empress, whom I considered a friend. To endanger the beautiful May-ling was unthinkable.

I can remember Ping telling me at one time she had never married and had no children. She had maintained this façade for years to protect her family during the Mao years.

As the rightful heir to the throne, she was constantly under threat of being killed. If they knew there was a line of descent, they would have killed them all. What a burden to live under.

I returned to my room for a restless night's sleep.

The next morning, I was admitted to the empress's presence. Normally, she had an ageless, vibrant look about her. Now, she looked tired and worn.

I passed on my condolences and those of the queen and President Kennedy. She accepted them with a tired nod.

"Richard, I need to speak to you alone."

At that, the room was cleared. She led me to another suite of rooms and then into a small room I recognized as a SCIF.

It was soundproof and electronic surveillance proof. I don't know what the letters stood for, but I had been in several built into embassies around the world.

"Richard, I have to ask a large favor of you. I know Ann has already asked you, but would you please investigate my son's death?"

"I thought you refused Ann's request."

"I did; if it got out that Haoran was suspected of foul play, what do you think would happen?"

"If nothing else, it would move his agenda up."

"Precisely. We need time to find out the truth, so we can't let on that we consider it to be anything but an accident. There is also the fact that Haoran is my son, and I do hate to think he would do such a thing."

"This must be very difficult for you."

"It is, but I must protect my China. While I don't think Haoran has done this, I know he would be a terrible leader and that to be that leader, he would have to kill me and the grandchildren."

"I'm unsure how to proceed, but I will do my best."

Chapter 11

I didn't have the faintest idea of how to investigate the crown prince's death. I did know someone who would—my dad.

He was a military police investigator in the Army. He even was involved in the investigation of the death of George Patton.

I went to the British Embassy and asked if I could use a secure telephone line. I had more influence with the British than the Americans, but that wasn't the only reason I was reluctant to go to them. Why, I can't tell you; it was just a feeling.

It only took half an hour to get a connection with my dad. I tersely explained the situation. He told me that two avenues of approach could be followed.

The first was establishing the movements of the crown prince as best as possible. Did he go to Haoran's hunting preserve willingly?

Next was Haoran's movements. Was he directly involved? According to Dad, if Haoran was seen in the crown prince's company, there was a good chance it was a hunting accident. If it weren't, Haoran would have kept himself at a distance.

He also suggested that I not talk to any official agencies about my investigation. Haoran would have people inside all the agencies. Even if he was innocent, he might get scared and have them act against the investigators.

For that reason alone, I wasn't to have anything to do directly with the investigation. Dad would hire private detectives through a cutout and have them do the leg work.

"How will you hire detectives in China?"

"I won't, the CIA will. They will be delighted to have us pay for retired agents in China to investigate the death. The problem will be getting them to share the information with us."

"Would it help if I called the president?"

"That would be a good start."

"I will let you know what he has to say."

I next had a call placed to the White House. It took me two hours to connect, but it was worth the wait.

President Kennedy told me that the CIA had briefed him on the crown prince's death being suspicious and that they would like to investigate it so they would have leverage in the situation.

I told him that my family would fund the investigation if we were kept in the know as to what they were finding. He was receptive to the idea and told me that Bobby would handle the financial end of things.

It made me wonder if the money would go to the CIA or the Kennedys. I decided I didn't care. It is not as though the CIA didn't have enough funding to start with.

He wanted to know why I was involved. I played it close to my chest and let him think I desired to know what happened rather than a request from the royal family.

I told him I could talk to Chia-Hao's wife, Ann, and see what his last known movements were. He told me to let him know directly. He would pass it on to the CIA. It would put their nose out of joint for him to have some information they didn't.

It would keep them on their toes in what they reported to him in all areas. I gathered this was a problem with all intelligence agencies. They would keep information compartmentalized to such a degree that they could work their agendas rather than what the top boss wanted.

They were bureaucrats who would be in their positions long after the current administration was gone, so they felt they were doing the best for their country by working the long game. In some cases, they might even be right.

After we hung up, I returned to the Forbidden City and asked to see Princess Ann. I was still confused about her title now that she was not the crown prince's consort. If it were England, it would be the crown prince's mum. That didn't roll off the tongue, so I doubted it would be that.

No matter her title, she agreed to see me. We met in a large garden near a water fountain where it wouldn't be easy to overhear our conversation.

I asked her what she knew about the crown prince's last movements.

"Rick, he left the palace to go to a meeting with the Port Authority. It was about the construction of the freight handling terminal. He was very interested in keeping it on schedule because he thought it was the future of China to be an exporter of products. With our lower labor cost, we could compete in the world marketplace.

"He talked of creating a huge chain of stores in the United States selling low-cost Chinese-made goods. Now that won't happen."

Maybe it would; that sounded like an excellent money-making idea. It would create the dilemma of raising the Chinese standard of living vs. lowering the American.

Lower-income Americans would benefit, but it would hurt the middle class. Since the middle class was the backbone of America, it could have a tremendous social cost. Maybe I should leave it alone. If it was to be, let someone else carry that burden.

In the long run, maybe I should be thinking about raising the Chinese internal standard of living without doing it on the backs of other economies. How do you jumpstart a country with such a high population?

Those were thoughts for other days. I needed to know if the crown prince had made that meeting with the Port Authority.

Ann told me his two bodyguards had accompanied him. I asked if I could speak to them. I couldn't, as it seemed that they had disappeared.

I told Ann that an investigation was just starting and that I would update her as things became clear. I didn't anticipate this would be a quick process, so I asked her to please be patient.

In the meantime, had they increased security around the children? Not yet, as they were in seclusion, but it would be done before they made any public appearances.

Rather than go directly to the Port Authority, I went to my local office. This was in the building the company had bought in the embassy district. I asked for a staff meeting.

During the meeting, I directed a conversation about the status of our projects since the death of Chia-Hao. This was my way to lead into a discussion about him.

"I understand he was on his way to a meeting with the Port Authority, and the next thing we know, he was on a hunting trip."

They agreed that it all seemed strange.

One of the field directors told us he had seen the crown prince arrive at the Port Authority office and enter the building with two bodyguards.

He remembered the time because he was just returning from lunch. No one else had any information.

Upon returning to the palace, I requested an appointment with the empress at her convenience. I was told it would be after the funeral in two days. The body was lying in state, and she wasn't seeing anyone until after the event.

I had to respect that; besides, there was nothing urgent in what I had to relay.

During my travels around Beijing earlier in the day, I had paid attention. I was being tailed, but whoever it was, was making no effort not to be seen. From that, I concluded it was the MSS just keeping up with all of us foreign devils.

I spent the next two days catching up with reports on Jackson Enterprises. No matter where I was in the world, the darned paperwork kept coming.

Of particular interest were the IC Chips. The teams I had put in place were working and had made some early breakthroughs. They hadn't doubled the number of transistors and associated elements yet but thought they had found a path to move forward.

At the same time, one of the large defense contractors was interested in licensing the manufacture of our chips for guided missiles.

I noted that we wanted this business at the lowest cost to them while we still profited. We needed to get a foothold with the chips, and I was interested in anything that would fly high and fast.

I had never lost my interest in space; I just never had time to do anything about it. By supporting others, I could enjoy it second hand.

The search company in California had identified candidates to start my air freight business. The trick here would be to find a good top man and let him build the business. This means he would have an ownership portion to keep him in the game.

How was I to interview them when I was in China? It would have to wait until after the funeral when I could return to the States.

Chapter 12

The weather on the day of the funeral was appropriate. Overcast sky in a somber grey. The priests had chosen the day after consulting the Chinese Almanac.

While Chia-Hao's children Chun-Chieh and May-ling were responsible for planning and conducting the funeral in the Confucian tradition of filial piety, they had the help of palace officials.

Invitations were sent out on white paper, which symbolized death. If Chia-Hao had lived to be over eighty, it would have been pink paper to celebrate living a long and prosperous life.

The invitations were for the ceremony, which would be held on the grounds of the Forbidden City.

Chia-Hao's body had lain in state in Tiananmen Square for three days, and over a million mourners passed by, each laying a white flower on the coffin. I watched the operation and realized it was a little cynical.

Single white flowers would be sold for a single small coin equal to the US penny at the entrances to the square. When the mourner reached the coffin, they would lay it on the coffin. When a significant number were piled up, a crew would gather them and take them out of sight.

I was curious about what would happen to the flowers, so I followed one gathering crew. They returned the flowers to the flower stalls where they had been purchased!

I thought about it and realized there was no way a million or more white flowers could be brought together for the funeral, so this was the only way tradition could be followed.

Still, it seemed strange to me. I bet FTD would have a fit.

A wake was started the night before the interment. The family would sit vigil all night. I was invited to the wake. Like all others, I brought a white envelope with an odd number of coins and a white flower. The coins were to help pay for the funeral. I don't know why it had to be an odd number.

Very noticeable in his absence was Haoran. He had sent a note declining to attend the wake as his back was bothering him, and he was bedridden. He would brave the pain and attend the actual funeral.

I had a few thoughts on that subject but kept them to myself.

The wake was not up to the standard of an Irish wake. That was probably because the Chinese were not great drinkers; well, most of them weren't.

The room was set up with pictures of the deceased, along with flowers and candles on the coffin. It was a somber, sedate affair.

I wore my army uniform and gave condolences to the family on behalf of the queen of England and the president of the United States.

The new Crown Prince Chun-Chieh looked bewildered about his new life position. He hadn't expected to be in this position for fifty years. Now, it was thrust upon him, and he was trying to process it.

May-ling was trying not to show her grief but wasn't successful. While keeping a serene look as was expected of her, tears would start rolling down her cheeks. I wanted to take her in my arms and comfort her.

That was me; she didn't even look my way.

The empress and the Dowager Ann kept their faces under control, but a tightness around their eyes gave them away.

To say the event was stressful would be putting it mildly. Coward that I am, I left as soon as it was polite to do so.

I, like all others, had RSVPed to the funeral invitation. It was being held in the Forbidden City, and Chia-Hao would be interred in the royal family's tomb.

The crypt had been opened and cleaned since there hadn't been a burial there since the 1800s.

During the funeral ceremony, a eulogy was given by a Confucian priest. It was odd, but the whole time, assistant priests would accept small items to be burned. There was a lot of fake paper money, houses, cars, and even TVs—everything Chia-Hao would need to be set up in the afterlife.

The burning of spirit paper and joss sticks filled the air until you had trouble breathing. Once the years-long ceremony was complete, we made a parade to the tomb. It was less than an hour; it only seemed like years.

A one-hundred-and-ten-piece marching band led the way. I tried to count the trombones but couldn't manage it. I kid you not; the parade started with a huge gong being struck.

The loud music was to scare away spirits and ghosts. I didn't know the difference between the two.

The immediate family followed behind the coffin, which was on a caisson pulled by six black horses. The men wore black suits and the women white dresses, both symbols of death.

We, the mourners, followed behind. The last group was the hired mourners who wailed in grief and ripped their clothes. I asked an attendant why they were there, as it seemed to be a full procession.

I had been briefed by the British Embassy staff on what to expect. The hired mourners were usually added when there were few family members and others. Millions would have been in the parade if they had opened the gates.

It was a matter of politics. The hired mourners had a guild and had made it clear that they had to be seen at such an important event so their traditions and livelihoods would continue.

Marching with the family was Haoran, who showed no signs of discomfort from back problems. While he, like all of us, wore a dark suit to show mourning, he also wore medals from the communist period.

These all had bright red ribbons. From a dossier I had read on him, he had not earned any of them. They were all political awards. The red of celebration was a not-so-subtle insult to the rest of the family.

Like all the other men, I wore a black ribbon on my left arm, which I would wear for one hundred days. Women would wear theirs on their right arms. Again, I had no idea why the different arms. There was so much of this culture I didn't understand.

The coffin was placed in a slot in the underground burial vault and the tomb closed. The vault wouldn't be opened again until the Qing Ming or Tomb Sweeping Festival. This tradition was held throughout China but had been forbidden by the communists for the royal tombs. They didn't want any reminders of the past rulers.

As we departed the area, we were handed a red envelope that contained a coin to see us home safely, a piece of candy to be eaten immediately, and a handkerchief. I was surprised when I saw the candy was M&Ms. I ate the candy and threw the coin in a fountain as others did.

None of these items could be taken home, so I blew my nose on the handkerchief and deposited it in one of the many trash cans stationed in the area for that purpose. It seemed crass to me, but when in Rome.

The last items in the red envelope were red threads. I had to take them home with me, or in this case to my suite in the palace, and tie them around the doorknob. This was to prevent any spirits or ghosts that may have followed me home from entering my residence.

I was glad to return to my rooms, take off the suit, and kick back. Like most people, I hated funerals, and this one had so many differences that I had trouble putting it into perspective. The wake was a celebration of life. The funeral seemed designed to bury him and to keep him in his grave.

It made me think of the Shawnee and their charms to keep Lew Wetzel in the ground. Maybe things weren't so different after all.

I wanted to update Dowager Ann on the situation. The embassy had informed me of her correct title. Now didn't seem the time.

No sooner had I thought this than there was a knock on my door by a messenger. The dowager wished for me to come to her rooms.

I had to scramble back into my suit as I didn't think calling upon her in blue jeans and a pullover would be correct.

The messenger waited while I changed and led me to her room. It wasn't a suite; it was a palace within itself. I just thought I was staying in a museum setting. This made Buckingham Palace look like a hovel. I wondered why the communists hadn't looted it.

I couldn't imagine the staff it would take just to dust the furniture. A painting depicting a vase of red roses made me think of Valentine's Day and that I had no one this year. Now, why did I think of that?

Chapter 13

I was admitted directly to find the royal family waiting, Empress Ping, the Dowager Ann, Crown Prince Chum-Chieh, and Princess May-ling.

All in comfortable clothes. The younger of the set wore jeans and pullovers. I thought about asking if I could run home and change but thought better of it.

The empress started the conversation.

"Rick, I have decided we must approach this situation as a family, so I have updated them on where things stand. Do you have anything to report?"

"Not a lot, but things are in motion. The US president is overseeing a CIA operation that is following the trail of how the crown prince went from a meeting of the Port Authority to Haoran's estate. I am funding it through them, so if Haoran learns of the investigation, he will not look beyond the US government."

"There has been no trace of his bodyguards."

"I'm sorry to inform you their bodies were found in the Yongding River."

May-ling spoke up, "At least we know they didn't betray father."

"I'm sorry, Your Highness, but they may have betrayed him and, in turn, were killed by their new master."

She looked at me with wide eyes as though seeing me for the first time.

"Do you think so?"

"At this time, we can't rule anything out. I would have the investigators check to see if anything had changed with the bodyguards' families or finances recently."

"Why their families?"

"They may have threatened to harm them or even kidnapped them as hostages to ensure the bodyguards' cooperation."

"Where did you learn to be so cynical?"

"My family has had to endure such events in the past, and we have learned that anything may be possible."

May-ling's mother broke in, "Dear, I will tell you more of the duke's history later."

The crown prince chimed in, "I loved your song, 'Rock and Roll Cowboy.'"

That confirmed that Oriental culture is different from Occidental culture.

"That wasn't my best moment. I can't sing. If the right song is picked, I don't sound unpleasant, but to sing any song, no way."

May-ling knew nothing about me.

"A singing duke, I didn't know British nobles did things like that."

"Sis, he is also an actor."

"As in the movies?"

"He should have won an Oscar for his role in *Over the Ohio.*"

She took a good look at me and gasped.

"You're Death Wind!"

"Guilty as charged."

"But you looked so evil in that poster."

"What poster was that?"

She looked a little flustered as she said, "The one in my dormitory at school. We all thought you were the perfect bad guy all girls are told to stay away from by their mothers but are attracted to."

"Make-up does wonders."

The dowager mother spoke up, "I'm still telling you to be aware of the bad boy. Stay away from him."

"Why, mother?"

"Because your grandmother and I have first dibs on him."

I don't think I have blushed so red in my life.

The crown prince had to laugh at his sister.

"He has been a hero many times over. All those medals on his uniform are for valor, not political."

I thought for a moment.

"Maybe the ones from North and South Vietnam."

"Not only that, but he is one of the richest people in the world. He has given China many millions of dollars. You could do worse than this bad boy billionaire."

He made it sound like some cheap romance.

All this teasing brought a smile to her face. It was the first I had seen since her father's death. She must have realized it because she became serious.

"I am sure that the Duke of Hong Kong is all that you say, but I have my duty to China. At the right time, I will find a husband who will be equal to my position as a princess."

Shot down in flames.

Turning to Empress Ping and the dowager, I saw them exchange brief smiles. I told them when I had something else to report, I would let them know.

"In the meantime, please put more bodyguards in place for the crown prince and princess."

The crown prince, who was three years older than me but with much less experience, told me he was fine with the two he had.

I bit my tongue. I almost said, "How did that work out for your father?"

Not the best thing to say on the day of his funeral.

I returned to my rooms and got comfortable again. I hadn't planned to be here in China for some weeks yet. I had other projects that needed tending. I had my flight crew notified that I would like to head back to the States in the morning.

The next morning, I was up and ready to leave bright and early. I was anxious to get on with it. As I left my suite in the Forbidden

City, I noticed the red thread on the doorknob. It had worked; no ghosts or spirits had bothered me in the night.

The flight across the Pacific was like all flights across the Pacific, long and tedious. I had to see about getting an inflight movie set up installed.

I discussed that with the head stewardess and chief pilot. They both agreed it would be a good feature. It could be installed to display against the front bulkhead in the forward cabin.

He said he would get it costed out. I told him not to worry about the cost, just to have it done. It is nice to have money, even if some Chinese girls aren't impressed.

I did get a night's sleep on the way home. This left me out of sync with the California time zone, but at this point, I didn't care. I just wanted off the plane.

We landed in Ontario, and a light plane was waiting to take me to the Forestry Service station. I felt fine but knew a trip as I had just taken could play heck with your senses. All I would need was to become disoriented at ten thousand feet.

At home, the family was sitting down for dinner. I think it was lunchtime for me, but I was hungry no matter what you called the meal.

The funeral was the main topic of discussion at the table. They wanted to know how it differed from an American funeral.

When I told them that the women wore a white dress as a sign of mourning, Mary piped up, "That is good to know. I will save my wedding dress so I will have something to wear if I have to go to a Chinese funeral."

I was still trying to wrap my head around that image when Mum asked about the crown prince's children.

I described them in detail. I noticed Mum and Mary exchanging smiles. What is this with women exchanging smiles like they know something that we men don't?

Dad told me to meet him in the library after dinner. He and I were there alone.

"Rick, things are all set for the CIA to begin its investigation. Their first report is about the bodyguards who were killed."

"Both of them were married with children. Each of their youngest children was kidnapped and murdered. They were told their eldest child would be next, then their spouse. These are bad people. Please be careful."

"I don't think bad even begins to describe them. The Soviets just think I held a grudge."

"Slowly, son, slowly. If you rush in, these things will go badly."

"I know, Dad. What has been done is so terrible."

"If our suspicions are correct, the empress or her grandchildren will be next. I hope they are taking this seriously."

"I know the empress is, but I don't know about the grandchildren. The crown prince took it lightly about needing more bodyguards. The princess, now that I think of it, did not comment one way or the other."

"What sort of a girl is the princess?"

"I don't know, just a girl."

"Nothing special?"

"Well, she is beautiful."

"I see."

He left it at that; he said he saw; I don't know what he saw. That reminded me of the old chant about what he saw, she saw, etc. I knew it was time to go to bed no matter what time of day my stomach said it was.

I did and was awake at two in the morning and couldn't get back to sleep. I tried reading but couldn't get into it. Instead, I slipped on a running outfit and took off across the back trails in the state forest behind the house.

It only took two spills to convince me this wasn't the best idea. Luckily, I hadn't injured myself, but I surely would if I kept it up.

I returned to my room, took a shower, and managed to get back to sleep until daybreak. I was then able to get my run in without killing myself.

Chapter 14

I interviewed the man who would be president and CEO of FreightExpress Airlines and ground delivery services. I was favorably impressed. He had a working knowledge of both industries but didn't profess to be an expert in either. Instead, he was an organization expert.

We had lunch together, which became a working lunch with us bouncing ideas off each other. I must say most of his were better than mine.

That is the reason I decided to hire him. He knew about Jackson Enterprises and wasn't reluctant to deal with me. I did explain this was to be a completely separate operation. The board of directors didn't think the idea had enough merit.

This was my operation and my investment. We talked about what would be needed to start an air fleet and truck line to service the entire state of California.

He did some numbers on the back of a table napkin and gulped.

"I can understand why your board doesn't want to proceed with this idea."

"How much?"

"Seventy-five million to start with."

"Okay, I will make the initial capitalization one hundred million and add to it as needed."

"I had been told you are rich, but this is a lot of money."

"It will be a billion when we go national and several tens of billions when we go international.

"Do you want the job?"

"I'm interested. What compensation are you providing?"

"Fifty-five thousand a year to start and five percent ownership based on your labor contribution plus an annual bonus depending on successes."

"I don't see any profit for the first few years."

"That is why I said successes instead of profits. Getting a working system in place will be a success."

"I can accept the position right now. I will give two weeks' notice at TWA, but they will let me go immediately."

"Your first objective will be to hire a person to run the airline portion and another the ground delivery. We have candidates identified, but they will be your choice and your hires."

I handed him a sheet of paper with a level organization chart, along with salaries and percent ownership. I was giving away twenty-five percent to the top management to help them buy into the company and its objectives.

"After you hire your top levels, select an area for your headquarters. The only thing I ask is not LAX. It is getting worse every day to get in and out of."

"Ontario airport would be a natural. Not far out, there are long runways, a low population in the area, and not much air traffic, and it's also near Interstate 10 for truck access.

"We can put up buildings fairly cheaply out there to sort packages. We will also have to provide aircraft maintenance there."

"What do you think we will need for aircraft when we start?"

"Something small, able to carry ten tons or so of cargo. Fuel efficient. Ease of maintenance. We will have to do a study based on the flight times to Ontario. I think there will be several different planes."

"Sounds like a plan. Here is my card. Meet me at this office tomorrow, and the papers will be all drawn up."

"Thank you. This sounds like a challenge that will be fun."

"I'm all for fun, especially if money is being made while having it."

I didn't want to come across as an amateur, only talking about having fun.

I went out to the country club and played a pickup round of golf. They were all duffers who didn't recognize me, and I didn't help them. It was a pleasant outing with no championship resting upon each putt.

Them not knowing who I was couldn't last. At the turn, enough people asked for my autograph that they twigged. After that, it was "What club should I use?" or "Good shot!" In other words, pain. They weren't so bad I wanted to quit. I did autograph each of their golf balls on the last hole and signed their scorecards so they would have bragging rights.

I guess the afternoon was okay after all.

The next morning, I met John Davis for the contract signing. After he signed his contract, I handed him a checkbook and signature card.

I had arranged for one of the Jackson Enterprises part-time accountants to take care of the new company's books.

Since they were part-time at JE, it would work well for them. It wouldn't take long for them to be full-time at FreightEx, which we were calling the new company.

Being home was pleasant and relaxing. I still received my company reports and spent an entire day signing notes and writing letters to employees and their families who had notable achievements.

There was one fly in the ointment—Mum's charity balls. She was having one every few weeks, and she thought I was her slave. Maybe not slave but dating service? I think the word might be gigolo.

I had to escort the young ladies who attended without escorts. At first, it had only been an occasional one that events had caught up with, like the one whose boyfriend dumped her the night of the ball.

Now the word had spread. If you wanted to meet the wealthy, elusive Duke of Hong Kong, that eligible bachelor, just attend one of Countess Jackson's balls needing an escort.

The first time, it was two young ladies. This week, it was five at the same time. I pleaded with Mum to let me skip the ball. She asked if I knew how many hours she had spent in labor with me while the bombs were falling.

How do you argue with that? Her solution was to set up a separate table for me to entertain the young ladies while we ate.

It was a wonder that a real catfight with scratching, biting, and hair-pulling didn't break out. I tried to have a pleasant general conversation with the young ladies, but they were a spiteful bunch. I'd had enough by the time dessert was served and walked out of the ball.

After everyone left, Mum was contrite. She thought that she had an elegant solution. It was elegant if you liked wrestling on TV. She accepted that I couldn't escort more than one young lady at a time. That is when she realized she could auction me off.

That was it for me. Dutiful son that I am, I had always obeyed my mum. Now, I told her I was done with her charity balls. She reminded me she knew where I slept. I told her that the street went two ways.

That was the first-ever fight I had with Mum, and I felt bad about it, but I wasn't going to back down. Fortunately for both of us, Dad came on the tense scene.

He listened to both our grievances and declared that I no longer had to attend the balls if I didn't want to. I was old enough to make my own decisions. Mum looked like she was going to tell him she knew where he slept but must have thought better of it.

The next day, I decided I should make myself scarce for a while. I arranged a flight to Spain to check on my holdings there.

So, instead of relaxing at home, I spent another day trapped in the aluminum tube in the sky. Halfway across the Atlantic, I had the plane turn around and fly to Atlanta.

Since I'm a member of the Augusta National Golf Club, I thought I might as well play a few rounds. I didn't feel like doing business; besides, I don't think Spain has any golf courses as nice as Augusta.

When I arrived in Atlanta, I called the Augusta clubhouse to see if I would have any trouble getting to play. From the response I received, I think they would have kicked people off the course to allow me to play.

The ever-present Harold and I, with a trunk full of clothes, rode in a limo to Augusta. He wanted to make certain I could be presented to the Queen of Sheba if she showed up to play a few rounds.

Those were his words, not mine. Being a female, I doubted the club would allow her to play.

We stayed at the same hotel as my last trip when I won the August National. Seeing that they had the same suite ready for me was slightly embarrassing. What was embarrassing was the plaque with my name on the door.

After my run and exercises in the morning, I stopped at the front desk and asked the manager about the plaque. He told me that they could charge a premium for that room. Now that I was staying there again, they would raise the prices.

I was able to eat my breakfast in peace, golf fans patiently waiting at the restaurant exit to get my autograph. Thankfully, I still carried some of my movie publicity pictures.

I accepted requests to have my photo taken, but they had to put five dollars in the March of Dimes charity jar at the cash register.

Chapter 15

I was at the first tee at Augusta when a golf cart approached us. The driver was yelling my name. I was confused about what was going on.

"The president of the United States is on the phone for you; he says it is an emergency. Hop in. I will get you to the clubhouse."

I had just met the other members of my foursome and had to wonder what they were thinking.

It was JFK on the phone, and it was terrible news.

"Rick, Crown Prince Chun-Chieh has been murdered. Can you get back to China and help keep the lid on? We are afraid there will be a civil war, and we won't like the outcome."

"I will fly directly there. Those are my friends we are talking about, not some abstract political game."

"Take care of your friends, and you will be helping your country."

"Yes, sir. Will you tell them if they need to go to another country, they will need passports in some other name so they can't be traced?"

"I will. Good luck."

I hung up and started making phone calls. The first was to Harold, who had stayed at the hotel since he didn't play golf. I told him briefly what was going on and to start packing.

Next, I chartered an airplane at the Augusta airport to fly back to Atlanta to my 707.

Then, I called the chief pilot to inform him that we had to leave for Beijing as soon as possible. I gave him my charter information so I could be met at the civilian terminal at Atlanta Municipal Airport.

I called Harold back to tell him to meet me at the Augusta private air terminal.

Then, I called my parents to let them know where I was headed. Mum answered the phone. She was all business and told me to be careful.

I met Harold at Augusta, and we flew in a four-seater down to Atlanta Municipal. When we landed and taxied to the private aviation terminal, a 707 was sitting on the main apron. It dwarfed everything around it.

Our pilot expressed awe and surprise at it sitting there.

"Whoever owns that must be worth a bundle!"

The stairs were in place, so I asked him to taxi right up to the plane. He gave me a look but did it. A couple of the crew came down and grabbed our bags. I had paid for the flight in advance, so we were good to go.

I smiled at the pilot as we were exiting the plane.

"A couple of bundles, if you are keeping count."

We hustled up the steps and were barely buckled in when we started to move. After we were airborne, the pilot came back and told me we were heading for Ontario, our home base, to refuel and pick up another crew.

Whenever we flew long flights like the Pacific, I paid for two flight crews so that each could have proper rest breaks. The commercial airlines didn't do this for cost reasons. It was legal, but I disagreed with their thinking. I knew the USAF had two crews onboard for such journeys.

I thanked him for putting this together quickly. He told me they called it a "snap-kick" in the Air Force. That term was self-explanatory. I liked it; I had done a few snap-kicks myself.

As soon as we landed in Ontario, the extra crew came aboard, and the catering service delivered enough food for a month, or at least it seemed like it.

The fuel truck was there and pumping in minutes. The new flight crew filed a flight plan and had the flight path weather reports and the latest NOTAMs.

Our downtime in Ontario was short, but my mum and dad met the plane. Dad carried a large suitcase. The way he handled the suitcase, it was heavy.

Mum hugged me. "Rick, this is going to be dangerous; don't trust anyone you don't have to."

She handed me an envelope. She indicated I was to open it. It contained two passports, one American and one British. They both had my pictures but had different names than mine.

"Just in case."

Dad, indicating the suitcase, told me, "There are some tools in here and some money that you might need. Heading into a possible civil war might get dicey."

I thanked my parents, and they left after a hug. They were no sooner out the door than it was closed, and the engines started to spool up.

We taxied out and had the first takeoff slot, so we never slowed down as we turned onto the active runway.

That had to be the shortest ground stop ever. Well, probably not, but it was a quick turnaround.

We landed in Anchorage for another refueling. I had told the flight crew that speed was of the essence, not fuel efficiency. You would have thought I had declared a snow day at school.

I had two meetings in flight, one with the stewardesses and another with the flight crew. I told them that the crown prince of China had been murdered and that we were going to help.

We would probably provide passage for the new heir to the Chinese throne, Princess May-ling, and her mother, Ann. I knew that under no circumstance would Empress Ping leave of her own volition.

There was the long flight down the Siberian coast with all its extinct volcanoes. At least, I thought they were extinct, but they don't call it the Ring of Fire for nothing. We took care to stay well out in international airspace to avoid attracting the attention of the Russians.

This time, I hardly noticed them. I was trying to play out scenarios in my mind. I realized the variables were too great to do a good job, but I had to do something.

I then remembered the suitcase Dad had brought on board. I took it back to my office and closed the door. It was heavy.

When I opened it, I saw why. It was stuffed to the gills. There were two big envelopes on top. I looked in them and saw stacks of one-hundred-dollar bills. A quick estimate resulted in one hundred thousand dollars.

Beneath that were racks of gold coins. American twenty-dollar gold pieces. I estimated it to be fifty thousand. That had to be almost a hundred pounds of gold at thirty-five dollars an ounce.

Under that was a Sterling submachine gun. That made me think of that actor who had me beat up. It had ten magazines of ammo. There was also a Colt 1911 .45 caliber handgun with a dozen magazines. There was also a magazine in the well. I looked, but there were no hand grenades.

No wonder the suitcase was so heavy. I replaced the 9mm I was carrying with the .45.

We refueled in Japan and set out on the final leg to Beijing. I had tried to sleep on the flight but had too much nervous energy to settle down.

I finally did get a long nap of four hours to tide me over. Not the best way to go into a possible battle, but you deal with what you have, not what you want.

We landed in Beijing in the middle of the night. It was raining but not a thunderstorm. As we pulled into our assigned spot, stairs were moved into place, and a van pulled up.

Six people started moving up the steps before they were even in place. I was watching out of a window near the forward door, so I got a good look at the Dowager Ann and Crown Princess May-ling. They looked miserable.

The other four people were carrying cases. I hoped they contained their clothes.

When the door opened, the lead figure, one of the bodyguards I had met before, told me we were cleared for immediate take-off to Hong Kong.

The chief pilot had come back to see what was going on. He looked at me, and I nodded, so he went back up front to get us moving. Doing rough arithmetic in my head, we had more than enough fuel to reach Hong Kong with safety margins intact.

All six new passengers were buckled in as we started moving again. I had the odd thought that we must be nearing some maintenance requirements by now. However, needs must when the devil drives.

After we were in the air, I sat back as our stewardess made our new guests comfortable. The ladies were shown the restrooms in the back of the aircraft, which were nicer than the ones up front. Those were configured the same as in commercial aircraft.

I was updated once they had all refreshed themselves and had a cup of tea in hand. Ann told me that Haoran had to be behind Chun-Chieh's murder, but he was a thousand miles away at the time in a public venue.

That just meant he had hired someone to do it. Empress Ping had finally declared publicly that Haoran would be questioned when he was brought in. An active search was ongoing, and if anyone knew his whereabouts, please come forward.

Chapter 16

I noticed one of the bodyguards kept looking around. I put it down to him doing his job no matter how safe his charge was. Still, it made me keep an eye on him.

About half an hour into our trip, I was glad. I saw him reach for his shoulder holster. I was sitting down, and my Colt was in the small of my back.

I had automatically buckled up, so I had to unbuckle, stand, and reach for my weapon. In the meantime, he had started shooting the other bodyguards. Later, I figured it was because he thought they were the only ones armed. The noise was deafening.

By the time I stood and had my weapon in hand, he had shot the three bodyguards and was turning his semi-automatic towards May-ling. I let out a shout and, as he was turning, shot him in the chest twice.

It was one of those events that were over before most of those present knew it had started. It had taken seconds, not even a minute.

I quickly checked the three bodyguards. They were all dead. So was the one I shot. I did a fast look around and saw that no one else had been injured.

I told a stewardess who had been serving more tea to take May-ling and her mother to my bedroom and stay there with them. Keep the door locked until I said otherwise.

Like most stewardesses, she was trained to handle emergencies coolly. With no questions, she guided the two ladies away.

That left me alone with four dead bodies. I used one of the in-flight phones to call the flight deck and asked the chief pilot to join me.

You could tell he was former military by how he reacted to the dead bodies or didn't react.

"What happened here?" he asked.

I explained about the one agent going rogue and shooting the others and that I was able to take him down before he hurt the crown princess.

He made a phone call up front.

"We are maintaining cabin pressure, so nothing punctured the fuselage. I will feel more comfortable if we can ascertain where each bullet ended up."

Using a pointer from my office, we traced the trajectory of each bullet that had been fired. With the pointer in my hand, I stood as if it were the guard's weapon. We had propped the dead men up so we could estimate where the bullets had gone.

We found the first man had two through and throughs, and they were buried in the seatback behind him. The second guy had only one exit wound, and it was also in his seatback.

The third guy had no exit wounds at all, so we knew his 9mm bullets hadn't done any damage to the fuselage.

My .45 bullets could be a different story. He had two great gaping exit wounds in his back. We were able to trace them to a restroom wall. Inside the restroom, they continued through the next wall into the cockpit.

In the cockpit, we saw where they came through that wall and buried themselves in the back of the pilot's seat.

I almost threw up.

The chief pilot gave a very nervous laugh.

"I guess I dodged two bullets tonight."

"I almost killed you!"

"But you didn't, and you saved those ladies and our lives. He would have had to kill everyone in the back end to have half a chance of getting out."

"I guess so, but that was closer than I like. I will get some sheets and wrap the bodies."

"Maybe you should call ahead to Hong Kong. We will be there shortly."

"You are right."

I went up front and used the radio to contact Hong Kong air traffic control. I identified myself and declared an in-flight emergency. The aircraft was safe, but I needed to talk to Her Majesty's governor, so would they patch me through on a landline?

One thing you can say about all air traffic controllers is that they don't get excited about anything.

In a surprisingly short time, the governor was on the line. I didn't try to explain everything to him. I requested that he have army troops surround the plane when it landed.

He knew I was bringing the heir to the throne in, so he didn't ask many questions. I said the important packages were fine, but four bodies were on board.

After that, I returned to the front cabin where the chief pilot had laid sheets over the bodies.

I continued to my bedroom, where I knocked on the door and identified myself. The door opened, and I found myself looking at the business end of a small pistol held by the dowager.

Once she saw it was me, and under no compulsion, she lowered it. I didn't say anything, but I approved of her action.

I told them that all was under control. All the bodyguards were dead, and the integrity of the aircraft had not been damaged.

We hadn't had a chance to talk.

"What were your plans after arriving in Hong Kong?"

"We thought we would be safe there, but now it seems Haoran has a long reach."

"I agree. Were you provided with passports in different names?"

"Yes."

Thinking back to my Siberian experiences, I replied, "It must be nice to own the government printing press."

That brought a strained smile to Ann's face. This woman had lost her husband and son in the last month, and now the same person was trying to kill her daughter.

"I think it would be best if you disappeared for a while."

"The empress suggested that, but where would we go?"

"Have you ever been to Spain? I have a large ranch there; few people know of it. You could stay there until Haoran is tracked down, and it is safe to go home."

The two ladies looked at each other. Like all women, they could communicate without using words. It must be in the woman's handbook.

"That sounds good. We will need new clothes for that."

As I said, there must be a handbook.

The ladies accompanied me back to the front of the plane. They avoided looking at the sheet-covered bodies.

We landed in Hong Kong and were led to a remote area of the airport. There must have been a hundred or more troops guarding the area.

When the ladder was pushed up to the aircraft door, the governor was the first on. The Chinese ambassador accompanied him. They both looked around.

The governor stated, "As I thought, I have a team here to remove the bodies and a cleaning crew to remove the blood and other matter."

This was a tough crew I was running with; bodies didn't faze them in the least. Maybe I was with the right crowd, as I didn't feel fazed by making the bodies.

While the teams took care of business, I and the ladies explained what happened. May-ling was most complimentary in describing how I had reacted so fast.

The Chinese ambassador told us he would provide the story to Empress Ping. He then asked where we were going. May-ling started to answer, but Ann stopped her.

"We would rather keep it a secret for the moment."

"As you wish. Will you contact the empress?"

I said, "Yes, I have a friend she knows who will contact her regarding our whereabouts."

He didn't seem to like that answer, but I wasn't trusting anyone at this point. Haoran had gotten to one of the bodyguards. Who else was his?

After the bodies were removed and the aircraft cleaned, the governor and ambassador departed the plane. I held the governor back a moment.

"Would you please tell Her Majesty we are going to Spain? She will know where. Ask her to call Ping and let her know the ladies are safe and sound and that they are to communicate directly with each other from secure rooms only."

I didn't know if Buckingham Palace even had a SCIF. I could see the queen in her crown and robes being escorted to Whitehall to make a phone call.

After the two officials departed, we taxied across the airport for refueling. While there, the pilots and copilots filed a flight plan to Tokyo and obtained the latest weather data. They all needed to stretch their legs.

Even Harold, with a stewardess on each arm, departed the plane for a stroll. It was not good operational security, but it was okay as long as the ladies stayed on the plane.

The nonstop flight was only four and a half hours, but I used it to sleep on the couch in my office. I gave my bedroom to the ladies for the duration of the trip to Spain.

I had no trouble falling asleep. I think the adrenaline had worn off.

Chapter 17

We refueled in Tokyo and headed for Anchorage. I would have to get off the plane there someday just to say I had been in Alaska.

Meals were served on that leg. After we finished eating, it gave me a chance to ask what had happened to the crown prince.

It was hard for his mother, Ann, but she told me that his bodyguards were picking him up, and one of them shot him dead. There was a gun battle between the bodyguards, resulting in the shooter being killed along with two other bodyguards.

The fourth bodyguard was wounded severely and was not expected to make it. That many guns firing that close must have been a mess—no wonder the result was so bad.

"Have they found any indication of why the shooter did it?"

"MSS is investigating, but they had nothing when we left."

"What agency did the bodyguards work for?"

"MSS."

"Who provides Empress Ping's bodyguards?"

"It was the MSS, but she had them removed, and now it is the army."

"That is a relief."

"Yes, Haoran's people seem to have infiltrated MSS."

"Maybe not; those guards were all on suicide missions. I wonder how their families are?"

"The families and their finances are being investigated."

"I bet the younger children were killed and the oldest threatened unless they did the shootings. That seems to be his pattern."

"Oh, those poor families."

"In the meantime, we have to go somewhere you aren't known and that neither MSS nor Haoran knows about. We will hide there until the funeral. Even if I tell you it isn't wise, I know you will be there."

"You are correct. The priest told me the almanac says we must wait two weeks."

"Then we need to keep out of sight for two weeks."

"Do you have someplace in mind?"

"I have a ranch in Spain, and few people know about it. MSS or Haoran could find it, but it would take them longer than two weeks to find and set anything up."

'So, you aren't ruling MSS out?"

"I'm only ruling out you, Empress Ping, and May-ling."

May-ling had sat quietly through our meal and the conversation. She seemed stunned by the events. Even in her grief, she looked regal.

The fuel truck took a while in Alaska to get to us. It seemed it was a busy time of day, whatever day and time it might be. I hadn't bothered to reset my watch. I had gone through so many time zones in the last week that my body clock was totally out of whack.

Since we had to wait an hour, I got off the plane and walked around it to say I had been to Alaska.

Next to the taxiway apron, there was a little stream. If I had a pan, I would have panned for gold, to say I had done it in the Yukon. Where is the Yukon, anyway? I was getting punch drunk.

I managed to sleep some more on the trip down to Ontario. Once there, we had a charter fly us to the Forestry Service Station and, from there, a Jeep to Jackson House.

Mum and Dad were waiting for us. Mum took the two ladies in hand and showed them the rooms that had been prepared for them. We only intended to stay for two days, but we needed the rest and time to sort things out.

I was wide awake at this point. Not thinking clearly, but wide awake. While the ladies were cleaning up and changing clothes, I updated Mum and Dad on the situation.

I told them the only positive thing I saw out of this whole mess was that Empress Ping had finally realized that it had to be Haoran behind the killings. We no longer had to worry about due process. He was dead if she could find him.

In the meantime, I had to keep Ann and May-ling safe. We would fly to Spain, but not on my plane. It was too well known. We would take a charter out of LAX. It was a large enough airport that one more charter flight wouldn't be noticed.

We all sat down for dinner together. It was dinner time in California, even if my stomach said breakfast. The ladies looked much better after having some rest and a chance to clean up and put on fresh clothes.

Mary asked May-ling if she was an actual princess. May-ling told her she was. Mary replied it was a shame she was so old, or she could model for her collection.

From their confused looks, neither Ann nor May-ling had a clue about Mary's clothing line. The explanation got convoluted.

Mum finally broke in and explained that Mary had bit parts in my movies, which led to her doing TV and radio advertisements. Then there was "Feed the Puppies." After that, the t-shirts and the clothing line expanded to the Princess Collection.

From their looks, you could tell the two women were wondering what sort of madhouse they had entered.

It didn't help when Denny asked if he could take their pictures for his portfolio and maybe use them in a photo contest or an advertisement.

Ann asked Eddie what he did to earn a living.

"Mostly run errands for Mary and then blackmail her about not telling Mum what those errands were."

I think the two littles were in deep doo-doo.

The next day, I felt a little more put together. When I was going down for my morning run, I met May-ling. She was dressed to go running. I asked, and she confirmed that was her goal.

I told her she could run with me along the state park trails. I thought I would have to slow down and probably end the run early. How wrong I was. That girl had stamina and speed. She had to slow for me.

At least she couldn't bench press as much as I could, though she wasn't shabby.

I asked her if she played golf. She didn't. I told her my next stop was the Forestry Service station to hit a few balls. She asked if she could come along. I told her it would be my pleasure.

Sam had the driving range open, and I had a spare set of clubs stored there, so I hit a bucket of balls working my way through the clubs. May-ling asked if she could try.

I won't say I was happy when she whiffed her first swing. I was a little concerned that she might be Supergirl.

I taught her how to line the ball up, the proper position, and how to swing the club. Yes, I had to put my arms around her. There was nothing to it.

Sam came out and watched her start hitting the ball correctly.

"You better watch it, Rick. She will take your titles away from you."

May-ling asked, "What titles are those?"

I guess she knew nothing about me.

Sam was glad to explain that I was currently the best golfer in the world. He took great delight in telling her about the Grand Slam of golf and that I was the first who had done it since Bobby Jones.

What she found impressive was that we were both amateur golfers and hadn't turned professional.

"Why didn't you, Rick? I have heard professional golfers made a lot of money."

Where do you even start?

I gave her a condensed version of my finances, which were based on my inventions and the businesses I had founded.

"So that is how you were able to help China. You gave us the money."

"Empress Ping didn't publicize it, but I underwrote the revolution."

She gave me a considering look. I had no idea what she was considering.

Back at the house, Mum gave her and her mother a tour of Jackson House. The ladies agreed it was a nice little home. When compared to the Forbidden City, it was. Mum didn't show them the sub-basement. That was closely held.

That afternoon, the women went shopping for clothes appropriate for a ranch in Spain. I wanted to ask if they had bought shit kickers, but I knew I would be in a world of hurt if I did.

I took the opportunity to call Mr. Norman and asked that it be relayed to the empress that we would be flying to Spain tomorrow. Only after I hung up did I realize I was asking the queen of England to be my errand girl.

The next day, from the Forestry Service Station, I flew us down to LAX, where we boarded a chartered 707 for Madrid.

Poor Harold had to stay home this trip. He must have been in a tizzy about what I would wear. I had a carryall with several jeans outfits and one suit. I feared the airplane might be overweight with what the ladies had bought on Rodeo Drive.

I didn't even want to consider the cost of being over the luggage allowance.

Chapter 18

We had one refueling stop on the way to Spain. Even though we had first-class seating, I realized that having my own 707 had spoiled me for commercial travel.

The service was good, but not at my every whim. The food was good but not the top-shelf quality I was used to. I could go on for hours. Why, they wouldn't even let me fly the plane!

I didn't ask if I could fly it, though if I had blown my Duke of Hong Kong cover, they might have. I was Edward Butler, a young man on holiday.

Ann and May-ling were a mother and daughter named Margret and Sarah Johnson. I had seen their passports, though on the trip, we weren't sitting together or supposed to know each other.

I kept a watchful eye on them during the flight. They both kept a brave face, but you could tell something was wrong in their lives.

They were sitting together, but a young man behind May-ling decided he wanted to get to know her better. Since they both had aisle seats, he kept leaning forward and tried to talk to her.

She ignored him as much as she could and even was rude in telling him to go away. The young Spaniard must have felt he was god's gift to women and wouldn't take "go away" for an answer.

I was about to get up and have a talk with the *caballero*. Though I doubt he was a gentleman.

A stewardess asked May-ling if the man was bothering her. When she said yes, the guy was told to sit back and shut up or move back to coach.

I liked the stewardess's style.

The rest of the flight was quiet and uneventful.

From Madrid, we took a local flight. I had a car waiting for us at the airport, as I knew Alejandro's SEAT wouldn't hold us, much less the luggage.

When we passed the intersection of 902 and 44, the new truck stop came into view. I owned it in conjunction with some Spanish businessmen and Colonel Frade from Argentina. How we ended up on good terms was a mystery to me, but I wasn't going to second-guess it.

We drove down the long road to the main house. When Jackson House *España* came into view, the ladies were complimentary. It met their expectations for a *hacienda* in Spain.

I described the *estancia* to them and all its products, including olives, grapes, almonds, walnuts, cherries, apples, quinces, and many acres of wheat.

They thought this was a very rich country, being able to grow all these crops. When I told them how many people lived on the ranch, they thought it was a waste. Fifteen hundred people were nothing; there should be fifteen thousand.

China is China.

I had sent a telegram warning of our arrival, myself and two female guests. I didn't explain more, so they must have been very curious.

At any rate, Mrs. Echevarria, Alejandro, and Elisa were waiting along with Fra Tomas. I introduced everyone—the royals by their *noms de Guerre*. I always wanted to use that phrase.

Mrs. Echevarria caught on quickly. There was no hanky panky going on or *Juegos de Manos*, as she would say.

It took Fra Tomas longer. From how he looked at Ann, I thought he would have an interesting time at his next confession.

Mrs. Echevarria and Elisa took the ladies to their rooms so they could rest and freshen up. Why do women always freshen up after a long trip? All I wanted to do was to pee.

After Alejandro showed me my room and I changed clothes into more appropriate attire for a ranch, we met Fra Tomas on the front veranda. He was anxious to show me the improvements made to the school.

The outside and inside had been painted, along with cracks in the walls being repaired. New desks were in the single classroom, with many new textbooks. I felt the money I had donated had been well spent.

I chose not to notice that the church itself had similar repairs. I hadn't designated the funds for the church, but I hadn't forbidden it either.

The good Fra told me that the bishop still wanted to meet me. I bet he would. I didn't reply to the hint.

At dinner, Elisa recounted her experiences as a model for Mary's clothing line. She found it to be great fun. She once again apologized for thinking that I was short. I didn't take it any further.

Mrs. Echevarria gave a very concise update on the *estancia*'s progress. Things were going well. The workers' homes were repaired and upgraded as I requested.

Regarding the crops, the fields and orchards had all been reconditioned with the new machinery and the proper fertilizers applied. It wouldn't be until next year that we knew how successful the efforts were.

I told her that since it was precisely what we foresaw in our planning, it looked like we were on our way back to making this an *estancia* we could be proud of.

I noted that it appeared the only place that hadn't had a lot of money spent on it was this *hacienda*. She replied that it was the leader's duty to see to their people first, and then, if anything were left over, they could enjoy the fruits of the labor.

You could see that May-ling approved of this attitude. She would be a fine ruler of China when her turn came. I hoped it wouldn't be for many years.

The next day, we took a horseback tour of the *estancia*. It was beautiful now that fences had been repaired and fields reconditioned. Almost all of the machinery that I saw was brand new.

I asked Mrs. Echevarria how many machines had to be replaced, and she told me almost all of them. She looked afraid for a moment as though I would chastise her for that.

"Good. I'm glad to see that you aren't being penny-wise and pound-foolish. As things progress, you should have a plan to replace the machinery regularly. Farming is hard on the machines."

"A breakdown at the wrong time of the season can cause a lot of problems."

That gave me a thought.

"Do we have a maintenance man with helpers to keep them in the best condition?"

"The crews look after their machines."

"An American practice is to have a maintenance shop with qualified repairmen performing preventative maintenance and repairs.

"It is a separate facility with the tools they need, along with the manuals on all of the equipment. They will also keep spare parts for those needing frequent replacement or having long lead times. This requires an extensive record-keeping system.

"I will have one of my American companies send an expert over to help you get set up."

Mrs. Echevarria exclaimed, "You would do that for us?"

"It is in my best interest. I want a successful *estancia* that will earn us all a living rather than trying to make money on the cheap."

We spent the next few days doing very little. I would get my run in in the morning. Sometimes, May-ling and I would arrive at the front of the house at the same time and run together.

It was never planned and only happened three days out of seven. Other times, we met, with me coming back and her going out.

Fra Tomas had me talk to the students at the one-room schoolhouse one day. I told them if their grades were good enough to get them into a university, I would pay for all their schooling if they maintained a C average.

You would have thought I was St. Michael descending from Heaven.

It was when I discovered that the school had no accreditation, either the school or Fra Tomas as a teacher. I had no option at that point but to make phone calls.

With the help of the British Embassy, I was put into contact with the Spanish Minister of Education. I explained my problem. From there, it became a mere matter of money.

I had to pay for six certified teachers—one for every two grades. Also, enlarge the number of school rooms. Plus, have all students tested to determine their appropriate grade level.

All those requirements floored me, but when I found out what the cost would be, it wasn't that great. The most significant cost would be adding to the current school building.

None of these items had been completed when it was time for us to fly to China for the funeral.

We took a charter with Harold on board to Madrid, where my plane was waiting. This time, we flew to Cairo for refueling, then onto Bombay. After that, it was straight through to Beijing.

Chapter 19

The flight was long, and the situation stressed everyone. Each of the ladies sat alone with their thoughts. There was no use in trying to lighten their moods, as occasional tears would run down their cheeks.

Anything I tried would seem to be a crass attempt to lessen the grief of their son and brother's death. That, on top of the recent death of the husband and father, was a heavy burden.

Add to that, May-ling was now a walking target. I made a personal vow to track down that SOB Haoran and kill him. While we had no direct links to him, he was the only one who would benefit from these deaths.

If I were wrong about him, it would be a shame. I didn't like him anyway. I stopped my thoughts in their tracks. What was I turning into? I wasn't one to kill on a whim. This left me sitting by myself, looking introspective for the rest of the flight.

After enough hours had gone by, we had to eat. The ladies picked at their food. I ate mine, not with gusto, but with a healthy appetite. I guess even potential mass murderers get hungry.

There was no talk at the dinner table, only polite remarks like, "Pass the salt, please." After dinner, we returned to our seats and our solitary thoughts.

I finally put it together that thoughts weren't actions. So, I didn't care for Haoran and wouldn't cry if he died. That was separate from his trying to kill his way to the Chinese throne.

I also realized that if I acted without more evidence, I was crossing a line that could never be uncrossed. So, I modified my vow to find evidence that he had ordered the killings. Then I would track down and shoot the son of a bitch.

That thought cheered me up. Now, the question was how to obtain the evidence. At this point, I had to rely on the CIA investigators. These were primarily retired CIA agents in China.

I had no way of knowing if they were even qualified to perform the investigation. Being a spy in place had to be different than being a police detective. I made a mental note to ask JFK if he had any idea of the investigative team's background.

We finally landed in Beijing. A whole army convoy was waiting to take us to the Forbidden City. We rode in an armored car. It was one of many vehicles in the parade, including tanks. We weren't in the lead or the middle; it was hoped we would be lost in the shuffle.

Halfway there, we were just entering the city proper when an anti-tank missile hit the middle-armored car.

I didn't see it but heard two tanks firing. There would be no one to question. The convoy picked up speed. They would have been run over if anyone had been in the street.

At the Forbidden City, we were immediately taken to an inner building different from any I had seen before. It was a solid construction that looked like a fortress.

Inside, we descended in an elevator. It was a long way down, but there were no indicators of floors along the way.

At the bottom, our accompanying bodyguards were turned aside. It was only the three of us that were allowed to proceed. We were escorted to another room where the empress waited.

There were hugs between the ladies, and many tears were shed. I stood there awkwardly, not knowing what to do.

The empress turned to me and thanked me for bringing her daughter-in-law and granddaughter safely home.

She then clapped her hands, and when a servant appeared, she asked that tea be served. By this time, I had a chance to look around. This room could be a reception room for an empress. On second thought, that is precisely what it was.

I think I figured out where we were.

"Is this the atomic war bomb shelter and command post?"

"Yes, it is."

"Then you are safe from outside attacks, but what about infiltration or corruption?"

"Everyone down here has been screened. Their families are all intact and have been moved to a safe army base for the duration."

I let it go at that. Hidden bank accounts and favorite mistresses could be a weak spot, but since there was no way to track all this down quickly, it was better left unsaid than create more stress.

I asked if I could make an international call from here. I was taken to the largest communication center I had ever been in. I think if they had phones there, you could call the moon.

I was put through to the White House in record time. They were using the identification words I had been provided. I was connected to the chief of staff, who in turn put the president on the line.

"Mr. President, I have some concerns about the abilities of the Chinese investigators. Being a spy and a detective are not the same. They require different skill sets."

"We are way ahead of you, Rick. Each of our Chinese operatives has been teamed up with an FBI agent to direct them. The only problem we have is communication. We have to be careful not to expose their identities."

"Why haven't you pulled them out of China before?"

"I'm told that these stay-behinds have extended families that would be at risk if they left the country."

"None of these are current agents, are they? They only worked against the communists?"

"That is correct."

"What if I asked the empress to protect them, as they have never worked against her? That would allow more effective communication."

"That would help."

"I will check right now; can we hold this line open?"

"From this end, yes."

I asked the officer in charge if this line could be held open. He nodded yes. I hoped he understood my broken Mandarin.

My escort took me back to the empress, where I quickly explained the situation. She gave her consent to my proposal and told me that a pardon would be issued immediately to each of the agents for past actions against the communists.

Any future actions would be a death sentence. I hoped they were truly retired.

Returning to the phone, I was put back on with the president. He said a list would be quickly convoyed from the embassy to the empress. He was putting all these lives at risk by trusting the empress.

If they were betrayed, it would do lasting harm to a relationship that was off to a good start. That thought hadn't occurred to me. I was playing dice with a lot of lives. I had better not be wrong.

Just before we were leaving for the wake, I was told the list of agents had been received and that pardons were being delivered. That was a relief, to say the least. I don't chew my nails, but I almost took it up while waiting.

I now knew we were three hundred feet down in bedrock. I timed the elevator ride at a minute and a half. I did that to keep my mind occupied as we were about to enter a large crowd.

It turned out that we didn't. The wake was arranged with us in a room with Chun-Chieh's casket. There were pictures and candles. People were escorted in to pay their respects after going through a security screening.

The empress sat on a small throne, with Ann and May-ling seated on either side of her. There was a lattice screen beside them and behind them. I suspected it was so they could make a quick exit to safety.

I was still nervous and viewed every group as potentially hostile. I would pick the order in which I would try to take down any aggressors.

After an hour of this, I was a nervous wreck. That, plus the adrenaline I had generated at the start was wearing off, so I was tired to the bone. The many time zones we had crossed didn't help.

That was when disaster almost struck. Even in my tired condition, one man in the next group stood out. His clothes weren't similar to the rest of the group's, and he stood aside from them.

As they were letting ten people at a time in, I figured he was an odd man out and let in to make up the numbers.

While I was putting these thoughts together, he lunged towards the empress. I dived after him in an American-style football tackle. I hadn't played football in high school, and now it showed.

I was able to grab one of his legs, but he slipped free. It didn't help him, as he was shot down by guards hidden behind the screens. At the same time, some mechanical device slid the ladies and the thrones they were sitting on behind the side screens.

The assassin was removed roughly from the room, and a clean-up crew came in. You would never have known what had happened in less than five minutes.

There were many photographs taken before anything was disturbed.

The other people in the assassin's group were all taken aside. They would be questioned and held until the wake was over. Not that they were suspects, but by keeping them from going back out, the viewing could continue.

Chapter 20

After the wake, the family got together. This time, I changed into comfortable clothes. When I entered the room, seeing how the family had shrunk since the last event was sad.

It was only one less person, but Chun-Chieh filled the room with his outgoing personality. Now, the room seemed to shrink in size, even though it was the same one.

This was the first time I could have a real conversation with Empress Ping. Once more, she thanked me for my actions in protecting her family.

Since I missed the tackle, I didn't think thanks were in order, but I guessed it was the thought that counted. I didn't express these thoughts but replied simply, "I see it as my duty to try when possible."

I continued, "What is the mood of the Chinese population these days?"

"The mood here and in the other large cities is ugly. The countryside doesn't hear of these events until much later."

"What is the mood ugly about?"

"There are several different factions. The largest is mine, pro-empress; they are happy with the country's direction. Then there are the old hardline communists. They want a return to communism.

"The hardliners are doing us a favor by identifying themselves. We are collecting names, and they will be rounded up as a group.

"The most troubling group are those that want a strong emperor rather than a weak woman. They propose that Haoran be made the crown prince instead of May-ling being next.

"We are picking these up and questioning them to find links back to Haoran.

"Then there are other factions that want many different things. One of them wants China to divide into many different states so they may live in peace."

I commented, "And I bet they have a peaceful warlord to run each of those countries."

"You are beginning to understand China."

"How is the absorption of Siberia going?"

I asked because Siberia now had a special place in my heart. A hard, frozen place in my heart.

We continued our talk for a while as we drank another cup of tea. I had to introduce Coca-Cola to the Chinese. It was strange that they didn't have it.

Rumor had it one of the secret ingredients in the Coke formula was from a berry that only grew in China. The Coca-Cola Company was smuggling it to the US. I have no idea if this was true or not. It made a good story.

I must have made a face when I sipped my latest cup of tea because May-ling handed me another cup, saying, "Try this blend; it is smoother."

It was much smoother and carbonated. If I didn't know better, I would swear it was Coke. When she winked at me, I knew it was. I thought I was in love.

I buried that thought. I had been in love too often recently, and it had gotten me nowhere.

While this byplay was occurring, an agent came in and presented a file to Empress Ping. She browsed through it and then made an announcement.

"The man who attempted the assassination earlier this evening has given us a name. We, in turn, shared that name with the former anti-communist agents. One of them recognized that name. Their homes and offices are being raided as we speak."

She then turned to May-ling and told her, "I would love to have one of your Cokes."

That brought a little laughter to the sad group. Even amid death, life would go on. I read that somewhere.

At breakfast in the empress's quarters, we were given an update on the raid carried out last night.

A link was found with a company that Haoran owned. A raid was being carried out currently on that company.

We retired to our rooms to get dressed for the funeral. This time, I chose to wear my military uniform with all my medals. I did wear the black armband.

I wanted to make a statement that while I was in mourning, I was prepared to act. When the empress saw me, she nodded in appreciation.

The funeral went off on time. Events didn't seem so strange to me since this was my second time around in a month.

I kept scanning the crowd, but since every other one was a soldier, I didn't think there would be any trouble. I didn't realize it then, but international news outlets were present.

They filmed me in my uniform against a backdrop of the many soldiers. It made it appear that I was in charge of the Chinese army. I didn't know about it until the next day when Mr. Norman called me and asked if I needed new uniforms.

When I questioned him, he told me what was being reported. In the stories that came out, my entire history was being brought to light. It made me sound like some international guy running things behind the scenes.

Just what I needed. I wondered if I hitchhiked from California to Ohio, I could rewind the whole thing.

These events were for later. The already clean tomb was opened during the funeral, and the late Chun-Chieh was interred. He had told me once that he had never thought he would be the emperor of China. Sadly, he was correct.

After the gifts were burned and envelopes handed out, still using M&Ms, and red threads kept repelling evil spirits and ghosts, we returned to the empress's chambers.

She asked me to take Ann and May-ling out of the country again to keep them safe while Haoran was tracked down.

It was official now: the company doing business with Haoran had his chief of security on their board of directors. He had used the company as a cutout to hire the assassin.

They had captured him at his home, and he confessed. I asked what would happen to him. The reply was, "Nothing, he didn't survive the interrogation."

China was still China.

We returned to the airport in reverse of the convoy trip in, but this time, no one tried to kill us. My 707 had been surrounded by troops the whole time it had been on the ground.

The crew had all stayed on the plane. It had been refueled and was ready to go. We boarded and once more got out of Dodge.

We flew to Hong Kong, where troops once more surrounded the plane. The only ground people allowed near was the refueling truck, and they were watched carefully. I hoped it wouldn't come to gunfire with all that JP1A around.

A man I recognized from the governor's office knocked on the aircraft door. He had a messenger bag for me. It had hundreds of messages for me, most looking like they concerned JE.

One of them caught my interest because it had come from Spain. As soon as we took off again after a brief ground stay, I opened it.

It was an update on my efforts to create an accredited school at the *Estancia*. Fra Tomas was pleased to inform me that Mrs. Echevarria had quotes from contractors to build the new schoolhouse and convert the old school building to housing for the nuns who were coming to be teachers.

Why did I feel used? I sighed and decided that I had to work within the system and that I was getting what I wanted. I just hadn't planned on being a supporter of the Catholic Church. Next, they would want me to convert.

May-ling had heard my sigh. I suspect the pilots up front heard it. When I explained it to her, she laughed. Her first real laugh in days.

"You are too used to having your way with everything. Learn to work with what you have rather than what you want."

Now, I thought that was unfair, as I thought that was how I operated. However, I was not going to get into an argument with her. Seeing her smile disappear wasn't worth being right.

Based on that, I drafted a return reply thanking the good father and asking him to help Mrs. Echevarria keep things moving.

See? I can work within a system.

Another was from Don Pearson, telling me he had dispatched a team to Spain to set up a maintenance program on the ranch. They were prepared to oversee putting up a building, ordering machinery, and stocking spare parts.

On a side note, he told me this was an excellent opportunity to reward some good maintenance staff. They viewed it as a vacation in Spain and had volunteered to rotate people in and out to hire and train workers. By the way, could I make sure there was housing for them and any families they brought with them?

So maybe it wasn't only the Catholics who were using me.

Chapter 21

I drafted a message back to Don that there would be room for visiting families. I also prepared a message to Mrs. Echevarria asking her to ensure the empty workers' cottages were updated and cleaned, as the maintenance trainers would likely have their families with them.

After thinking for a moment, I also suggested she buy at least one van and two more cars for transportation to and from the airport. Then there was the problem of food and things for the families to do.

I asked her to treat it like a dude ranch, though she didn't have to have a rodeo or bullfights. This was getting more complicated all the time. I added a note for her to find out if any American-trained doctors were in the area. If so, we should have them on call. Maybe we could run a clinic at the *estancia*.

What was I getting into? Maybe I should revisit my thinking about an even larger ranch in the Australian outback.

Once more, I must have sighed loudly, and May-ling heard me. She raised an eyebrow, but I didn't bite. I had about enough second-guessing for the day.

The next batch of mail was from JE. It was mostly about the IC Chips. We had our first licensing agreement in place with a defense contractor. They were designing ground-to-air missiles for the US Air Force and needed a lightweight solution for their electronics package.

If ours worked correctly, they would more than meet their requirements. The test units we provided worked as advertised, so I didn't see any reason full production wouldn't.

There were also exploratory talks with IBM about providing chips for a computer that would sit on a desktop for office use. I could see them migrating to the home in short order.

In this case, there was a hold-up because of software. They needed a user-friendly operating system because not everyone was a programmer. Without this system, the user would be limited.

IBM had been caught flatfooted on this deal. They didn't plan to have a desktop computer until the 1980s. That is what their development people had told them.

With the advent of our IC Chips, it was the first one to market wins. I did write a note to Jim Williamson asking him to see if any startup companies had the capabilities.

Maybe we could back them for a percentage of the business.

There were normal updates on the business. Dockworkers were striking in Sydney. Popeye was on his way to straighten it out.

Mark Downing wanted to expand DF once more. My reply told him to proceed. He also told me that Anna Romanov would renovate several bathrooms in the White House.

I just hoped she and Jackie didn't meet up.

In other news, Queen Elizabeth invited May-ling and her mother to stay at one of the royal residences. I thought that was an excellent idea but wanted to cut our trail. I had an idea I wanted to pass by Mum.

After another long flight in which my logbook kept adding up, I now had almost a thousand hours on the 707. I would have to take a check ride someday to get my ticket punched.

When we finally landed in Ontario and returned to Jackson House, I asked Mum if we still owned the house in Bellefontaine. We did, and it wasn't occupied.

She thought my plan was a good one. We would fly into Dayton and stay in Bellefontaine for a week, making no real effort to hide. We would then take a limo to Cleveland and fly a charter to Ontario, Canada. From Ontario, another charter went to London; from there, we went wherever the queen directed us.

After seeing Ann and her daughter to safety, I would go somewhere else, maybe Australia—anything to confuse the trail.

When Dad got home, we shared it with him. He thought it was a great idea. He tried to picture Chinese agents sneaking around the town. He kept laughing when he thought of it. In small-town Ohio, they would stick out like a sore thumb.

We rested for a night. We invited the ladies to join in on a family game of Monopoly. They did. Mary and May-ling teamed up and took us all to the cleaners. They kept whispering to each other during the game. Mary couldn't get me in any trouble, could she? I would have felt better if they didn't keep looking at me and giggling.

The next morning, we flew to Dayton where a limo was waiting. Dad had called his realty office in Bellefontaine and had them check the house out and make sure it was clean and the utilities turned on.

It was strange going into my old bedroom. Nothing had changed. Well, the bed was made, but that was it. I was never into posters, but my old favorite books were spread everywhere.

There were a few ribbons from my high school golf outings and pictures from the various dances that I went to. May-ling thought my prom picture was cute.

I made two phone calls. The first was to the Bellefontaine Police Department. I was lucky as the new police chief, Chief Woodruff, answered the phone. He remembered me.

I told him I was in town for a week and would be out and about with several women. One was Chinese, the other her English mother. He should be aware the Chinese girl was May-ling Ping, the heir apparent to the Chinese throne.

Talk about dead silence on the other end. I asked him if there were any reports of Chinese men showing up in town, to let us know. We would leave immediately.

I could tell he would rather have a tooth pulled without Novocain rather than go through this, but he said they would keep a lookout, and he would have extra patrols pass by the house.

My next call was to George Weaver. I asked George if he was interested in a story that would give him an international byline. Of course, he said no.

What he really said was that he was on his way.

I intended to talk to George but asked the women if they wanted to. They did.

When George arrived and I made the introductions, I thought he would wet himself. He managed to control his excitement and performed a professional interview.

The ladies told him of the attempted assassination attempts, giving me more credit than I was due. They next filled him in on our journeys around the world. As a good reporter, he tried to find out what was next but didn't press the issue. It may have had something to do with when I told him, "We can tell you, but then I would have to kill you."

I was joking; it was more like kidding on the square. I asked him if he could embargo his story until after we were gone. I thought he would resist.

Instead, he was excited. He could see the first paragraph stating the story had been embargoed at the request of the future empress of China.

Sometimes, the devil makes you do things. While he was talking to the ladies, I called the White House. When JFK came on, I told him what I needed. He thought it was a keen idea.

I handed the phone to George and told him it was for him. This time, I swear I saw a drop of pee stain his pants when the president of the United States asked him to embargo the story.

All work and no play makes Rick a dull boy.

After he hung up, George told me he didn't know if he loved or hated me.

May-ling spoke up quickly and said, "Rick is very loveable."

She also blushed as she said it and ran out of the room. I think she just said what popped into her head and wasn't serious.

Her mother had a slight smile.

The next day, we walked down to Don's Hamburgers for lunch. It was a Saturday, so school was out. A typical March day, it was blustery, but we had found coats in the hall closet that fit.

At Don's, there were kids that I recognized as being two or three grades behind me. When we walked in, all conversation stopped.

A boy who looked familiar spoke up, "Are you Rick Jackson?"

"Yes, I am."

"Oh wow, wait until I tell my parents I met you! You are a legend around here."

By this time, we had found an empty booth and sat down. I could see that this may not have been the best idea I could have had, but we were here, and we were hungry.

A waitress came to our table. This was new; in the old days, we had to go to the counter and place our order—the old days, four years ago.

Chapter 22

I finally put it together that the kid I had come up to us was Tom Morton's younger brother, Bob.

After we ordered, I waved Bob over to our table. It was strange; everyone in the restaurant was watching us. As Bob was coming over, I heard one kid say to another. "She is Chinese. I just know it."

The other kid said, "No way, China is on the other side of the world."

Bob arrived at our table, and I invited him to sit down. His friends sitting at the counter were all turned and staring at us. Was I ever like that?

I briefly introduced Ann and May-ling. He nodded his head shyly to them.

"How is Tom these days?"

"He's going to Ohio State. He is doing okay, but from what I hear Mom and Dad say, he is enjoying the partying too much."

"That's a shame. If you see him, tell him I told him to straighten up and fly right."

His eyes widened as he said, "Okay, can I tell my parents you said that?"

"Certainly."

May-ling couldn't keep her mouth shut.

"Is Rick a big deal around here?"

"The biggest! When he won the golf Grand Slam, it was great. Now he is running around with the crown princess of China!"

You could see it in his eyes when the coin dropped.

"That's you; isn't it?"

"Yes."

"Are guys going to come here and try to kill you?"

I told him, "I hope not, at least not until after I finish my cheeseburgers."

Ann spoke up for the first time.

"We will be gone from here soon. They won't catch up with us, so Bellefontaine is safe."

That had to be the moment when Chief Woodruff entered the restaurant and made a beeline toward our table.

"I just got a call from the FBI. They have agents on the way, but they want you to go to the airbase. A load of Chinese just left the Dayton airport heading towards Springfield."

"Thanks, Chief. Eat up, ladies."

We quickly finished our food and rode back to my house in a police cruiser. Before we left the restaurant, I made an announcement.

"Sorry to eat and run. I had hoped to stay longer, but the bad guys have found us. Tell everyone I said hi."

We hadn't unpacked yet, so it was easy to grab our clothes and go. The waiting police car took us out to the airbase.

When we reached the front gate, one of the airmen got on the phone and announced that Cowboy had arrived.

As we walked to the Base Commander's office, May-ling asked what all that was about. I replied in a very off-handed way, "That is a holdover from when I saved the US from the Soviets trying to drop hydrogen bombs on us."

That was fun; I could see her confusion. Was I lying?

We were escorted right in when we arrived at the commander's office.

It was the same commander who had relieved Colonel, now General Hawthorne. He shook my hand and gave a half-bow to the ladies.

"It has been a long time, Rick."

"A lot of the water over the dam since then."

"Yeah, I bet the Soviets still regret that stunt they pulled. Little did they know that night was going to be their downfall."

"They started it."

"And you finished it. Did you know there is a memorial stone out back with the dates of the incursion inscribed? It doesn't say anything else, just the dates."

"Who had that put up?

"President Eisenhower. He couldn't give you public recognition but wanted something done. If you dig it up, on the bottom side is your name. Weirdest memorial I have ever heard of."

"I have always liked Ike. I even have a button that says so."

The commander just shook his head.

"I'm not supposed to talk to any strange women that may show up here so that I may deny any involvement with them."

"Then I won't introduce Crown Princess May-ling or her mother, the Dowager Ann."

"It was nice not to have met them."

The two ladies stood there amazed.

"If the colonel is questioned later and he is careful with his answers, he will not have to tell them you have been on an American military base."

"Won't they just beat it out of him?"

"America is America, like China is China; no, they won't."

The colonel's phone rang. It was the front gate, and the FBI was here. As fate would have it, I recognized both of them when they entered the office.

They were the same two agents who, on the day of the incursion, told me I was just trying to be a hero again, that I hadn't seen anything.

They remembered me, too. I decided to let it go. This situation spoke for itself.

"We are ready to take you wherever you want."

"The Cleveland airport; we have a charter flight waiting for us."

They didn't groan. I had just told them they had another five hours of driving and then three more to get back to Columbus, just in time to go to work.

Sometimes, things in life work out.

As we were leaving, Chief Woodruff, who had been sitting in his cruiser, waved us over.

"A report just came over the radio that a carload of Chinese just passed the state patrol office on 68."

"Can they be slowed down?"

"The wing tire salesmen have pulled them over for speeding."

"Thank the state police for me."

"Will do. Also, I'm pretty certain they will be speeding when they go through the Mary Fulton school zone."

"Thanks, Chief. I owe you. Now we have to use this head start."

We settled in for the long ride to Cleveland. Both of the ladies slept most of the way there. I sat there with many and no thoughts going through my mind.

They centered around how I got in this pickle and what was next. I managed to nod off.

At Cleveland, there was a flight waiting for us. We were barely out of the car, and it was wheels up. In Canada, we all presented diplomatic passports and let it be known we were in transit.

This was reinforced by the 707 that taxied up next to our small charter plane.

The plane had no decorations—just the tail number.

The tail number meant nothing to me. We boarded the aircraft, and I was home, or at least my home away from home. It was my aircraft; someone had thought to have the fancy paint job removed from my jet.

I didn't know how they were able to have a new tail number assigned. When I asked the chief pilot, he told me it was a privilege given to Queen's Messenger Flight One.

The plane had been fueled and catered, so we left for our short hop across the Atlantic—a short hop compared to the Pacific crossings we had made.

Both women knew their way around and headed for my bedroom. That was okay because I headed to the hold for one of the little sleeper cabins there.

That was when I found out that even Harold was on board. At least I would have clothes to wear.

We landed in Aberdeen and were driven to Balmoral in a limo with tinted windows. This was to be our home for the next while.

I had read that this is where Victoria and her faithful servant, John Brown, spent much of their time. There were many rumors about them, but I consider them the ravings of jealous people who didn't have any true friendships.

Even if they did, get over it; they are both long gone.

Balmoral can best be described as comfortable. Though described as a castle, it was built as a home, not a defensive work. Prince Albert had torn down the original castle after building the new home. No cold drafts here.

While there, I was able along with the others to tour the flower gardens, including the Garden Cottage for Victoria's children, Baile-na-Coille for her Highland servant, John Brown, and Karim Cottage for her Indian Secretary, the Munshi Abdul Karim.

The entire estate of fifty thousand acres, surrounded by the Cairngorms National Park, is privately owned by the royal family. There would be no stray Chinese here even if they found out where we were.

We were settled into large suites of rooms for our stay. Mine was so large you could park a car in the bedroom.

On my first morning there, Harold won me forever. He had a kilt in the Jackson tartan. He also had all the other gear with it.

I wanted to wear it to breakfast, but he talked me out of it. There was a private event with the royal family this weekend, and I should save it for then. He was correct, as usual.

Chapter 23

We settled in at Balmoral. It is beautiful. The climate is pleasant, and the land surrounding it is scenic. Most of all, we could move around without looking over our shoulders.

Friday, the royal family came to visit. They had ridden their train to Edinburgh, and then a caravan accompanied them to Balmoral.

I dressed for dinner in my new kilt with the Jackson tartan. Harold helped me dress. I learned once more that a valet could sometimes be a lifesaver.

The plaid was typically Scottish, with red being the dominant color, with black and navy-blue stripes.

He helped me into a white collared button-down shirt with cuffs. I used my solid gold cufflinks with my coat of arms. Next, he positioned my kilt to the correct height at the waist and knees.

I then donned my socks with garters and flashes in the Jackson colors. The brogues were tied in the high front style.

He made certain that my kilt pin with my Hong Kong coat of arms was in the correct place to keep the kilt from flapping open at the wrong moment.

My sporran had the Jackson coat of arms on the front. My small *sgian dubh* was in my right sock. The emblem on its haft matched the kilt pin.

Lastly, I put on the vest and then the jacket, both dark blue. I had a tam in the colors but elected not to wear it in the house.

As to underwear, it's none of your business.

I must say, I looked quite spiffy.

When I entered the anteroom to the dining room where we were gathering for dinner, all eyes turned to me. You could have heard a pin drop; they were in such awe.

At least no one snickered.

The queen saved the occasion.

"Duke Richard, you look finely dressed for dinner suitably. Some of these other gentlemen should pay attention."

Since the only other gentlemen dining were husband and son, I thought she was going too far. She had saved me from ridicule, at least from May-ling, who had to put her hand in front of her mouth.

Her mother Ann saw nothing wrong with what I was wearing. It was telling that the wait staff approved of my attire, as they were deferential in their treatment. I have never heard so many "Your Graces." They were only outdone by "Your Majesty."

Prince Phillip was a real brick about things. He made a point of complimenting my turnout and then describing his first time wearing his. He said I was blessed since I didn't have knobby knees like most Scots.

Other than May-ling looking like she would burst into laughter whenever she looked at me, dinner was lovely.

I was seated across from the queen, with Phillip on one side and May-ling on the other.

The queen kept up a lively conversation with May-ling. You could tell she was taking her measure. I was sitting between Ann and Princess Anne.

The princess was not interested in talking to an old guy like me, though she did want to know if I had any advance knowledge of Mary's next collection release. When I didn't, she lost interest.

The Dowager Ann spent her time listening to the conversation across the table. I could understand her wanting to know how her daughter was faring, so let her be.

It was not an exciting dinner, but the food was good.

The following day, I was awoken by the most ungodly sound on earth. Bagpipes.

I rose and performed my morning rituals and then dressed to go for a run right after I tracked the piper down and killed him.

A coffee service was set up outside of my room, so I delayed the planned murder to enjoy a cup. Two cups later, I decided that going to the headsman wasn't worth killing the piper.

He was safe for another day as I started my run. It was a beautiful day for running. The temperature was just right, and the sun was shining. A trail headed towards some woods, so I took that.

On my way, I passed a shooting and an archery range, so I knew where I would spend time. I was making mental notes about this place for when I established my country retreat.

They had over a hundred years to get it right, so why try to reinvent the castle?

The royals departed Sunday, so we had time to ourselves. I soon developed a daily routine of using the ranges. There was a gillie in charge of them who had a stock of weapons that made me drool.

The longbow he loaned me was a work of art. He told me they didn't know its provenance, but it had been here since day one—almost a hundred years.

I swear I couldn't miss the target with it. I wondered if I could pinch it but realized that would be poor repayment for the hospitality. It did make me want to start a search for another bow like it.

Ann and May-ling would watch me at times. May-ling even asked if she could try my bow. I handed the six-and-a-half-foot-long bow to her, knowing full well that the one-hundred-and-fifty-pound draw weight was far beyond her.

It was fun watching her struggle for a minute. Snicker at my kilt, will you?

Things were different at the shooting range. I wasn't that proficient with firearms. I could point and pull the trigger slowly. Well, that is unless the other guy was shooting at me. Then it was fire away.

I suppose that is why so many shots are missed in gun battles. When the other guy is shooting at you, there is no time to aim; just pull the trigger and be surprised by the weapon firing.

The gillie in charge of the range walked me through rifles, shotguns, and handguns. I fired off hundreds of rounds. I thought I was getting pretty good.

Then May-ling came along. Once more, she borrowed my weapon, a handgun, and wasted the target. She also blew my theory about aiming out of the water as she pulled the trigger as fast as possible.

The recoil would draw the pistol up, but she had it back down faster than I could see. She blew the center out of the target.

I knew when I was beaten and complimented her. She told me that her father had insisted she become proficient with firearms, starting when she was six years old. She had fired tens of thousands of rounds in her life.

We did go horseback riding several times. She had a good seat. That is, she rode well. I wasn't thinking of other things.

We talked about our futures. She had to abandon her school plans as she would never be safe in an uncontrolled public setting. This was even after Haoran was captured.

I asked her about who she saw as a future husband. This was more of idle curiosity, as I knew I would never be eligible. Heck, I didn't even know her that well.

She told me that her husband would probably be picked out by her mother and grandmother. He would be a high-ranking Chinese, as they didn't have the traditions of the Europeans in bringing royalty in from other countries.

She seemed fine with that thought, and I had no interest, so I let it go. We continued to enjoy our ride together, sharing this wonderful countryside.

We received an update on Haoran, and it wasn't good. He appeared to have disappeared off the face of the earth. Like us, he had found a haven.

At least we were in a position of being able to communicate with our families. Saint Patrick's Day came and went—the staff celebrated by wearing orange.

I listened to Ann explain the holiday to her daughter. She agreed that any man who could chase snakes out of a country should be a saint.

I received updates on my businesses regularly. I was even given an office to work out of. This settled life was wonderful. I worked, ran, or practiced weapons when I wanted.

There was even an expert in unarmed combat available. All I can say is that I was rusty. He knocked the rust off and about a yard of my skin.

When we practiced, we only wore tight pants. Barefoot and shirtless, we went at it. We started drawing a crowd—mostly the young ladies who worked on the estate.

The first time May-ling saw my fans, she was a little snippy, but her mum had words with her, and she kept quiet after that. Tightlipped but quiet.

As for me, I appreciated the pretty young ladies. They took to flirting in the hallway with me. One even went so far as to deliver me a cup of hot chocolate at bedtime. Enough said.

Chapter 24

Our days at Balmoral can be described as idyllic. My family even came over for a week. The kids thought it was great because it got them out of school.

Denny spent his time taking pictures of the castle and its environs, or snaps, as the locals called them.

He became popular with the young ladies of the staff, and he freely took pictures and had them developed locally. I don't know if he got served late-night hot chocolate, and I didn't want to know.

I did have an embarrassing, for me anyway, conversation with Dad. The box of condoms he had given me several years ago when I went to Hollywood was now exhausted.

Where could I get more? He told me a good valet would take care of that problem. Just leave the empty box where Harold would see it, and a full one would appear.

I did, and it did. Wonderful.

I did ask Dad about Denny. He told me that Denny was on the verge, and he would take care of it.

That was good because I still remember Mum's horrid threats if I made her a grandmum too early.

For some reason, during the conversation, Dad asked how I was getting along with May-ling. I told him she was okay, and we were getting to be friends.

"Why do you ask, Dad?"

"Just wondered; you two seem to spend a lot of time together."

"That's just circumstances. We will both be going in different directions in life."

"Total change of subject. Have you kept up with the new space program?"

"A little bit. It is exciting, but this new NASA is already becoming a bureaucracy."

"How would you speed it up?"

"They appear to be doing most things linearly."

"They are trying to get a man in orbit, which is good, but they should be building moon habitats, so when they land, they can stay. They are working on a manned mission, but it is there and back.

"There are no plans to create an enormous stockpile in space to support a permanent outpost on the moon.

"Furthermore, this drive to declare no national or private ownership of any portion of the moon or other planets is ridiculous. It removes all incentives for private enterprises to do anything other than to make a profit off supplying services to the government. It is being argued in the halls of the UN, but I would have it a done deal before they can act."

"What would you do?"

"Set up my own mission and be damned to them!"

"Those are pretty strong words and could cost you a lot if you tried to carry it through."

"Dad, I'm rolling in money, and it keeps coming in. Until just now, I didn't know what to do with it."

"How can you even start such a project?"

"That part, I know. I will hire people and give them my objectives, and they will develop a plan to meet them. Once we have a plan in place, we will hire people to work it."

"Who can develop such a plan?

"The expression, 'Amateurs study tactics, armchair generals study strategy, but professionals study logistics,' is attributed to Omar Bradley from lessons learned in the Spanish-American and World Wars. I would have a military group take the first look at logistics after defining the mission."

"Who will define the mission?"

"I will."

"Rick, you could be throwing away millions of dollars."

"Before it is over, it will be billions."

"Where will you base your efforts?"

"Not in America. The government will not want any competition at this point."

"Then where?"

"My first thought is China. That would serve several purposes. I need to help China build an internal economy, so they don't lower the rest of the world's economies, and it has the natural resources needed. I don't know if they have the intellectual power the project would require."

"It sounds like you have a lot of thinking to do. Don't be afraid to say you can't do it. Don't let pride lead to your downfall."

"I think it can be done, and now that the Soviet Union's space program has collapsed, the Americans will not have the pressure to get to the moon first. They will start playing games with their government agencies, and we can get ahead of them."

"Who will you talk to first?"

"Queen Elizabeth. The British military is used to providing logistics throughout the entire world. They will be my first stop."

Actually, it was Mr. Norman who was my first stop. I had to explain to him why I needed to speak to the queen. Not even my status as a godson and duke allowed me unfettered access to Her Majesty.

I had to make a trip to London to talk to the queen. It was done on the quiet. When I explained my grandiose idea, she smiled.

"You have never thought small, have you?"

"I guess not. Things just seem to follow one after the other."

"I will put you in touch with General Booth, who oversees logistics for all British armed forces. He will be able to get you going in the right direction. Have you talked to Empress Ping about this?"

"Not yet, Your Majesty."

"Let me make the first approach. I think England and China could be good partners in this project."

"All right, but remember, this is only in the exploratory phase. The mission is to set up a permanent base on the moon. I need to learn what problems have to be solved to achieve this?"

I stayed overnight in the palace to keep a low profile. General Booth came to the palace, and we had a private discussion in a secluded office.

When I told him what I had in mind, his eyes glowed. Well, he demonstrated great interest.

"This project could be one of the greatest in human history. I would love to be part of it."

"What would it take to get it started?"

"Not that much, really. Did you know that your General Eisenhower planned the invasion of Normandy in its broad strokes by himself with a couple of support secretaries?"

"No, I didn't. I don't think we could get Ike; he is showing his age."

"I wasn't proposing that. I was trying to show how large projects can be described by a small group. It is when the details are looked at it becomes an enormous endeavor."

"How would we even start?"

"You know you will need a rocket to get to the moon, something to land with, space suits to wear, etc. We will detail a couple of bright young things to work up a list. They will research the body of literature out there to see what has been developed, and at the same time, they will come up with a host of other problems we haven't thought of."

"How can we begin?"

"The initial costs are low; I will budget for them. When we have to start hiring others and putting infrastructure in place, you will have to handle that. I advise you to start a new company to handle these matters."

Thus, the Jackson Enterprises Space Division was founded. This didn't happen in a day. It took months for the initial data search and for a new division to form within JE.

In the meantime, the queen talked to the empress, and a verbal agreement was made for cooperation between the two countries.

At this point, the brainpower would come from England. This would employ the British aerospace and supporting industries, lessening the brain drain.

When actual manufacturing was started, it would be in China. They would also host the launch facility.

I returned to Balmoral. Ann and May-ling had become tired of the bucolic life and wanted to return to China. Since Haoran had gone to ground and there had been no word of him, they thought it would be safe to return.

I didn't think it would be safe while he was still alive, but I also realized that he wouldn't be the only one who would want them dead. It was a condition of their position.

I didn't argue with them about going back. They wouldn't have listened anyway. The empress was consulted and agreed with them, so my thoughts were moot.

Taking the caravan back to Aberdeen to meet my plane seemed strange to them. They had been in the countryside for months now.

At the airport, I was pleased to see that my plane had been returned to its original paint scheme. The time for sneaking about had passed.

As we started the long polar flight back to Beijing, I wondered how I had become the personal taxi service to the Chinese royal family.

I'm afraid I have done it to myself. I shouldn't have agreed to pick up that dry cleaning.

Chapter 25

The glamor of flying I had felt several years ago was long gone. I still enjoyed piloting a light aircraft, but traveling in a jet was old hat to me.

Even sitting in the left seat was more like driving a bus than flying. Maybe I wouldn't bother to take the check rides. It isn't as though I would be working for an airline.

Now, the thought of a rocket ship was a different animal. I was smart enough to know that my size worked against me, but I could dream.

During the flight, we sat separately, for the most part, wrapped in our thoughts. Dinner was served in my conference room, so we did talk there—nothing of import.

Upon landing, we were loaded into an armored car and convoyed to the Forbidden City. There, the empress welcomed us. The ladies exchanged hugs.

You could have knocked me over with a feather when the empress hugged me.

"Thank you, Rick, for bringing my girls safely back to me."

"My pleasure, Your Majesty."

"Elizabeth and I have been talking; I love your space plans. They will allow China to enter the modern world without doing it on the back of cheap labor."

"It is early days yet, so don't count your dragon toes yet."

I was proud of that response; the more toes on a dragon, the luckier it was. A five-toed dragon was best. The empress laughed at that.

"I will use that with some of my ministers who always predict success."

"Be my guest."

May-ling butted in, "Maybe we could make a song about that and have Rick sing it."

"Now, that is just plain mean!"

There was more laughter; I think it was a release of tension from the stressful days behind us.

"Rick, what are your immediate plans?"

"I don't have any."

"May-ling and Ann have to take up their official duties so that they will be busy."

May-ling asked, "What official duties?"

"Learning to be an empress. You will have to sit in on many of my meetings."

It was my turn to laugh. I received a sharp elbow for my effort.

I told them, "I think I will leave China while I'm in one piece."

"Seriously, Rick, you are welcome to stay as long as you want."

"I do need to get back to the States to take care of my business and to see to the creation of the new company."

"When will you leave?"

"Tomorrow, if you have no objection."

"I have none."

"Then I will say good night, ladies."

"Rick, take care."

"I will, May-ling, and you be careful. Haoran is still out there."

Empress Ping told us, "We have seized Haoran's business and properties. His bank accounts are frozen. Many of his supporters have been arrested as we investigated his business practices. Most importantly, the people of China hate him for what he has done. He could never take power. Let him rot in whatever hole he is hiding in."

There was no reply to that, but I thought it would be best if he left this earth. I nodded and went to my suite. I didn't even need a guide to get there. I was starting to know my way around the palace.

As I headed to my plane in the morning, it seemed strange not to have May-ling by my side. I missed her already. I felt positively Shakespearean.

When I got to the plane, it was once more unto the breach. Henry V, I do believe. My time at Oxford wasn't a complete waste. It's what we shouted when we wanted another round at the pub.

I sat at the controls on the way home. Maybe I would get that certification after all. I wasn't feeling as gloomy as I was the other day.

Landing in Ontario went smoothly. The immigration officer who came aboard welcomed me back from my trip to England. I let it go. It's not as though I knew where I was half the time.

The stamps on my passport showed only the trip to England. I had used my British diplomatic passport for most of my back and forth.

At home, I had to update Mum and Dad on my latest. I told them about my arrangement with General Booth. It was still too early to get any results from the literature searches.

The first morning home, after I was ready to start work for the day, I called the R&D Center to see where the IC Chip project stood.

They were surprised to hear I was in the country. They asked me if I could come over. They had a demonstration ready.

It took me two hours in the horrible LA traffic, but I finally wheeled my T-bird into the parking lot. When they said they had a demonstration ready, I had no idea what to expect.

There was a breadboarded operation set up—bare boards with no enclosures. There were numerous IC Chips on the board. The board was attached to a CRT screen and a funny-looking typewriter keyboard.

I say funny looking because there were keys but no strikers. There was also a strange little square box with a cord coming from its back. I could see where they got the name mouse.

They had me sit at the keyboard and gave me a list of commands to enter. I followed the list, and a program opened. The program performed math. I entered numbers, highlighted them with the mouse, and clicked, and they were added up.

The program could add, subtract, divide, and multiply. They told me more complex formulas could be entered and the results found just as quickly.

They had one set up for standard deviation. I learned how to calculate the standard deviation of a population in school. Doing it by hand would take ten to fifteen minutes for a group of thirty numbers. This handled it in seconds. The longest portion was entering the data.

This alone would revolutionize business. Next, I opened a program for typing memos and other text. Not only could you type something in quickly, but it was also easy to fix if you made an error. When you were finished, you typed in the command to print, and you got a clean copy printed out on the large printer next to the machine.

To say this was a breakthrough in computing was putting it mildly. My thoughts immediately went to the complicated math needed for orbital mechanics.

I congratulated them on their success and told them they had met my condition for an annual bonus. They excitedly told me of plans to replace the complicated commands with what they called icons. You would click on those with the mouse and execute the command.

That would make it useable at a mass-market level. Having to know all those commands would limit the market. I could see the day when every home would have one.

There were other improvements underway. The typing program could have a dictionary to catch misspellings. The math program could have charts and graphs added.

They even had plans for a program to replace those transparencies I hated. I told them full speed ahead on this project.

Also, to start looking for other companies to manufacture the computer sitting on the desktop. They picked up on the phrase and started calling it a desktop computer.

My damage for the day was done there. I went surfing.

When I got home, a very shamefaced Mum approached me.

"Rick, I have a problem."

"I will escort her."

"How did you know?"

"That look you had could only be because you had to ask me to do something painful, and that was the worst that I could think of."

"Thank you, Rick."

I didn't tell her that Dad had caught me in the driveway and told me Mum was in a real bind and not to give her a hard time.

At dinner that night, I escorted the daughter of a major donor. There had been a last-minute breakup. Why was that always the case? I hoped the girls weren't breaking up so they could have me escort them.

I even asked Sue Long what happened. She told me her boyfriend was so late picking her up that she walked two blocks to his apartment and used her key to get in. He was in bed with another woman.

That qualifies as last minute and not breaking up to be with me. I asked her, "What did you do?"

"I dumped a pitcher of cold water on them and left."

"When I got back to my apartment, the phone was ringing. It was him telling me I didn't understand. I told him I understood all that I needed to know.

"Mom and Dad insisted I join them tonight. They don't know about Tom. I just told them he had to cancel at the last minute. The tickets to this cost so much, they didn't want to waste two of them."

I told her I would try to make her evening as pleasant as possible. She smiled and said, "How about all night?"

Chapter 26

In the morning I replayed in my mind the events with Sue Long. I had turned down her advance in what I had thought was a graceful manner. She was good-looking, and all that, but something screamed at me that the situation was wrong.

What was wrong was that she was a psycho. When I told her I wouldn't return to her apartment with her, she started screaming at me. Thankfully, it was when I was walking her out to her parents' car.

Fortunately, they hadn't valet parked, so we had to walk around the house where no other people were nearby.

Her parents were walking in front of us but stopped dead when she started. Her mother rushed to her side and held her. Her father came up to me.

"I'm sorry this has happened, Rick. Sue has real problems. We thought they were under control, but she must be off her medications or had a severe mental shock."

I decided to tell him about her finding her boyfriend in bed with another woman. That would set anyone off, and if she were off her medications, murder could have been done.

"Thanks for telling me. It will help that her doctor knows the truth. With her mental state, she could forget it and not understand why she now hates the guy. This, in turn, could lead to other problems. You, sir, are a gentleman."

What do you say to a guy who thanks you for telling him why his daughter is a nutcase?

What a weird night. I was going to tell Mum about it so she would realize, I hoped, why I didn't want to escort strange women. I managed to pick up enough trouble on my own.

Live the life of fame and fortune and have gorgeous women hanging all over you. Sure.

In the morning, I went for a longer run than usual. I usually didn't think a lot when I was running. I just pounded the miles out. Today, I reviewed where I was with all of my projects.

With too many balls in the air, I was sure to drop one. Thinking it through, there was one that I could turn over to others.

When I returned to the house, I called the R&D group and told them I was on the way over and wanted to meet with Craig Miller, the head of the IC Chip project.

When I got there, Craig was waiting for me in the lobby. We went to his office, where I turned down an offer of coffee.

"Craig, I realized this morning that this IC Chip project is getting out of hand and that I have too much personal involvement. I'm spread pretty thin, so I would like to break the project down into smaller increments.

"After that, farm out the small increments where possible. Your mission is R&D, but I have put you in charge of commercialization without thinking about it. My first question is, which do you prefer, R&D or bringing a product to market? There will be no loss to you with either choice."

"No question, I prefer R&D."

"That's settled then."

"Now I have to find someone to take over the commercialization."

"May I make a suggestion?"

"Sure, at this point, any help will be appreciated."

"Dump the problem on JE management. Tell them the structure you want, then have them make it happen."

I made a mental note to ensure Craig received a very healthy bonus.

"Let me bounce this off you. I know it won't be in your wheelhouse. But by speaking to someone who has a clue, it will help me clarify my thoughts."

"I'll listen and give you my thoughts for what they are worth."

"First, we need an outside company or companies to handle the software, just like we are hunting for companies to build the mechanical components."

Craig replied, "My first thought is that you should do that, but do it under an umbrella. Have one company in charge of the whole project, and then other specialized companies develop the individual programs, such as a math group, a word processing group, etc. Then, task the umbrella company with ensuring that the same keys achieve the same results no matter the program.

"For example, the same keystrokes or icons to copy or paste something. That way, consumers only have to learn one basic set of commands for all the programs. Of course, each program would have some unique commands, but if you used that program regularly, they would be easy to learn."

It would be a healthy bonus.

"I understand and would have never thought of it like that; thank you. Now, the next one is out there:

"If this becomes as big of a deal as I think it will, we will become huge. The entire operation: software, computer assembly, and chip manufacturing would allow the government to come after us as a monopoly.

"I think these operations should be spun off as different companies, so I'm a significant investor but not the sole owner. That way, they are separate companies and couldn't be accused of being a monopoly."

"I can't even comment on that; I do not know that area of the law."

He is not afraid to admit he doesn't know everything. A significant bonus. Maybe part ownership of the new companies.

"Craig, have you ever thought about retiring young?"

"I have and will work until you put me out to pasture. I love what I'm doing. This job has me and my family in a good place. Why would I quit?"

"Just checking."

I didn't want to throw so much money at him that he could walk away.

Not wanting to let all these thoughts get away, I drove back to the main office with Bobby Rydel blaring on the radio. Since I had the T-bird top-down, everyone nearby could hear. The old folks would glare at me. You could tell they couldn't understand why I liked that noise and had to play it so loud.

Jim was in one of his meetings when I got to the office. He seemed to be in meetings all the time these days. Better him than me. I let his secretary know I was there but to let him finish his meeting first. I will be in my office.

I spent about an hour in this office before my business meetings. It was a wonder it wasn't covered in dust, but they kept it clean.

I spent the next hour and a half signing congratulatory cards and writing notes to my employees. It was getting harder to keep up with all the time, but I felt like it had to be done.

I loved the Eagle Scout notices; I could sign them from one Eagle to another. I got a kick out of that. Now that JE was manufacturing in other countries, I could sign it with the Eagle equivalent from that country.

I had honorary Eagles from almost every country in Scouting. I had to keep a list of the award titles for each country. I could remember the UK's St. George Award and sometimes the South African Springbok Award, but I had to look up Portugal's Cavaleiro da Pátria every time.

Jim rescued me after an hour of this misery. The misery was my hand starting to cramp. I wondered if I could file a workmen's comp claim on that basis.

He had to reschedule a meeting to spend time with me. There are some perks to being the boss.

I explained my conversation with Craig Miller to him. In his methodical way, he had a yellow pad out and was drawing organization charts. He appreciated the umbrella concept with the software. He started calling it an Office Suite. That was good but not catchy. It would have to change or be shortened to Office. I would leave that to marketing.

When I got into the monopoly concerns, he brought in several staff lawyers. They were experts in corporate law, but not necessarily those involving monopoly. They did agree that my approach would derail that possibility. It would also give tax advantages. This was within their expertise.

From that information, I told Jim to proceed on that basis. Keep me posted on the progress, but have management handle it. I had done my part.

Jim did take me aside and asked if I planned a bonus for Craig. When I told him I thought a bonus plus small ownership in the new operations would be appropriate, he agreed, especially after he learned that Craig had no desire for early retirement. That had become a real problem for us, as we were making our management rich.

Jim sighed when he realized what all I had dumped on his plate. I told him to do what I had just done: find someone to dump it on or hire more staff.

He brightened up a bit at that.

"Rick, that brings up another subject; we are bursting at the seams. We need more office space. What we really need is a campus."

"Okay, do it."

"Just like that?"

"Do we have the need and the cash flow?"

"Yes."

"Then do it."

"Yes, boss."

He said that as though he meant it—the boss part, I mean. I went to my car, thinking I had put in a good day's work. Maybe I would play a round of golf.

Chapter 27

The next day, I had a message to call General Booth in England. He wanted to give me an update on where they were at. The biggest news was that the old Soviets had a rocket ready to come off the design board. They called it the Proton.

The Russians needed the capital to finish it and were willing to give launch rights to whoever came up with the cash. If successful, the rocket would solve all the lift issues.

I told him I was interested and would come up with the cash if his people reviewed and approved the design. Imagine getting a rocket to go to outer space for under five million dollars. Such a deal!

There were no other near-miraculous breakthroughs on the horizon.

I wondered how the Chinese integration of Siberia was coming along. A call to Empress Ping's chief of staff brought me up to date.

They were proceeding with their plans to complete the Trans-Siberian Railway with a single gauge, double track its entire length. There would also be a roadway following the right-of-way. The emphasis would be on the railway. There would be spurs built for every modest-sized village.

I couldn't believe the schedule they were predicting. When you have an on-site labor force of over a million men and more on the way, you can get a lot done.

The only hold-up was the steel rail. Plants in China were running full out and unable to keep up with the demand. They were importing it from South Korea, Japan, and the United States.

There was no shortage of sleepers, as the Gulags were still chopping down trees. I would have to look into that. I wasn't in favor of slave labor.

There was gravel galore in Siberia from all the glaciers grinding the place down. The right of way was being cleared at a rapid pace.

The four thousand miles they controlled were being cleared at a rate of ten miles daily. This meant they should have the right-of-way clear in a little over a year.

Before they cleared the right-of-way, it had to be surveyed for the proper grade. If it was too steep, the locomotive couldn't move the cars. Since there were already tracks in place most of the way, that shouldn't be too much of a problem.

The same goes for drainage, though more would have to be added for the second track. The same held for the bottom ballast of medium-sized sand. The sleepers and rails would go down fast at that point.

The top ballast of medium-sized stone is dumped from special gondola cars and would be as quick. Eighteen months was the timeline for double track of the same gauge the entire length.

Once that project was done, the Chinese would hold all of Siberia. Russia would never be able to take it back.

The chief of staff also told me they were using old records for guidance but had exploratory teams out hunting for minerals and the various commercial ores.

Coal and iron were high on their list. Strangely enough, gold wasn't. I asked why, and he told me there would be plenty of independent prospectors out there, and they would cover more ground than the empire's crews ever could.

There was still no sign of Haoran.

While making phone calls, I checked in with my office in Hong Kong. All was on track there. The local improvements in quality were beginning to gain international attention. In the meantime, Dr. Deming had finished there and moved to my operation in Pittsburgh.

A quick call to Don Pearson let me know that it was early days with Dr. Deming, but he had already made believers of the staff, and they were investigating processes full speed ahead to optimize them. In one case, they found a step that could be eliminated.

I was burning up the phone lines. It was early in the day in Germany, so I called my new office there. They told me that the land for our new plant had been purchased, and the surveyors were laying the campus out. The Germans were holding up their end of our bargain and were building railway sidings to our site.

England was not so good. There were already labor problems at the manufacturing site being constructed. They claimed we were unfair in our wages. They wanted double and the workday reduced from eight hours to six. I saw the fine hand of the communists at work here.

I called the Prime Minister's office. He didn't want to take my call. Since the Labor Party was currently in power, I wasn't surprised.

After thinking about it, I decided to let the situation go and see where it went. If they were so darned stupid, let them cut their own throats.

I got tired of making calls, so I hung up with the idea of cadging a snack in the kitchen. The phone rang, and it was for me. The one person I hadn't thought to call was the president of the United States. Now, why would I forget him? Everyone must call him daily.

After the usual short wait, JFK came on the line.

"Rick, I understand you are buying a lot of steel for railroad tracks, so much so that it has caused a ripple in the marketplace."

"Not me, sir. It is the Chinese."

"I consider you the Chinese banker and the force behind everything happening over there."

"You are giving me too much credit, especially in this case. The Chinese had asked me what I would do in Siberia. I told them control of Siberia is determined by the rail system. I suggested they lay a consistent gauge double-track its entire length with many sidings and spurs to outlying towns."

"What are they doing?"

"Laying a double-tracked...I get what you are saying. It hadn't occurred to me that I would be considered the planner of that project. Anyway, I'm not funding any part of it. The Chinese are doing it on their own through their central bank."

"Where did the central bank get the funds?"

"Borrowed, based on their gold reserves."

"Who helped put them into a hard currency based on gold?"

"Criminently, I did."

"And you wonder why I consider you the father of modern China."

"I never looked at it that way. The empress has asked me to help in a few areas and give my opinion. Other than my initial gift, I thought my contributions had been minimal."

"Who has she trusted with the life of her granddaughter and heir?"

"Me and a mechanized division of the Chinese army. They have bigger guns and can call in airstrikes."

"Point taken, but she still calls you when May-ling is threatened."

"That is because China has yet to buy or build a fleet of planes that can cross the Pacific. Why don't you contact Boeing and have them try to enter a partnership with China? I could ask the empress to put her imprint on it."

I don't know why JFK broke into laughter. I thought it was a good idea.

"I will do that. Rick, please give the empress a heads-up. It will take a while, but Boeing will call. Who should they contact?"

"Try the empress's chief of staff. I will call him back; I have talked to him once today."

For some reason, the president started to laugh again. When he settled down for the second time, he asked me if I had any idea how much steel the Chinese intended to buy, as it would help keep the US marketplace on an even keel. I told him I would make inquiries.

"Who should my Chinese contact talk to?"

"Have them place a call to the Secretary of State Dean Rusk. I will alert them that a call will be incoming. Have your contact tell them that they are calling on your behalf."

"I can do that."

He then wished me a good day and hung up. Darn, I wanted to hang up on him again. What bragging rights.

I did call the chief of staff back and shared my conversation with the president about a partnership with Boeing. He told me they had been trying to contact Boeing but never could get to the right person. He would inform the empress that I had helped them once more.

He would have to find out the foreign steel purchasing plans and have a call placed to Dean Rusk's office.

The chief of staff asked, "Rick, who is working for whom here?"

"What do you mean?"

"We are making calls to high-level officials on your behalf. Are you now running China?"

"No!"

"At times, it seems like it. On another subject entirely. What must we do to jump-start the Chinese economy, especially in the outer provinces?"

"Eisenhower did it with the US interstate system. Take a look at that."

"Yes, boss."

"What?!"

I never knew that Chinese men could giggle, and then he hung up on me.

Chapter 28

At dinner, I shared my telephone calls as everyone related their day. Denny asked a good question.

"Do you keep a log of all your calls and what was discussed?"

"No, why should I?"

"I had an assignment in my Political Science class to report on congressional investigations, how they were conducted, and what evidence was acceptable. Phone logs were high on the list."

"Do you think I will be investigated?"

"Yes, it might not be you, but you could be called to testify 'who you talked to, when, and the subject matter.'"

"That is a good thought, Denny; I will start doing that."

"Besides, knowing you, you will get yourself into trouble one of these days."

"Mum, Denny is picking on me."

"And a good job of that; keep up the good work, Denny."

"Dad, now Mum is picking on me."

Dad refused to answer. Mary asked if she could have a turn.

"Sure, shortcakes, go for it; everyone else is doing it."

"Before you go to jail, will you do some modeling for my company? They wanted me to ask, but I didn't know you would get locked up so soon. I thought it would take at least a year."

"Mrs. Hernandez, they are all picking on me."

"*No hablo inglés.*"

"Eddie, you are my only hope."

"Who, me, Kemo Sabe?"

That did it; we all roared with laughter. I did tell Denny that a phone log was a good idea. It would also be an excellent historical record as I was considered the father of the Chinese Empire.

We won't go into the grief that statement got me.

The next morning, after my workout and breakfast, I dressed up to go to the studio. I hadn't been there for a while, and I was curious as to what, if anything, was going on.

The sticker on my car was still good, so I was allowed to drive onto the lot. Walking to the stunt area, I saw a few people I knew and waved at them.

Most of the crew was at the stunt area. There wasn't much activity on the sets today requiring their presence.

A Coke machine was handy, so I paid a dime and opened a bottle. I was saying hello to all the guys and shaking hands when Mr. Monroe pulled up in his golf cart. It was distinctive. It had a front end that looked like a Rolls Royce front end. That had to cost a pretty penny, or farthing, or whatever.

"Rick, this is my lucky day. We need your help with some archery work."

"Rod Bell has quit here; he has moved to the east coast and is working full-time for some outfit called the Central Institute for Archery."

I had just taken a swig of Coke, so it came back all over the place as I gave a huge laugh."

"Rod's working for the Central Institute for Archery, otherwise called the CIA?"

"Yes, oh, I never put it together. I know he went with you when their training people wanted to talk about your escape."

"They were very interested in his skillset; it seems he could contribute a lot in field skills."

"My problem is that we now have no one who can shoot a longbow. We can't even fake it properly. Can you help?"

"Since I'm invested in the movie, I certainly will."

After a stop at makeup and costuming, we went to the outdoor set where they were filming the scene where I set the Black Maria transportation center on fire."

The director wanted a continuous scene where I pulled and shot; they kept me in the scene while the arrow flew to its target. It would be a wide-angle shot and be effective. At least, I thought so.

They had the twerp who was playing me on the set. He would be shown in the close-up, drawing the bow. I would take the actual shot.

A thought occurred to me, not that I cared, but there was someone I wanted to tweak a little.

"He will have to stand on a box. Our height difference will stand out since the scene will shift quickly from him to me."

The director agreed with me. Twerp was just under six feet, not short, but I wanted to send stills to a young lady in Spain.

There was always a still photographer on set, so I approached him and told him what I wanted. These weren't for distribution so I would pay separately.

"These will be free. That guy is a pain in the rump to work with."

Twerp didn't like it; it would hurt his image as a tough guy if the stills got out. I didn't intend to share. I didn't know about the photographer. I hoped the tabloids paid him well.

It got funny when Twerp decided he could shoot the longbow. He tried and tried and couldn't pull the string back. Giving him a few minutes to look foolish, the director finally called for me.

I made sure to bend the bow in one smooth motion. I could hear cameras clicking in the background. There would be more than one sale made tonight.

I shot three arrows to make certain I was on target, and then we had the money shot. That was where the whole place blew up when my arrow landed. Hollywood can do better than real life.

I had started a series of fires. They made it go boom. No one would have survived if I had done that in real life.

Everyone but Twerp cheered when the scene went off perfectly.

Mr. Monroe, who had been watching, asked if I could do one more scene for them. It was where I stepped from the signal block to the moving train.

I told him sure. That meant another trip to makeup and costume, but it didn't take long.

In Moscow, the train was moving five miles per hour, if that, creeping along. They had it moving twenty miles an hour, so the cars would be rolling back and forth as they do at speed.

I don't blame Twerp or his insurance company for not wanting him to do this stunt. I had said I would do it, so I did. Playing on boxcars in Bellefontaine paid off. The trick was to step from a stationary platform to one moving away from you.

To not fall on your face or to get hurt, you had to launch yourself into a run and keep it up after you had landed for three or four steps until your body momentum was the same as the train.

If you did that, it looked easy. The director had me do it four times just to be sure he had a good shot.

I asked if I would be paid scale for my work today. That took Mr. Monroe by surprise, but he said yes.

Hey, I'm a professional who works for pay.

From there, I went back to the stunt area. One thing I wanted to do there was practice my sword work. I hadn't done any in a long time. I had to be rusty.

I was, but not as bad as I thought I would be. After a sweaty half hour, I called a halt and moved on to quarterstaffs. I wasn't as rusty at that as I thought I would be either. Maybe using a rifle with a bayonet attached in close quarters was enough to count. That trip to the Siberian frontlines was rough.

After that, it was boxing. That I hadn't done in a long time, and it showed. I was lucky not to be knocked out, even though I had a head protector on. I would have been spitting teeth if I hadn't had a mouthpiece. I made a mental note not to get into any pure fistfights.

Unarmed combat, yes; fistfights, no. I had no rust at unarmed. Somewhere along the line, I had filled out even more. I hadn't grown any taller, but I was bigger overall and stronger. Someone even mentioned I ought to try out as a lineman with the Green Bay Packers.

That was a laugh, me and football. Not being able to play football was one of those things that started me down this path in life.

My very, very good friends, the stuntmen, had a little surprise for me. I don't know how they did it, but I backed right into a water trough.

They were all sorry about that, Your Dukeship, but I still swore to get even. I had changed clothes to practice, so I didn't have to drive home wet. I did think evil thoughts about what I could do to them.

About halfway, the humor of it all caught up with me, and I started laughing. What are friends for if not knocking you down occasionally?

I still thought I would get them back, but I was beyond burning the studio down.

Chapter 29

I even shared my day, including the water trough, with the family at dinner. They agreed that it was nice to have friends like that, but some form of revenge was in order.

After dinner, I went to the library, and using a yellow legal pad, I made a list of all my projects and their status. Everything was under control. Maybe not moving as fast as I wanted, but under control.

The one that gave me the most heartburn was the space program. I had very little control over that. It was still in the investigation phase, and I couldn't hurry that along. I wanted to blast off and do it now.

Feeling self-satisfied about how business was progressing, I moved on to my personal life or lack thereof. Even there, I couldn't make things happen.

Maybe I could. How about ads in the paper: lonely, rich, titled actor looking for a girlfriend? No one would answer that—maybe not so good an idea.

I knew it was time to go to bed when a huge yawn escaped me. I was looking forward to a solid night's sleep. I never slept as deeply on planes and had certainly spent enough nights in the air in the last month.

I was asleep for two hours when the phone in my room started ringing. It took me a while to wake up enough to figure out what was going on. The phone kept ringing.

I managed to stumble over to my desk and answer it with a mumbled, "Hello."

I recognized Empress Ping's voice on the other end.

"Rick, Haoran has tried to kill May-ling again. I have her on a plane to Hong Kong right now. Could you pick her up and take her someplace safe?

"Of course. It will take almost a day to get there."

"I know, just hurry."

"I will."

After hanging up, I started making calls. The first was to the flying service. I told them I had to be wheels up for a trip from Ontario airport to Hong Kong as fast as possible. They told me the plane was fueled and catered, so all they needed to do was roust out the crew. They should be ready to go in two hours.

I thought about leaving Harold here. When I thought that, he appeared dressed and ready to ensure I was dressed properly. How does he do that?

I called England and got the night desk at Buckingham Palace. I asked for a message to be passed on to Mr. Norman. I needed a haven for May-ling. Could we use Balmoral again?

I thought about letting my parents sleep but then thought better of it. I knocked on their door and let them know what was going on. They told me to be careful and to be safe.

I said I would. How do you remain safe when a maniac is trying to kill someone you are traveling with?

The quickest way to Ontario at this time of day was to drive. It would take about an hour, so the crew might not even be in place when I arrived.

Harold and I rode in the back of one of the limos. One of the guards was driving us. From the pictures taped to the back of the front seat, I realized it was Mary's. I hoped they would return it in time for her to go to school. If not, I would pay for it. If it were only cash, I would be getting off lightly.

Maybe I could forestall her by buying her a new horse trailer for Ajax. The current one was getting to look shabby. I wrote a note to that effect and asked the driver to pass it on.

Since I hadn't even folded it, he read it. He laughed, "She has your number, sir."

"Yes, she does."

We arrived at the airport as the pilots were doing their walk-around of the aircraft. Nothing had fallen off, so they thought flying might be safe. The weather reports were fine, so we were good to go.

We were wheels up less than two hours after the empress had waked me. I did the only logical thing and went back to bed. I slept through our refueling stop at Anchorage. By the time I cleaned up, dressed, and had breakfast, we were landing in Japan for more fuel.

A hand-carried message was waiting for me in Japan from the Japanese emperor's staff. It was an invitation for May-ling to take refuge there if no place else was deemed safe.

I drafted a quick reply stating that this was a great honor the emperor was extending and that we may have to take him up on that. It depended on what I found in Hong Kong.

This was enormous. The relations between Japan and China had been strained since the 1930s. The change in Chinese leadership must have triggered hope for the Japanese—the Emperor's Club, you know. I wondered if Queen Elizabeth was eligible for that club.

I did wonder how the Japanese knew. I soon found out. An English edition of the *Straits Times* had the attempt on its headlines. The whole world knew. From the story, I gathered that May-ling had been in a convoy to a meeting.

She and her mother Ann were hidden in a trailing car in the equivalent of an armored box. The ruse worked; an anti-tank weapon destroyed the vehicle that she appeared to be in. All in the car were killed.

The car they were in immediately went to the airport as per its instructions, where she boarded a plane and left. It was not known where the plane had landed at press time, but they would keep us posted.

Damn journalists, they don't care who they endanger as long as they can print something. I knew she was in Hong Kong at the governor's mansion, and Haoran would, too, if the papers had their way. They would even report what room.

We took off and made the relatively short flight to Hong Kong without problems. The governor, along with May-ling and Ann, met me at the ramp. We boarded the plane. The governor told me we were welcome at Balmoral, so I told him that was where we were going.

May-ling herself looked exhausted. She stood there wearing what she had been wearing for many hours. I wrote out a note for the governor to send to my mum.

I informed the flight crew we were to leave for Edinburgh immediately with a quick stopover in Ontario.

We took off. Our total time on the ground was less than half an hour. Even the press would have a hard time keeping track of us.

Harold, the perfect valet, told the two ladies that he had several comfortable outfits they could choose from after they had a chance to rest and clean up.

They grabbed the offer like a lifeline. Then May-ling surprised me. She hugged me tightly and whispered into my ear, "My knight to the rescue once more."

You could have knocked me over with a feather. I knew I was a knight, but *her* knight?

I decided now was not the time to pursue that thought. It was probably the stress speaking.

By the time they had slept, cleaned up, dressed, and eaten, we were almost back to Anchorage. May-ling wore slacks very nicely. I had never really seen her shape before. Let's just say she is shapely.

After a year or two of travel, we landed in Ontario. Mum was waiting as I requested with several suitcases of clothes for May-ling and Ann. The nice thing about Rodeo Drive was that they kept your size on file.

May-ling, Mum, and I had a quick conversation while they were refueling. Mum had been working the phones but had nothing to add. The person who fired the rocket got away. There was no sign of Haoran.

We flew to New York City, then on to Reykjavik, Iceland, and after that, to Aberdeen, Scotland. Our sleep and meals were so messed up it would take days to get straight.

There was a limo waiting for us in Aberdeen. The security guard accompanying us told me that it was felt that a lower profile was best. A convoy for the trip might be safer, but it would also advertise that an important person was in residence. It was decided that this was the lesser risk. I agreed.

No one tried to kill us on the way, so I counted it as a win. The staff was ready and had "our" rooms waiting for us. What a trip.

The first thing we did was to call the palace and ask them to let the empress know that we had arrived safely at the same place we had hidden before and would be staying there for an indeterminate amount of time. I had deliberately not said Balmoral.

I wondered if I could finally get a good night's sleep. I thought it was in the cards until that bagpiper started in the morning. There should be an open season on them, with no limit.

Chapter 30

I got up for my daily run after the horrid shock to my system—bagpipes in the morning. I always wondered about the Scots. Now I knew. They are insane.

It was a wonderful day, discounting the wake-up call. After being cooped up on the plane for days on end, it was a delight to get out and stretch.

I must have run ten miles instead of my usual five. It felt good until it didn't. Suddenly, I was tired, and I felt my legs start to cramp. I needed water and salt.

That's when I realized I had no idea where I was. I was still on the grounds or in the national park, but beyond that, lost. At least I was on a trail. I could turn around and backtrack.

It would be a long and slow slog, but it had to be done. I walked slowly with a slight limp for about a mile when I heard bells jingling behind me. It was a pony pulling a cart.

The driver was a lassie, and I don't mean the dog. She had auburn hair, a fair complexion with freckles, and a cute button nose.

She pulled up beside me and asked if I would like a ride. I thanked her for stopping and told her I most certainly would accept the ride.

I climbed aboard her little pony cart. I could see that she was hauling baked goods in the back. Not only could I see them, but I could also smell them. They were heavenly.

She told me her name was Nicola MacGregor. I started to introduce myself, but she interrupted me, "We all know who you are, Your Grace."

That took me aback a bit. I didn't realize that the general public would recognize me. I said something to that effect.

She laughed, "One of my stops is at the kitchen at Balmoral. The staff wags about you all the time. They follow you in the papers. Besides the royal family, you are their most interesting guest.

"Though you might have to step up your game now that they have met Princess May-ling."

"I now understand why the queen refers to the unruly MacGregors. Troublemakers all."

She laughed at that.

"Aye, we have done that a wee bit."

"You say some of these baked goods are going to the kitchen at Balmoral?"

"Yes."

"Since I'm staying there, would it be okay if I ate a bun or two? I'm starving."

"I suppose it would be okay, but you have to tell them, so they don't think I'm one of those unruly MacGregors trying to short the count."

"I'll do that."

With that, I turned and opened a bag of cinnamon buns. She reached into a small box beside her and offered me a slab of butter and a knife to spread it.

"This is my favorite way to start my daily trip."

As I daintily ate the first one in two bites, I told her it was a shame she had no coffee.

"The thermos is under the seat if you don't mind sharing a cup."

I think I fell in love at that moment. We continued down the road at a sedate pace for another mile or so. There was a small shop at a crossroads.

"This is my first stop."

I helped her carry bags of bread, rolls, and buns into the shop. A tall young man was standing behind the counter. He scowled when he saw me.

Nicola said, "Now be off with you, Robert Sturgeon. I'm just giving His Grace a ride, as he has strained his leg."

She turned to me, "Your Grace, I would like to introduce you to my intended, Robert Sturgeon."

We shook hands. He was no longer scowling as she had made her position clear.

I still loved her for the coffee. I did tell him he was a lucky man. If he hadn't been her intended, I might have whisked her away as they did in so many of those Highland Romances.

He laughed at that. "Me mum reads those; I'll have to tell her I about lost my fair Nicola to a duke."

"Give me a head start; she may try to chase me down."

We had a good laugh at that. We all thought those books were silly. Always the wealthy noble and the poor young lass.

This wealthy noble and poor young lass returned to the pony cart and continued down the road. After another two stops, we reached the tradespeople's entrance at Balmoral.

A guard at the gate told me that people were looking for me. An emergency hadn't been declared, but the questions were coming more frequently.

After stopping at the kitchen and confessing to eating a full dozen of the cinnamon buns, I went to the lobby, where I knew I could find a footman to spread the word that I was back from the wilds of Scotland.

I didn't even make it to the lobby when Ann spotted me. She and May-ling demanded to know where I had been. I told them about pulling up lame on my extended run.

I'm not sure they believed me because I had walked it off. I even took them to the kitchen to introduce my savior, but she was pulling away in her ponycart.

It even got a little tense when they saw Nicola give me a cheerful wave as she left the grounds. May-ling was muttering about reading about those Scottish girls meeting wealthy nobles.

I let that one go. I wasn't going to try to convince her she had it backward and that it was English girls meeting a wealthy Highlander Laird that was the trope.

It wasn't even lunchtime on our first day here, and I was in trouble. I don't know why May-ling was upset; it is not as though she was my girlfriend.

After my outing, I had to clean up and change, so we didn't meet again until lunch. They had decided to go riding for the afternoon. I had enough outdoor exercise for the day, so I told them I would spend my time in the library.

That worked for about half an hour. It was too lovely a day to spend inside. The book on Scottish farming practices was easy to put down.

I went for a stroll in the extensive gardens. The place is gorgeous. There were several gardeners at work pulling weeds. I kept angling deeper into the gardens when I rounded a corner and saw a Scotsman sitting on a bench. I was pretty certain he was Scottish, as he wore a kilt.

"Good day to you, sir."

"And to you, young man. What brings you this deep into the gardens? Most young people get bored and go back."

"It is so beautiful here, and I was in the library. It felt stuffy, so here I am."

"Vicky was like that; she was always wandering around."

"I don't think I have met her."

"She has been gone a long time. I keep hoping she will come back, so I linger here. I think she met up with Al and chose him over me."

"I'm sorry to hear that."

"It is the way of the world."

I hadn't stopped walking as we talked. I was just about past his position when he was gone—not got up and left but was just gone. I looked around and found no one.

When I asked back at the castle, I was told it must have been John Brown. His ghost had been seen more frequently in the last decade. It was felt that he was about to give up on Queen Victoria coming back to him.

If that were true, it would confirm a lot of rumors that had been spread about. As I was leaving the lobby where I had asked the question, I saw two younger footmen elbowing each other as though they had played the greatest joke of all time. Maybe they had.

I went back to the book on Scottish farming; at least it keeps me out of trouble. It did, as I fell asleep with it open in my lap. I had to be woken to change for dinner.

As Harold assisted with my coat, he informed me that there would be a ball at the castle on Saturday week. If Mum hadn't used phrases like that, I wouldn't have known he meant a week from Saturday.

Several other guests were staying at the castle. I think they were all poor relatives that were living on the queen's charity. When I entered the reception room where we gathered for dinner, two men and three women were chortling at a joke that had been pulled early today on that Yank upstart.

They became quiet when I walked in.

Now I wonder who and what they could be talking about.

Chapter 31

I decided what was good for the goose was good for the gander. I was banking on the fact that the older generation revered the memory of Queen Victoria and wouldn't want anything to sully her memory.

"I had the most interesting afternoon in the garden.

"I talked to the ghost of John Brown. For being dead, he is talkative. He told me how he and the queen were lovers, and he missed her so."

Now, the prankster had said nothing of the sort, but if the dinner crowd denied he said that, they would be giving the game away, so they kept mum. One gentleman harrumphed and stated that Brown had to be lying.

"Why would a ghost lie?"

Now, here is where the fun starts.

"I'm going to tell the American press what he said. I'm sorry that will blacken her reputation, but the public must know the truth."

Put that in your pipe and smoke it.

One of the ladies was the first to crack, "Reggie, tell him the truth."

"What truth is that?" I asked.

"It's a prank we play on all newcomers who walk in the garden. The footmen are in on it. When a new person goes out there, I dress up as John Brown. I put on a false beard and all the other kit."

"It is hard to see, but the way one tree grows in front of another, you can 'disappear' by stepping aside. I never said anything about Brown being the queen's lover."

"I know it; I just wanted to smoke you out. I would never talk to the American press unless forced. Much less degrade Queen Victoria. You shouldn't still be laughing when your victim enters the room.

"Now let me tell you some real ghost stories."

I regaled the dinner table about my visit to New Orleans on that publicity tour.

May-ling and her mother were sitting there open-mouthed. They couldn't believe Americans would let the spirits and the ghosts wander about. What was the priest doing?

China is China.

The next day, I spent a lot of time with the huntsman, who was an expert at unarmed combat. He knew his stuff. I was younger and quicker, but experience and muscle memory count. He mopped the floor with me time after time.

Our bodies were glistening with sweat. The young ladies of the castle gathered around. At one point, my opponent had something to say to me. As he had me pinned once more, he whispered.

"You're a sneaky sod, aren't you? This isn't about training at all. This is to attract the birds."

"And a pretty lot they are."

My plan worked.

The next morning, with a smile, I went to the archery range and worked for several hours. After that, it was the firearm's turn. I was improving. I was nowhere near May-ling's level, but I wasn't competing with her. Was I? Where did that thought come from?

While cleaning the .45 pistol I had been firing, I heard a familiar clanging and banging. Someone was using swords. Well, two people.

I hadn't noticed it before because hedges surrounded it, but there was a squared-off area where two people were going at it with claymores. Those are those great two-handed swords the old Scots used.

I had to watch those guys go at it. I'm classed as being excellent with one-handed swords, only fair with two-handed. These guys were fantastic.

I declined a chance to take on the winner. Who wants to get beaten with a six-foot-long iron bar?

I told them I would love some single-handed exercise. They replied that that was for Southerners. I had to think that through. They meant Englishmen.

That's how I spent my days at Balmoral, other than dialing back my running to my normal five miles. In the middle of the week, one of the gillies asked me if I wanted to go on a hunt.

I thought that would be interesting, so I agreed. It was a hunt for a particular stag. The herd needed thinning so they wouldn't starve over the winter. This stag was getting up there in years, and a younger one had replaced him as the herd leader.

We got up in the middle of the night to be above a pond the stag was known to frequent. I was loaned a Lee-Enfield rifle that shot a .303 round. As the British army had phased them out in 1957, plenty of these were floating around.

The estate management hunting license covered me, so all was good.

We lay in wait for almost an hour when this magnificent beast came to drink. I had been told that they went up to five hundred pounds. This one was every ounce of that. It had a breathtaking antler crown.

The gillie nudged me to take the shot. I couldn't do it. I could kill people in battle. I couldn't execute this wonderful creature.

When the hunter realized I wasn't going to shoot, he did. To him, it was culling the herd for their betterment, just a job.

After we field-dressed the deer, he asked me how many men I had killed. He knew some of the things that I had done. I told him that I had lost track.

He shook his head at this silly American being sentimental over a deer while being able to kill men.

I'm sure he would enjoy telling the story over a glass of whisky.

Speaking of whisky, I had a tour of the whisky distillery. The Royal Lochnagar Distillery is only a mile from the castle. I'm not a whisky drinker, but the sample I tried was smooth as silk. That is, until I took too large of a sip, and it burned like fire all the way down.

Harold was in a tizzy; from hunting in the morning until the ball tonight, I would wear five different changes of clothes. I would shower between every change, so it seemed all I was doing was changing.

First off was the hunting outfit. Then jeans and a pullover for breakfast. We could get away with this as the guests hadn't started to arrive yet.

Lunch was more formal, with a sports coat and tie. This must have been to impress the early arrivals, as we usually stayed in jeans and pullovers for most of the day.

After lunch, it was back to jeans and pullovers until it was time to dress for dinner and the ball. This was to be a holiday, but I found out that my afternoon was to be a series of meetings with British industrialists who wanted a piece of the Jackson pie.

All I could do was take notes on each proposal and ask them to send a more formal presentation to Jim Williamson at our head office in the States. This whole exercise was futile. Why would I be interested in a company that made sweets for poppers?

Saturday was the day of the royal ball. That meant Queen Elizabeth was its official sponsor. Being it was at her house, that seemed appropriate.

I thought there might be a few local couples, the upper crust, if you will. There were gobs of people, most coming up from London.

There was a security screen set up five miles out from the castle. You had to have a written invitation to the ball to get any closer.

Vehicles were parked in a barnyard about a mile from the house, and a bus sat waiting to take the attendees to the castle.

Guests would be staying overnight in one of the fifty-two bedrooms. Upon arrival, they would be escorted to their room by one of the many staff. Tonight, there would be one hundred staff on duty.

Usually, there were fifty or sixty full-time. The extras were part-timers from the estate. You would think the guests were moving in from the sizes and numbers of suitcases they had with them.

I hope the staff had workmen's comp for their backs. I made the mistake of being in the lobby when one group arrived. The eldest son of the family summoned me over. I went thinking he knew me or something.

"Boy, take these to our room; it is room forty-two on the second floor."

You would think he would realize that I wasn't in uniform. All the footmen seemed to be very busy at the moment, so I grabbed two bags. I was told to be gentle with them. I have no idea who he was, but that was a bit too much. I dropped the bags with a resounding thud.

"I say, I will have your job for that."

His parents turned at the commotion. Father knew who I was. He rushed over and started to apologize.

"You don't owe me an apology, sir. You weren't the rude one."

He turned to his son and told him to apologize to His Grace, the Duke of Hong Kong. It was a still and quiet moment in the lobby, well, except for the peals of May-ling's laughter.

Chapter 32

I had a thought some weeks ago and had acted on it. The Chinese Empire was new, so it had little in the way of traditions. This included clothing and crown jewels. When compared to the riches of the British Crown, they had nothing.

When I visited General Booth in London, I stopped at the House of Garrard to order two pieces. They were to design a tiara for May-ling and a crown for Empress Ping.

They had designed the pieces and sent me drawings. With the contrivance of the serving staff at the Forbidden City, I was able to ascertain their hat sizes. I thought it was a hoot that they came with lifetime repair warranties. Not the lady's lifetime, but the lifetime of the Chinese Empire.

The cost was north of ten million dollars, but I thought it was well worth it. Why did I do it? I'm not sure; it just seemed like the thing to do at the time. It was not as though money seemed real to me anymore.

I'm just glad I haven't ended up like Tommy Manville or the way Howard Hughes was heading. They were disasters, though at least Hughes had accomplished things.

On the day of the ball, an armored car with a police escort came to Balmoral with a representative from the House of Garrard to ensure the tiara fit correctly.

The royal crown wasn't ready yet and would be shipped directly to China. Were there armored airplanes for delivery?

I had told Empress Ping what I was doing. If I had given the tiara directly to May-ling without the empress knowing, all sorts of things could have been misconstrued. I made certain that it was understood these were part of the Royal Crown Jewel Collection and owned by the empire, not the family.

She thought that was wise. When she asked me why I was doing this, I told her it would be tacky to give my class ring to May-ling to show we were going steady.

"Are you, going steady, with May-ling that is?"

"No, she has made it clear that she will be marrying for China so her husband will be a rich, powerful Chinese."

"I'm glad she has her head on straight and not confused by this romantic nonsense you Westerners believe in."

"So, I wander the earth looking for my true love."

"That's what I mean, Rick. Have your parents find a suitable girl for you. You are still young, but it is time to start looking."

I shuddered to think what sort of woman my mum would pick.

Before we hung up, she asked me if I still carried my Chinese passport. I told her it was always in my case with my American, British, and British diplomatic ones.

"Oh, we need to get you a Chinese diplomatic one. It will make things easier when you come into the country as a Chinaman.

The ball was unusual, at least to me. There was no purpose to it rather than a bunch of people getting together for a good time. Mum's Charity Balls required you to bring your checkbook.

At least I knew that I would be escorting May-ling tonight. I didn't have to worry about it being some psycho like that one in California.

I will wear my Coldstream Guards dress uniform tonight with all the full-sized ribbons and sash with knightly orders. In other words, in full fig.

Harold hovered over me all afternoon, making certain all was correct. He had even arranged for a barber to come to my room to give me a haircut and a shave. He had mentioned a manicurist, but I put my foot down at that. I don't know if I should be insulted, but he checked my fingernails to ensure they were clean.

I couldn't say too much as I hadn't got all the dirt out from under them from picking up and pulling arrows out of targets from my morning session on the archery range. Maybe I should have had a manicure. Who needs a man card anyway?

I went to May-ling's room with the present in hand. The tiara was in a fine, leather-tooled box. The leather was deep red, with the five-toed dragon embossed in gold on the lid. The hinges looked like they were made of real gold. And that was just the box!

The lady from Garrards was with me. I had tipped off the Dowager Ann of what was going on so she wouldn't be surprised. For some reason, I was as nervous as I was when I went to my first prom.

This wasn't like a date or anything. Heck, she was nice to me, but that was it. She had made it clear that I had no chance with her.

May-ling looked up in surprise when I walked into the room, followed by Phyllis Jones from Garrand's. May-ling hadn't started to change yet, as it was too early.

I didn't mess around.

"May-ling, here is a present to the Chinese throne."

I then handed her the box. It wasn't dramatic or romantic, whatever you want to call it, but I just wanted it over and done.

Not knowing what to expect, she opened the box. Her gasp was all I needed. It was a success. Inside the box was the tiara. The platinum-wired frame held over two thousand diamonds with a two hundred-carat diamond at the center.

The large stone didn't rival the ones in the British Crown Jewels but was the largest fine stone on the market at the time.

The lady from Garrand's helped her put it on for the first fitting. The platinum could be twisted some to give a better fit. I thought the experts could do that. I would hate to break it on its first day.

I explained that they weren't her personal property but that of the Chinese throne and its heirs. She didn't have to worry that it was something serious like my class ring.

She gave me a funny look at that. I understood; it was a dumb thing to say. I explained that I had also commissioned a crown for the empress, which would be sent directly to her when completed. The empress was aware of everything.

"And she approved you presenting this to me?"

"Yes."

"I know you are wealthy, but this is incredible. I don't think until now I knew how wealthy. It is a shame you aren't Chinese."

Suddenly, I felt very uncomfortable.

"It is, isn't it?"

I left the room to start dressing for the evening. I remembered the conversation with the empress about my passports.

Considering I could put on a shirt and pants in five minutes or less, it took forever to get dressed. Harold fussed and fretted about the hang of my uniform. In one case, he opened a seam in my shirt and resewed it, so it hung better.

I must say, the hour and forty-five minutes it took to get dressed were worth it. I had never looked better, dressed, that is.

Hat under my arm, I marched to the crown princess's suite. You don't walk in a uniform like this; you march.

The crown princess was ready. She was stunning in a dark blue empire waist dress, her hair hanging down in ringlets by her ears. It was done high in the back. This arrangement highlighted the tiara for the whole world to see and admire.

She wore high heels, bringing the top of her head even with my chin. Her necklace was made up of diamonds of the first water. I didn't know it, but when I informed the empress what I was doing, she commissioned a matching necklace for the tiara.

Not only was she the crown princess, but she also looked like a crown princess should.

Official photographers took our pictures as we gathered at the head of the stairs, which descended to the grand ballroom. While there were no official representatives from the press, several people in attendance would describe what was worn.

When it was our turn at the top of the stairs, the majordomo announced to the world: "The Crown Princess May-ling Ping, heir to the throne of the Empire of China, escorted by Colonel the Duke of Hong Kong, Sir Richard Jackson."

We were a long way from Kansas.

My biggest fear going down those steps was stumbling. I lightly held May-ling's hand to steady her, but we both looked straight ahead as we descended.

The applause started halfway down and grew louder as we came down.

After we were safely down, we took our position at the foot of the stairs and awaited the true stars of the evening.

"Lords, gentlemen, and ladies, Her Majesty the Queen, escorted by her consort, Prince Phillip."

I'm glad they didn't use all her titles, or we would still be standing there.

Chapter 33

Elizabeth and Phillip descended the stairs with the ease of long practice. We all bowed as a sign of respect, even May-ling. I was murky about the etiquette in her case, and I suspect she was, too. Better safe than sorry.

The royals proceeded down the length of the room, allowing everyone to give their greetings. The first event of the evening was dinner. It was a light repast so as not to interfere with the dancing.

May-ling and I kept each other company through dinner; we both were strangers in a strange land. Instead of withdrawing for port and cigars, the men had to put the best face on it and start to dance.

I knew better than to expect them to play the twist. It was all dances from the 30s and 40s. None of that jitterbug stuff, mind you. Waltzes, rumbas, and sambas. No adventuresome tangos.

One naughty young couple tried a black bottom to a rumba. Kinda weird. An elderly man spoke to the girl, and they settled down for the rest of the evening. Her grandfather, I suspect. If it had been her father, there would have been words.

May-ling and I kept to waltzes. She accepted other requests to dance all evening but only sedate ones. When she was dancing, I would look for a young or not-so-young lady who stood against the wall looking as though they would like to dance.

My dance partners were all pleasant and enjoyed the dance, but I could tell it was the dance they enjoyed, not me.

At one point, I ended up where the queen was sitting surrounded by her ladies in waiting. The queen thanked me for being thoughtful and asking those without partners to dance. I didn't reply that it was better than standing around. I'm not a complete fool.

May-ling's tiara was the talk of the evening, at least in the female set. They wanted to know the details. She would answer technical details and that it came from the House of Garrard, but not that it was a present from me.

I was thankful for that as it would send the wrong message.

During one dance I had, the young lady got very close, so close she could tell my interest. She returned the signal with a slight grind of her hips. When she asked where my room was, I was delighted to tell her.

After that dance, I was pulled into a corner where the men were talking business. I was quizzed as to my plans and what opportunities they might have. I played it close and only gave general answers.

I gave my card to one gentleman who told me his company was testing different materials for high heat resistance. They thought they might find a market in the US with the space program.

As the night wore on, people departed the ballroom. I escorted May-ling to her room. Ann had not attended as she was still in deep mourning for her son and husband. May-ling and I were able to get away with the black armbands.

I did have a late-night visitor. Lady Grey was a pleasure in all senses of the word, but there was no real interest between us.

The next morning, I was up early for my run. May-ling was just coming in from hers. She stopped and asked if Jane and I had a good time last night. She had seen her walking down the hall early this morning.

I felt embarrassed but decided I shouldn't. May-ling and I had an understanding. She didn't want me, and my feelings for her came and went. She was a friend, and that was it.

In reply to her question, I gave a simple "yes" and left it at that. I don't know how May-ling felt about that response. She didn't talk to me for three days.

After showering and putting on my second outfit for the day, I went to breakfast. There was a small, hung-over crowd there. Most were sitting by themselves morosely drinking coffee and smoking cigarettes.

Being the kind person I am, I gave a loud, cheerful, "Hello everyone!"

None responded in kind. There were some mutterings that I pretended not to hear. What rude people!

Since no one was up to a good conversation, I went to the archery and gun ranges. I spent most of the morning practicing them. My archery was in top form, and I doubted it could get any better. I wished I could enter the Robin Hood event at Sherwood Forest again. I bet I could do better than a bronze medal.

My ability with the long guns had improved dramatically. Pistols were okay. I could hit anything within ten feet. In my experience, that was all you needed with a handgun, or a shotgun, for that matter.

When I expressed that opinion to the range master, he gave me a long look.

"As you Americans say, you have seen the elephant."

I had, but I considered it interesting that I was still considered an American, even though I was in the British armed forces and hadn't used my American accent in so long I may have lost it.

The Mandarin I spoke even came across as British.

The next day, my business mail started catching up with me. I now would spend the time between lunch and dinner reading and responding to my correspondence.

I did get an update from General Booth. They had just identified a product with the necessary heat resistance, so now we could consider having a reusable spaceplane that could land on a runway rather than a capsule that would have to land in the water.

I had a chuckle when I recognized the name. It was the same company that I had met at the ball.

They had also established that a company in Dover, Delaware was making space suit designs for NASA. NASA was so slow at making decisions that they were desperate for cash flow.

General Booth recommended that I invest in that company to ensure a supply of suits and have us as a preferred customer. I called my business office in London, instructing them to contact my broker and buy at least five percent of ILC.

Once the purchase was in hand, they were to provide a loan at a low rate to stem their cash flow problems. Another box ticked.

That made me feel good until I read the report from his eager young researchers who had listed all the obstacles to be overcome before we could successfully fly to the moon. It was enough to make you want to cry. Instead of crying, I requested what had to be done to overcome these obstacles.

Who would have thought you would have to have exercise bikes in space? It made sense once you thought about the lack of gravity and loss of body mass. Hundreds of these details would have to be addressed.

One good note was that the concern about food poisoning in space was being addressed. A group headed up by Pillsbury was investigating how to keep foods from going rancid. They had a program underway called HACCP: Hazard Analysis and Critical Control Point concept.

I didn't see what the big deal was. They had to establish things like the fact that chicken can go bad quickly, so the entire processing cycle had to be in a building that was a giant refrigerator. I thought they had always done it that way. I guess not.

Things were going ahead well in Spain. The maintenance program was up and running. They had decided it would need US expertise for a long time, so Don Pearson would continue to rotate people in and out, along with their families.

I would allow him to continue his little boondoggle. It wasn't him directly benefiting; he obviously could see a benefit for some critical employees. I just hoped it didn't work its way to other departments.

In the meantime, Fra Tomas was happy to report that with the nuns added to the teaching staff and the deacon approved by the bishop, they could now say a mass for me daily.

Also, the bishop would still like to meet me. I had no trips to Spain planned.

There was the usual stack of congratulatory cards to sign. This was even after the bulk of them had machine-signed signatures.

They always included a sample of the many letters I had received from the general public. This was to give me a good idea of my public image.

Currently, I was Satan incarnate, and would I marry their daughter? Satan because I was helping those godless Chinese.

They had never listened to a priest at a Chinese funeral. They could go on with the best of them.

Marrying their daughter was what any right-thinking young man would do to ensure that his new family lived the life they deserved.

Chapter 34

The IC Chip business was skyrocketing. The first manufacturing units were coming online at three different licensees. They were sold out for months in advance. This allowed them to borrow more money to increase production.

Companies that could build CRTs, keyboards, printers, and mice had been identified. My brokers in London were quietly buying an interest in each company. I didn't want to go over fifty-one percent and have majority ownership in any of them.

Once this was accomplished, orders would be sent to them from the assembly company of which I owned forty-nine percent. Employees owned the balance.

The assembly company would sell to the umbrella company, which would install the software purchased from the various companies that wrote the programs. These programs would come together as a suite called Workplace and run by a View operating system.

I owned a significant portion of each of these companies. We would keep the whole thing honest looking by putting out bids for the various products. The bids would be written so that only our companies could qualify. I learned this by watching how the US federal government released its Request for Proposals.

The RFP would have statements like, "must have previous experience with the US Army Corp of Engineers," when they had only ever worked with one company.

These companies we chose would eventually be taken public. Since the only relationship they had was that I owned a minority portion of them, my lawyers assured me that there should be no monopoly concerns.

My sister Mary had taught me that when the word monopoly appeared, you should always be concerned.

I felt comfortable with how things were going and was happy with my life at Balmoral.

I even played several rounds of golf at the castle golf course. It is a nine-hole course with eighteen tee blocks to give a different look on the back nine. It is a short course of 4,825 yards, with par being 67. It is beautiful and well-maintained.

It is open to the public but has restricted playing times. As a castle resident, I was allowed to play with no one else around. They provided a caddie who I tipped well. The tips were to keep silent about my scores. He told me my 49 one day blew the course record out of the water.

No one needed to know that.

Life was all settled and at ease. I was feeling rested for the first time in months when things changed. The ladies wanted to go home.

Haoran was still on the loose, but they wanted to return to China. They had called the empress, and she agreed with them. They couldn't hide forever.

A grim fact was that he couldn't be caught unless they exposed themselves as bait. After I made certain that they understood the risks involved, I agreed to fly them home. I certainly wasn't going to stay here if they were gone.

The place is lovely, but I, too, wanted to get on with life.

It took two days to put everything together. For once, it wasn't fleeing in the middle of the night hidden in the boot.

The trip was long, boring, and uneventful. Just like I liked them. A small convoy was waiting, which escorted us to the Forbidden City.

Empress Ping was delighted to see us. She received us in the formal throne room. I wondered why she was doing this when it hit me. The crown had arrived. It was stunning. It matched the British crown. The central diamond wasn't as large, but there was a cluster of 200-plus-carat diamonds as a centerpiece.

The ladies had to try it on. It fit all of them. May-ling sent for her tiara so she could show it off. Again, all the ladies had to try it on. From the wistful look I saw on Ann's face, I knew what her Christmas gift would be.

Still no news on Haoran.

We were tired from our journey, so we took it easy for the next two days. Easy meant no public appearances. Behind the scenes, it was one briefing after another.

Why I was invited to attend them, I don't know. I knew better than to decline an "invite" from the empress.

Along with May-ling, I learned more about the inner workings and the state of the Chinese government than I ever wanted to know.

What impressed me about them was that the empress was an active participant but didn't pretend to be the holder of all wisdom. She would listen to her advisors and even take mild criticism of her thoughts.

I noticed that the criticism never went beyond mild; after all, she could have their heads. Unlike Queen Elizabeth, her parliament was the figurehead, not her.

Every decision that was made had one central thought. How can we create a larger middle class in China? She had studied the West and understood that the middle class is the true wealth of a nation.

The poor had little to give. If you stripped all their wealth, the rich couldn't support the country. Only with a large middle class could enough wealth be created to have a self-sustaining economy.

She understood that a "rising tide raises all boats." She also understood that all boats needed to rise, not just the wealthy. The wealthy could only hire so many servants and create so many jobs.

Once a person is rich, they can't spend the money fast enough to have it trickle down. The trickle-down effect would only work when trickling down from the middle class to the poor.

I had never thought of it this way, but it seemed that the truly wealthy of a country were a detriment. They locked up the wealth of a country, not because they were greedy, but because they couldn't spend it fast enough.

As one of the wealthiest people on earth, this gave me a headache. I needed to keep my money flowing. Tying it up in stocks and bonds contributed to my growth but didn't allow enough to trickle down.

I needed to spend more on building things. Putting the money in motion would help create the middle class, which was the true support of a nation.

I needed some time to sort this out. I'm sure that others have looked at this. There had to be a middle ground between capitalism and socialism. I'm thinking of socialism in the pure sense. Taking social responsibility for all citizens, not as a means of central controlling authority to aggrandize a few, as the communists have done.

After sitting in on these meetings and having these thoughts, I realized I was confusing myself. I had to sort these thoughts out. I needed to identify a path for myself that would help people in a good way, not make them dependent.

If there were an easy answer, it would have been written about a long time ago. I had never heard of it in all my reading. Did I need to reinvent society?

Once I got to this point, I started laughing. What an ego. I reinvent society! It would have been better if I hadn't had that laughing fit in the middle of a presentation of projected grain shortages.

I had to apologize to the group and told them my mind had wandered in a funny direction and that it had nothing to do with the grain shortages. As a sign of my contriteness, I would donate ten shiploads of grain from the Canadian wheat fields.

Thus, my laughing fit cost me several million dollars. I chose the Canadian wheat fields because they were still family-owned farms. The US had a new term, agribusiness, which was large companies taking over the farming industry. It was either help the Canadian middle class or US big business.

I thought I had begun to identify a route to take.

Later in the day, when it was just a small group of the empress and her top three advisors, I explained what led to my laughing fit. I called it a fit because it wasn't a chuckle or brief outburst, but a true belly laugh that continued.

They agreed that I had identified the crux of their issue. The biggest question was how to funnel funds to a small middle class and have them spread it around rather than hoarding it to become wealthy.

The American Founding Fathers had a similar problem. Theirs was how to spread power to all the population rather than an entitled few. They had to dance between the power of the mob and the power of the few. They had some success, but even they had missed out on slavery and women.

If we could do as well the Founding Fathers, I would be satisfied.

What is this, "if we could do as well?"

What was my role in all of this?

Chapter 35

After wrestling with these thoughts for a day or two, I realized that smarter people than me had thought about these issues for a much longer time.

Since no magic bullet had been published, there probably wasn't one. Even if one were published, it would only be an unproven theory. All I know is that by creating infrastructure, other people would have a chance to use it to improve their lives.

I wasn't going to give my money away. I would offer low-cost loans and issue bonds on their behalf. I would expect to get my money back and hope to beat inflation.

That would be better than letting my money sit in stocks or the bank gathering interest. I could buy bonds issued for infrastructure in places that needed it.

Even my money for the space project could be considered infrastructure. I would expect a greater return since I would pay for it directly, and the risk was much higher.

The only things I was involved in that I could see having an immediate direct impact on people's lives were the IC Chips, the computers, and the software. They were pure money-making ventures. Maybe they could improve people's lives. Time will tell.

In the meantime, the backbone of my fortune, Jackson Enterprises, with its container and freight divisions, would support me as I made a dumb decision or two. By dumb, I meant throwing my money away on a bad project.

After reducing my complicated and probably messed up thoughts to something I could understand without needing a Ph.D. in Economics, another in human behavior, and another in Politics, etc., I had a meeting with the empress's chief of staff.

"We talked about implementing the US interstate system in China. Has a decision been made to proceed?"

"The empress wants to do it. We just don't have the funds."

"What does it take to issue a bond?"

"The first step is to approach the bank and explain the need for financing. This is not a problem here because the Bank of China will be underwriting it at the empress's orders.

"Then a rating analysis needs to be performed. Again, no problem as this is a sovereign debt against the Chinese government, which is on the gold standard.

"After that, there needs to be a presentation to investors; they call it a roadshow. This establishes if there is interest in the bonds. If there is enough interest, then they can go on the market."

"How is interest shown?"

He answered, "If investors commit to buying ten percent of the bonds on the roadshow, then we can proceed. To put the backbone of the interstate in, we would need a billion dollars in bonds."

"So, one hundred million would get the ball rolling?"

"Yes."

"If the roadshow is held successfully, I will make that commitment. Every time I give China money, you insist on paying it back. My financial team is always on me to find places to park the money. This may find me peace for a while."

He smiled and replied, "At least for the thirty-year life of these bonds."

"What will the entire project cost?"

"Over ten billion is the closest we can figure. But as the project succeeds, the global market will happily buy them."

"Who will buy them now besides me?"

"The empress will let the one hundred wealthiest families in China know that investing is in their best interest. We just didn't have anyone with enough to kick it off."

"You should have come to me first."

"The empress forbade it. She said you have done more than enough for China."

"I will have to speak sternly to her. I will help who I want."

He got the most horrifying look at the thought of speaking sternly to the empress.

"When I say speak sternly, first I will lie on my stomach and grovel and beg to underwrite the bonds."

"Oh, your Western humor, I never have understood it."

"My family says they can't understand my humor either."

I wanted to play some golf, but there were no golf courses in China. When I let it be known that I was flying to Hong Kong to play a round of golf, you would think the world was ending.

The empress summoned me and wanted to know how one got a golf course constructed. I had never built one, but I knew someone who did. That is how Sam ended up in China, laying out and building their first golf course. It was based on an Arnold Palmer design, which Arnold licensed to China.

The name of the course was The Royal Course of the Middle Kingdom. That meant it was the national golf course of China. The invitation-only club dues would be a hundred thousand US a year and have all the amenities.

They asked me if I knew how to run a golf club, and of course, I didn't, but I knew who did and put them in contact with Augusta National. They ended up being reciprocal, which saved me a bundle.

It took a while, but I figured out that China was building a golf course so they wouldn't lose face by me going to Hong Kong to play. At this point, I doubted a hundred people in China could play golf.

I probably was correct in my initial thought, but it didn't take long for several professional golf schools to open and other courses to be constructed. Why the communists thought they could succeed in this capitalist culture, I will never know.

That all occurred in the near future. I did fly to Hong Kong to play golf. That is when I found out that someone still wanted to kill me. Haoran was on top of my list, but a disgruntled Soviet or member of the Stasi could have been on the list.

Whoever it was had good inside information on my movements. My car was approaching the Government House in Hong Kong when someone threw a Molotov cocktail at the car.

Their aim wasn't very good because it hit high enough on the roof that most of the contents were spewed into the air. There weren't many people around, so none were hit directly.

The bomb thrower got away.

The driver had been trained well. He managed to get the car several blocks down the road before he had to stop. If there was an ambush, we had driven out of it.

The driver, my security guards, and I were all bailing out of the flaming vehicle. I was aware that this might have been a ploy to get us out of the vehicle.

A trailing police car was there immediately, and I was hustled into it. With lights flashing and sirens blaring, we proceeded to the Government House.

When informed of events, the governor told me I wouldn't be making any public appearances and that golf was out. What a waste of a trip.

I decided to check in on Jackson House Asia. I hadn't been there in several months. Boris welcomed me at the door. I had called him from Government House, so he was current on events.

I asked him how he was liking life here.

"Much better than Poland. I am warm and getting fat; it is wonderful."

We all have different expectations in life.

"Your Grace, I will now finally have a chance to show you the secrets of this house."

"What have you found other than the secret passage down the hill, a hidden subbasement, and a wine cellar below that?"

After I said that, I was sorry. He looked like his candy had been taken. He was looking forward to showing me these wonders.

"How did you know?"

"This house was built by the same man who built Jackson House in the US."

"That explains it. Would you like a tour?"

"I most certainly would."

The escape passage was exactly as I thought it would be. It came out in the garage of a house several hundred yards down the hill from mine. It was on my property, but no one was living there.

Boris had his suite of rooms, so it wouldn't do to move him there. I would have to give it some thought. In the meantime, it wouldn't hurt it to sit empty if we maintained it.

The subbasement was reached by similar hidden staircases from the main bedrooms and the elevator system. There was some equipment in the subbasement that I had to explain to Boris. He was shocked.

He took me over to a large safe.

"We haven't been able to find a combination, and I didn't want to bring a locksmith down here without your permission."

"Let me try something."

I remembered the combination of the safe in the US. I wonder if it would be the same. It certainly would be more convenient.

Chapter 36

The safe opened to the same combination as the US safe. Jason Talmadge probably did the wrong thing in having the same combination on both safes, but I wasn't complaining.

The safe had a small fortune in gold and silver, a larger one in old one-hundred-dollar bills. What was amazing was a stack of one hundred notes from the Bank of England. They were each for one hundred million pounds. If they were real, they would be for ten billion pounds. A fortune, no matter how you look at it.

How did Talmadge get them if they were real? What would the Bank of England do if I turned up with them, and they were real?

I quickly closed the safe before Boris, who had wandered away, could see what I had found. He had seen the gold and silver bullion. He would have no idea of the worth of the old one-hundred-dollar bills; my guess was several million at auction based on the last ones we had found in the other safe.

I went upstairs and placed a call to Mr. Norman at the palace. It was the middle of the night there, so I wouldn't hear from him for some hours.

After that, I asked Boris to take me down to the hidden wine cellar. This one was full of old bottles of distilled spirits. I wondered what an authentic Napoleon brandy would sell for. I would let Dad take care of all this. He enjoyed it and could advise me on what I should keep for gifts.

There was no stolen artwork. My parents had the stuff found at Jackson House returned to the last legal owner or insurance company if it had paid out. The rest had found its way into museums through anonymous donations. Talk about being hotter than a two-dollar pistol. Most of the paintings were well-known and couldn't be sold.

The museum donations had set off a frenzy in the art world. Surprisingly, while my parents had hired experts to trace down the rightful owners, those that ended up in museums had several would-be owners crop up. Seven people came forward in one case, telling how it had always been in grandma's parlor.

For some reason, I was very tired. It couldn't have anything to do with being almost burned to death earlier in the day and then finding a fortune. That fortune didn't even include the British banknotes.

Mr. Norman returned my call at a civil hour for both of us. I asked him if he could ask a question of the Bank of England for me.

He said he could. What was it about?

"Did they ever print one hundred-million-pound banknotes?"

On the line, I heard an intake of breath.

"Don't tell me you have found the Titans."

"What are the Titans?"

"Notes of that denomination were lost in the sacking of Bombay in 1897. It has been thought they were destroyed somehow, but we have never been able to account for them. As such, the Bank of England has had to keep them on their books as a liability."

"How many were lost?"

"One hundred of them, ten billion pounds worth. It represented the Bank's treasury in India."

"Well, if these aren't fake, the treasury can have them back. That or I could keep them and spend them. I can see it now at the checkout counter at Marks and Sparks."

"Rick, how fast can you get these back here?"

"My plane is fueled and ready to go on short notice, so if it is that important, I could come right away. I must let the empress know I'm making a side trip so she doesn't worry, especially after yesterday."

"What happened yesterday?"

"It hasn't made the news. My car was firebombed here in Hong Kong. I won't mind leaving here at all. They won't even let me play a round of golf."

"If those are real, we will let you play free at St. Andrews old course for the rest of your life."

I called the Forbidden City, the Governor's House, and my chief pilot. I asked Boris for a briefcase. The banknotes were A5 in size, so they were like a fifth of a ream of typewriter paper—no big deal to carry.

That is why I double-checked the load in my .45.

Boris excused himself to make certain my car and driver were there. I took the opportunity to retrieve the banknotes without him knowing.

It was a nervous ride to the airport. I had people trying to kill me and potentially ten billion pounds in a small briefcase.

While seeming an eternity, it took the normal amount of time to safely arrive at the airport. The governor was waiting for me and wanted to know why I had to go to England suddenly.

I wondered how he knew that since I had only told him I was leaving Hong Kong. When I asked him, he told me all he had to do was ask about the flight plan.

Silly me, almost getting worked up about nothing. I told him that it was a request from the queen and that I couldn't share the basis for the request. He took that with a stiff upper lip. What he actually said was, "Oh, okay." I just like the term.

When I boarded the plane, I immediately stuffed the notes in my small safe. I spent the rest of the flight fretting and fuming about what I should be doing next.

At least Harold had caught up with me. The poor guy had to fly commercial to Hong Kong from Beijing and almost took a cab to Jackson House Asia when I asked for a trip to England. He was at Government House at the time, as that was my announced destination, so he heard the revision of the plan in time to be on the 707.

As usual, anymore, the flight was long and boring. I had a couple of fiction books and even some non-fiction on world economics, but I couldn't get into them.

I did manage to get some sleep, so I wasn't a total wreck. When I cleaned up, put on a suit suitable for the palace, and had breakfast, I was ready to face the world. Almost twenty hours after leaving Hong Kong, we were landing in London.

Usually, I was met by a car and driver from the palace. This time, I was met by an armored truck in which I rode in the back with a police escort. I would have felt silly if it weren't for the banknotes I had with me.

I bypassed palace security through a side door I didn't even know existed. There was a group waiting for me in a conference room. Included were the queen and the prince consort.

I was introduced briefly to two men from the Bank of England who were experts on the notes in question. They even had a similar note with them for comparison.

I wondered aloud about how many of these there were. The answer was that there was a total of forty in the vault of the bank on Threadneedle Street.

There were drawn breaths all around. I may have the real thing. They felt the paper, dripped some chemicals on a small corner of one of the notes, and looked at them under a large magnifying glass.

The two experts mumbled back and forth for ten minutes. The crowd in the room held their breath.

The lead expert, or at least the one to talk, announced: "It is the correct paper, the correct ink, and imperfections in the printing are the same as the known note. These are real."

I had to ask, "Now what?"

The queen countered, "You found them; what will you do with them?"

"Oh no, Your Majesty, you aren't going to dump these on me. They go back to England."

"I know, Rick, but your mum suggested the question. She thought it would be fun."

"Was it?"

"Yes, the look on your face was priceless."

She continued, "This is like found money for England. It is now carried as a liability; we can erase that and be ten billion pounds richer. If the politicians get wind of this, they will go on a spending frenzy like never before.

"We are going to lock them away and bring some out only at need, a rainy-day fund if you will. Since the money will be to settle an emergency, the Pols won't be able to run our debt up as usual."

"Can a secret this big be kept?"

"We have bigger. You can have no recognition for an event that has never happened, but I think the Crown can arrange a tee time at St. Andrews whenever you want."

"More than enough, Your Majesty."

I was taken to my suite at the Plaza, which would raise the fewest questions on my trip. I spent the ride wondering what other significant secrets the Crown was keeping. If they were on the order of ten billion pounds, they had to be big.

Chapter 37

Now, I was in England at loose ends. I was getting cynical recently and thought I would only be here until summoned back to either spirit May-ling to safety or attend her funeral.

There wasn't much for me to do. If I returned to China, I would have to stay in the Forbidden City for my safety. I wasn't even safe in Hong Kong.

I decided that the only reasonable thing was to visit my grandmum. A hotel limo took me to Oxford. Once at the Meadows, I could use one of their cars.

Grandmum was glad to see me, especially without any Eurotrash in tow. I decided for the 707 to be moved to Oxford so it would be available when I dashed off to China again.

I spent several days with Grandmum and Mr. Hamilton. They seemed to get along very well. I thought more power to them.

I did call the Oxford boys, and we met at our favorite pub. Things had changed between us. When I updated them on my most recent adventures, I noticed they held me with a certain reserve.

I asked what was wrong.

"Don't take this bad, Rick, but I feel like I could be killed any minute just because I'm sitting next to you. The tabloids have taken to calling you the bloody duke."

I hadn't known that because I had quit reading them long ago.

"While there is no direct evidence that you have done anything, where you go, bodies turn up."

I thought the assassination attempts had been covered up, but apparently not.

"There is this Chinese guy who wants to be emperor, Haoran, one of Ping's sons, but not in the direct line. He has been trying to kill May-ling. He has killed her father and older brother. She is the only heir to the throne before him."

"Why don't you go all bloody duke on him?"

"I would if we could find him. Teams of professionals are looking all over China for him."

"Why don't you give him an irresistible target to lure him out?"

Out of the mouth of a mildly drunk Oxonian.

"Thanks, guys. I have to make some phone calls. Here's the money for my shout, but I have to go."

Back at the Meadows, I called China and asked for the empress's chief of staff. It was one of my luckier days that I got put directly through, both the call and him.

I went right to the point.

"Can we find a double for May-ling to lure Haoran out, or at least capture his hitmen to get them to lead us to him?"

"We have already tried that. We captured the hitman, but the information we got didn't pan out."

"What did he have to say after the information failed?"

"He didn't live that long."

China is China.

I was discouraged after that. After lunch the next day, I called the White House. The chief of staff told me they were having no luck tracking Haoran. It was as though he wasn't in China at all.

Maybe he wasn't; if not, where would he go?

I made another call to China; Grandmum would have a fit when she saw her phone bill. I would leave a couple of hundred quid with her for my portion of the bill.

This time, I asked if Haoran had any country in particular he did business with or visited. It turned out he was one of the few Chinese who was free to come and go to North Korea.

Bingo.

I placed another call to the White House. I told the chief of staff about Haoran's many visits to North Korea. They didn't have many assets there, but they would ask if anyone was aware of him being there currently.

I ordered my plane so I could return to China. I suspected all the action was going to be on that side of the world.

The flight took just as long as all the others but didn't seem as tiring this time. I was heading towards some possible action. It was also acting rather than reacting.

I continued to mull over what I could do best for the world. I decided once more the best I could do was build infrastructure at a reasonable profit and hope that others used the improved infrastructure to help themselves.

Upon arrival in Beijing, I was placed in the usual escort, but we took a different route into the city. I inquired why and was told it was to try to prevent ambushes. There were a dozen possible routes. The convoy leader would pick three at random just before they started. His immediate subordinate then would choose one of the three. This prevented individual bias.

There could be group bias, but no system is perfect. It would take a machine with enormous computation power to create a truly random number. Hmm.

I was allowed to see the empress upon arrival. She knew that every resource they had was looking for Haoran, now concentrating on North Korea.

The only problem was there was a good chance that he had subverted the MSS agents responsible for watching North Korea. They had doubled the agents up so no one could work alone, but he could remain hidden if two bad apples were working together.

The Americans made the breakthrough. Whenever Haoran flew into Pyongyang, he was picked up in a limo. They had a permanent watcher at the airport who took down license numbers and the names of passengers.

Haoran had taken the same limo so often that the watcher had sent a picture of him to Washington. They traced the license number of the limo and found it to be a government agency.

The agency provided entertainment to high-level officials. It seemed they had an official brothel department in the North Korean government. Now the Americans knew where to look, it was easy to locate Haoran.

Despite the legend of prostitutes with hearts of gold, they are a corrupt bunch willing to do almost anything for money. The Americans had penetrated the brothel a long time ago with the Yankee dollar. They just had never thought to check to see if Haoran was there.

The brothel was about fifteen miles outside Pyongyang in a secluded park-like setting. Besides the women, it was set up as a complete resort for the North Korean elite.

Once his whereabouts were known, the question was how to get at him. The empress didn't want to go to war with North Korea over this, and there was a chance he could once more get away.

It would have to be a stealth mission. A small group would parachute into North Korea and assassinate him.

I told the empress I knew just the group, SEAL Team 2. She wasn't aware of my venture into Laos, so I told her of that mission. I hadn't signed an NDA with the US government about my involvement, so I felt free to relate the details.

She had a call placed to the White House. It went through much quicker than any I had ever made. I then learned a secret: there was a line kept open permanently between Washington and Beijing. This was to avoid misunderstandings expanding into incidents. They were cute about it. The phones used were red.

The empress and JFK talked for a while. When they got down to business, he asked to speak with me. The speakerphone was turned on.

"Rick, I can make SEAL Team 2 available, but there is a problem. They will not know what he looks like for certain. I don't want to blow this up any more than we have to. There will have to be someone along who can personally recognize him."

"No problem. Can I ask that Harry Beal's element be the one that goes with me? We know each other."

"You would go on this mission?"

"I'm the only one who knows both the SEAL team and Haoran. It's not like I haven't done work like this before."

"I will tentatively okay this mission. I have to check if the SEALs in question are even available. Their command will have the final say on whether or not they think the mission is feasible."

"That sounds good. How long before we know?"

"I will be calling back in two hours with a preliminary report. The insertion plan will probably take longer."

"Okay, we will be here."

The empress inquired, "Rick, you will do this for us?"

"I'm the only one who knows both parties. Plus, I'm getting sick and tired of reacting to Haoran. He only has to get lucky once."

"You are amazing. China owes you so much. I don't know how we will ever repay you."

"There is only one problem."

"What is that?"

"I've never parachuted before."

Chapter 38

With my brilliant statement about not parachuting before, I just about ruined everything. I hadn't jumped before, but the new parasails were like the homemade parasail I had used to escape the Gulag.

To use each of them, you had to jump off a high place, twist your body, and pull on the cords to go in the direction you wanted. The only thing different really was remembering to open the parachute.

The empress insisted that I talk to a parachute instructor about this. I was taken to an air force training base where they taught pilots how to bail out.

Their army didn't have any paratroopers, so this was the only source of knowledge. I was introduced to a hard-bitten instructor. He had no English, and my Mandarin, while better all the time, was not up to the task.

It was fortunate that my escort spoke both well. Maybe it wasn't good fortune but good planning.

When I explained what type of parachute I would use, the instructor shrugged. They only used the round style; these were probably World War II surplus!

He agreed that my parasailing experience was equal to the Rogallo wing parachutes in use today. They didn't have any of them. If I had one left over, could he have it so they could learn how to make them and practice with them? They seemed to be the chute of the future.

Even if they had one, he wouldn't recommend my trying to practice. The incidence of injury in first-time jumpers with any type of chute was high. The fewer jumps, the less chance of injury.

That made some sense, but I would feel better if I could practice. We had time before this mission could take off. The SEAL team had to be in position, the area around the resort where Haoran was staying spied out.

A jump zone had to be identified. Then how were we to get out of North Korea? Also, just because Haoran was there didn't mean he would come out to where we could get at him.

The place was too big and had too many people to try to go inside. We had to be able to get him while he was outside and at a distance.

We needed the SEAL team element here before we could make plans. The CIA was doing high-altitude overflights, taking pictures of the site. These would be made available to the SEAL team.

This gave me enough time to call the states and have ten Rogallo wing parachutes shipped from Little River to Beijing. They would be on military aircraft with a high priority.

In two days, we had them. I was told it would be a whole week before the team arrived. This gave me time to get comfortable with these chutes.

My instructor was extremely happy to get the chutes. He immediately had one put aside in a locked room as the prime example. If there were any questions later, he would refer to this unopened, unused parachute as the master chute.

Two more were taken by an armed escort to the best and, as far as I knew, the only parachute manufacturer in China. They would open one, take measurements, determine the materials used, and reverse engineer them.

I wondered briefly about the moral and legal issues involved, but I didn't wonder very long since my life might hang in the balance with these chutes someday.

That left seven chutes to practice with. The first thing that the instructor had his riggers do was to open one chute on a long table. As they opened and unpacked the chute, they would draw the chute at each stage. They wanted to be able to repack it exactly. I approved of this idea.

Once they had the drawings in place, they repacked the opened chute. I accompanied them to a plane very familiar to me, a C-47, the military version of the DC3. There were some differences between the two.

The DC3 had a rounded tail, while the C-47 was squared off. This allowed the C-47 to tow gliders with an attached shackle. There was a cargo door that could be removed to make it easier to jump out of.

There was also an astrodome for the navigator. I was told the floor was strengthened for heavier loads.

None of these changed the aircraft's flight characteristics, so if push came to shove, I could fly it. Not that I wanted to on this mission. If I had to, it meant we were in a world of trouble.

We went up in the plane with sandbags attached to the parachute harness. There was a static line to pull the ripcord after the chute was clear of the plane.

We went up to ten thousand feet. We had safety lines attaching us to the aircraft. They were short enough that we couldn't get out the door. I liked that feature.

I was able to get right to the edge of the door and look down ten thousand feet. When sitting inside the plane, I never felt uncomfortable about the height. Looking straight down ten thousand feet was a different feeling altogether.

My instructor moved around freely as though he was in his living room at home. I kept a hand on the safety rails all the time.

When we reached the height, he tossed the sandbags out of the plane. We watched them fall and pull the chute out of the plane; then, the static line pulled the ripcord. The chute opened flawlessly. At least they could be safely repacked. That was good to know!

I was wearing one of the unopened new chutes. Now that the first test was passed, I thought it was my turn. Instead, a young pilot in training went first. It seemed I was considered too valuable for the first human test in China.

Since the pilot's chute opened as promised, we circled until the ground radioed that he had landed okay. Then I was allowed to go.

When the instructor who was acting as jumpmaster signaled, I stepped out into nothing. It was but moments until the static line pulled my ripcord.

While I was falling, the wind rushed by, creating a lot of noise. When my chute opened with a yank on my body, the world became a lot quieter.

The instructor had fussed over my harness, making certain that it was on tight and in the correct places. He told my translator that men had been castrated when their harnesses were not correct.

I made sure that mine was tight in the right place in my crotch and that nothing important was trapped under the straps.

The force made by the sudden slowing when my chute opened made me a believer in having the equipment adjusted correctly.

Now that my chute was open, I was able to take a moment to look around. I was to land on the airfield, a big enough target, preferably on the grass rather than a concrete runway.

It made sense to me.

I was facing away from the airport, and the wind was drifting me further away. I used my parasailing experience to turn my direction of fall.

The professionally made parasail was so much better than the homemade rig, I wondered how I hadn't killed myself.

I landed within a few feet of the target zone I had selected. I bent my knees and took a couple of steps to try to land upright but went down on my butt anyway. It didn't matter. I had done it.

I was taken up three more times that day and jumped successfully. Each time, I was given a new unused chute. I even managed to stay on my feet on the second and third jumps. I was feeling cocky on my fourth one, so of course, I bumped halfway across the runway when I didn't spill my chute fast enough.

After dark, I was taken up one more time. To be qualified, I had to make a nighttime jump. It was a moonlit night, and the airport runway lights were on, so it wasn't much different from a daytime jump.

It would be a different animal if it were cloudy with no moonlight or ground lights. That is where preplanning would come into play in our mission.

After my night drop, I was awarded a set of parachutist wings. They had the Imperial Dragon centered on them. I had never seen these before. I commented on that.

I was told that the Chinese Air Force didn't award parachutist wings; only the army would. The empress had ordered such a group be created. Since they didn't have an airborne group, I was parachutist number one!

I wondered if I could wear them on my Coldstream uniform. I thought I could but on my right, rather than the left. I had seen other officers with their British set on the left and foreign ones on their right.

Chapter 39

There would be a one-week delay in getting the SEAL team element in place. Something about recovering from an insertion. No details beyond that.

With the mission first place on my mind, I asked to see all the aerial photographs taken. Not that I would be able to interpret them as well as the professionals, but I wanted to become familiar with the area.

Hundreds of them showed all the terrain from the resort area to the Chinese border. There were all sorts of annotations about what the maps were showing. The one thing missing was an escape trail.

It appeared that was for us to pick out, which made sense. I spent many hours looking for ways in and out. It was relatively easy. You had to pick a route that would have the least radar coverage and be prepared to fly low all the way.

It looked like the best route was taking off from Fengcheng, China, crossing the border near Gulouzi, China, and turning towards Phyongwon before jumping out near Pyongyang. But that was my opinion.

I had wondered about a submarine insertion and pick-up off the coast as it would be the shortest distance. I was disabused with the idea quickly. The North Korean coast in that area was almost shoulder-to-shoulder with coast watchers.

My flight plan would be under three hundred miles, so distance wasn't the problem. The obstacle was parachuting in the dark with no lit landing zone.

Where would we land, and how would we keep track of each other?

Once we were down, we would have to accomplish the mission, which I didn't have the faintest idea how to do, but experts were on the way.

Then there was the exfiltration, getting out of Dodge. Several things in our favor would be the many forests. We could keep a low profile going through those. I had learned that in East Germany.

I was sent a CIA briefing on North Korea. If they kept on the course they were going, they would denude their forests in the next thirty years. This was due to the need for firewood and farmland. They were leeching the soil without replenishing it. They would starve their people if they weren't careful.

Not so good was the mountain territory we would have to travel through. While the elevations were not that high, the mountains were new and rugged.

I penciled in several possible routes to share with the SEAL team when they arrived. They would probably have all sorts of objections, but it gave me something to do.

I spent a lot of time at my offices. The Bank of Guangzhou was doing well. Almost too well. They were making so many loans they were causing inflation in their area. I had to force them to tighten up their loan requirements to limit the yuan loaned.

When a market got as hot as this one was getting, the collapse would be nasty. It was past time to cool it down. As soon as the requirements were instituted, ten percent of the loans defaulted. This was no surprise. I was relieved that it wasn't more.

Those books I had been reading had taught me a few things. While the bank lost money on the defaulted loans, the properties seized would have future value, so the losses weren't as bad as one would think.

What impressed me was that all the defaulters were arrested. After investigation, a few were let go, many sent to prison, and, in one blatant case, executed.

That seemed draconian by US and UK standards, but it sure did send a message.

The Chinese Department of Transportation, or whatever title they gave themselves, announced that an expressway network would be constructed.

It would be a "freeway," in the sense it was free from cross traffic. They were calling it the National Trunk Highway System or NTHS.

When completed, one would be able to cross China at 75mph without encountering one traffic signal. Most freight was by railway, but it would be less expensive in the long run to use trucks to reach many towns and villages.

There would be many rest areas and fuel stations along the way. Newly licensed drivers would be restricted from using the NTHS until they gained experience.

Unlike in the US, passing on the right or speeding would lead to severe penalties.

I had to wonder if this included a beheading.

After all, China is China.

This program was to be paid for by the gracious Empress Ping, who was issuing bonds that would be purchased by the wealthiest Chinese willing to improve the Middle Kingdom.

Willing, my Aunt Martha's aching knees.

I received a letter in my mail pouch from Mrs. Echevarria. She was concerned with Fra Tomas and his actions. He and his Bishop had declared the *estancia* a special part of the diocese and that a surtax would be charged.

It looked like it was time for a reformation in Spain.

I wrote back to her that she was to charge the church a rent equal to the taxes imposed. Taking care of the children of the ranch was one thing. I wouldn't support the bishop in his efforts to become a cardinal.

That shows my simplistic view of the Church, but I wasn't far wrong. I learned along the way that someone would always try to have their hand in my pocket.

I got to choose the hand.

Another letter was from Mr. Monroe informing me that the movie *Escape from Siberia* had finished filming and was now in post-production. They hoped to have it in theaters by Christmas.

He had also sent the stills that I had requested to the young lady in Spain. It was unfortunate that they had leaked out to the tabloids. While helping the film's publicity, they did nothing for the lead actor. Mr. Monroe didn't even bother to express regrets that it happened.

That was good; I hated crocodile tears.

I spent several evenings with the imperial family. I have never met a more vicious group of Monopoly players in my life. That even includes my sister Mary.

I wanted to do more parachute jumping or skydiving, as it was now being called, but it was forbidden because the chance of injury increased with each jump.

I asked Whitehall what British parachutist emblems I could wear because I had earned the Chinese "Dragon" with five jumps from an airplane, one being at night.

I was informed that since the Coldstream Guards were not a parachute regiment but a regiment of the foot, I could only wear the "Lightbulb," this being a parachute without wings.

Bummer.

The long wait was finally over on a Friday. The SEAL Team 2 element made it to Beijing.

They were in mufti, civilian clothes to the uninitiated. This mission was so black that I don't think even those of us going on it were cleared. The US government was never, ever involved in assassinations unless they were successful and had a good result. Then, it was statesmanship by different means. Something like war is diplomacy by other means.

I was glad to see Harry Beal. I considered him a good-luck piece.

They were a tired-looking bunch, not just from the flight but from their last mission. I was glad that we had no timetable. There were eyes on Haoran, and there was no indication he was coming out of hiding. Reports were that Haoran had gained weight and looked like he spent his days drunk.

Maybe we would get lucky, and he would do himself in; I wasn't picky about how he went.

The team took the next two days to rest up. They looked a lot better the next time I saw them. This was in a conference room at army headquarters.

Harry told me they were finding this weird; they had always thought they would fight against China instead of on joint missions.

The aerial photos were all laid out. I kept my mouth shut and let the experts do their thing. I was glad I did. My plan to fly in wasn't that far off course. It was the delivery system that I had wrong.

They proposed using a glider made of canvas and wood with an extremely low radar profile. We would glide in and not have to jump at all. That was the plan.

The Chinese Air Force tore that plan apart. The mountains along the border would have many unpredictable winds, and the North Koreans had many single-engine aircraft patrolling the border zone just for such incursions.

It would have to be a parachute jump, after all. I had mixed emotions. Gliding in would reduce the risk. But dang it, I had earned those jump wings and wanted to use them. Probably childish, but it is what it is.

That was my take. Harry Beal said, "They didn't hire us to do easy."

Chapter 40

I did find out how we would keep track of the person who jumped before you. We would have a light on top of our helmets pointing up. If we jumped with the proper separation, we could see at least the person in front of us.

Weather and clouds permitting, you might see everyone in the stick. The only fly in that ointment was that the more and lower cloud cover, the better, at least for concealing our jump.

We performed several jumps at night to make sure I knew how to do it. They'd had many jumps like this. It was easy to follow the others in when the sky was clear. The more clouds, the harder it was.

Even SEALs had limits on what they could do. It was decided that the perfect cloud cover for our purposes would be fifteen hundred feet. We would fly most of the trip two hundred feet above ground level.

This would keep us invisible to the older type of North Korean radar.

We would rise to fifteen hundred feet at the last minute to allow a safe distance to jump. The downside is that it might put us on the North Korean radar.

We were going to sacrifice the aircraft. The C-47 had a rudimentary autopilot. I would fly the plane with the help of the SEALs, one of them acting as the copilot to provide muscle on the controls.

It took a lot of strength to operate them. While only three hundred miles, it would still be a hairy hour flying at low altitude. When we were in line with our jump-off point, I would line the plane up so that it would cross the landing zone and then head out to sea.

We hoped it would make the coast before being shot down by North Korean air defense jets. Since the collapse of the Soviet Union, they may not even have many jets in flying condition.

There would be two fresh corpses on board, young men killed in auto accidents. At least, that was what I was told.

China is China.

The bodies would be dressed in civilian clothes, and there would be two hundred kilos of heroin onboard. If shot down over the sea, the plane might sink and be a mystery. If it didn't sink or was shot down over land, then we had set it up to make them look like drug smugglers.

Our weight for each jumper was almost at the maximum. Including our body weight, we were jumping at three hundred and sixty-five pounds.

Since Harry was the lightest of us, he had the most gear. He told us to be nice to him, or he wouldn't share the K-ration packs. If it took longer than a week to hike out of North Korea, we would have to supplement the food locally.

Knowing that, I made a point of having my longbow and several dozen arrows as part of my load.

The bow wasn't my normal bow. It was a composite using fiberglass. In the center of the bow, it had brass screw fittings so that you could break the bow down to half its length. So, the bow and the arrows would fit in a package three feet long.

I had it made special by a friend of Rod Bell's, Wilber Allen, Jr., who was experimenting with new types of bows.

He called this one a compound bow. It had pulleys on both ends of the bow to reduce the needed pull weight, allowing for a shorter bow.

Rod had introduced us one afternoon while at the archery range at the studio. Will, as his friends called him, was there to help Rod do some stunts.

Later, over a couple of beers, Will described what he was doing. I had to open my mouth and ask why not make a true longbow into a compound bow.

Will pointed out the idea was to reduce pull weight to what ordinary people could use.

"Well, I'm not normal. Can you make me a compound bow that is also a longbow?"

In theory, that would increase the power of my longbow spectacularly.

The idea intrigued Will, and I committed to paying for the materials for a test bow. The result was a three-hundred-pound pull bow. It took one hundred and fifty pounds to draw but was released with three hundred pounds of energy.

We played around with it and found that we could shoot an arrow and hit the target as far as we could see the target. We even experimented with a small side-mounted telescope on the bow. It was incredible.

If you could shoot that accurately, it would kill a deer at five hundred meters. This was shortly after my return from East Germany, and I didn't have deer in mind.

We had to wait ten days for the weather to be as we wanted. The CIA had pictures of the site, and it looked good. The large flat plain near the river was clear. We hoped to get enough reflection off the river to help.

The evening of the flight in, we gathered at the airbase. I walked around the C-47 to make certain it was okay. It was my third walk around the aircraft that day.

I double-checked the fuel to ensure no water was in it. The oil sumps were full with no sign of leakage.

As I walked around, a truck pulled up, and two body bags were unloaded. They were placed near the front of the aircraft. The SEALs and I would have to wrestle them into place before jumping. There were also several large cases that I assumed contained the heroin.

Harry led the team in the last check of their gear. All was good, so we boarded. I was now checked out on this aircraft, so taking off wasn't as hard. I lifted the tail as we went down the runway.

Steve, one of the SEALs, was in the righthand seat. My hands were on the controls along with his. He was doing the heavy lifting of the controls. We had agreed that my strength had to be husbanded so that if there was an emergency, I could handle it.

The first leg was easy from Fengcheng, China, to Gulouzi, China, as there was radio guidance from one airport to the other.

We had to navigate from Gulouzi to Phyongwon, North Korea, before jumping out near Pyongyang. The weather was good; the cloud cover was thin and low. I kept us flying just above the various hills and mountain peaks we saw.

Fortunately, the peaks not only stuck up above the cloud cover, but they were also good navigational aids. Harry Beal, holding a chart, told Steve and me when and where to turn. We flew from peak to peak.

Even so, I was still nervous about our course until we saw a few lights ahead, which had to be Phyongwon or Seattle. I was hoping for Phyongwon.

The river we were hunting for came up exactly at the right time. We studied the terrain below, hoping to get a hint of the flat land we wanted to explore.

Two things happened. First, a jet, probably a MiG, came rocketing by us. Next, we saw lights below. We had found our field, and from the lights, it looked occupied by a North Korean regiment.

We had to make a quick decision. The jet had a large turning radius, so we could drop below the cloud cover and hide for a minute or two. I did that.

Without any prompting, the other SEALs started unpacking our deadheading passengers: grim times, grim humor.

I followed the river north, hoping to find another large open field. Two minutes of flight brought us to one. I yelled, "I'm bringing around to go on autopilot. Get ready to jump."

I turned and brought the plane back on a course on what I thought was the large open field. A corpse was placed in the right-hand seat. I set the autopilot, and one was put in the left seat.

For some reason, I told the dead pilot, "Second star to the right and straight on until morning."

We rushed to the back of the plane. All were kitted and hooked to the static line. Harry, who was to be last in line, checked me out as far as correct connections. I returned the favor.

When I said he was good, he yelled, "Jump."

We went out the door one after the other. We each had our equipment bag hooked to one of our feet below us. We had to push them out the door. There was no jumping as such; the bags pulled us with them.

It was a clear night, and I could see the lights on the back of all their helmets. After the shock of my chute opening, it was a pleasant night for a ride.

Chapter 41

All good things must come to an end, especially a parachute ride to Earth. No sooner had the chute in front of me collapsed than I was coming in hard and fast.

It seemed that way in the dark. Not having the proper depth perception was a hindrance to a standup landing. It turned out that what we thought was a flat field was a rice paddy. That was good and bad.

The mud made the landing softer; the water got us wet. That didn't slow us down from the immediate objective. Gather the collapsed chutes and get as far away as possible. We had no idea if we had been spotted bailing out of the doomed C-47.

With an armload of parasail silk and our equipment bags slung over our shoulders, we headed north. It was the direction of the Chinese border. If you measure by air, we had a little over a hundred miles to go. It was more likely two hundred by ground.

We trudged through the ankle-deep water for several hundred yards before we reached dry ground. After that, we marched inland until we reached a forest. In the dark, we had no idea how large it was.

We had two small entrenching tools, folding shovels to us civilians. We used those to bury the parasail silk. Careful not to leave a trace of the hole we had dug, we spread downed leaves over the freshly turned earth. One good rain and you would never know it had been disturbed.

I asked Harry if he had any idea how long it would take us to walk north to the Chinese border.

"I don't know; it depends on how long the mission takes."

I had forgotten. These were SEALs on a mission. They weren't about to let a mere North Korean regiment get in their way.

We had a good idea of where we were, as we had come down near the river. All we had to do was follow it south, and we would get back to our target.

Keeping to the woods and its concealment, we headed south using compass headings.

At the hint of daybreak, we started looking for a place to hide all day. There was nothing good nearby, so we went under the low-hanging branches of a large evergreen. The branches brushed the ground, so we couldn't be seen easily when we got against the tree trunk.

If dogs were hunting us, it was all over.

We ate, took care of our physical functions in a cathole, then slept in our lightweight sleeping bags. The SEALs set up a watch rotation. I got to sleep most of the day, catching the last watch as the day faded.

We went south for most of the night until we reached the edge of the woods. In the distance, we could see the lights of the resort that was our target. We set up the same style of camp as the night before.

The next day was spent observing the North Koreans who had moved into the field that had been our jump target. They showed no sign of moving. If anything, it looked like they were settling in for an extended stay.

The SEALs spent five days and nights snooping and pooping, as they called it. They scouted out the area. During the day, I kept watching to see if Haoran appeared. I saw him twice with my binoculars. Each time, he was on the same patio.

The NK troops had any shot at him blocked.

After a week, we all decided that the mission couldn't be accomplished without committing suicide. We weren't into that, so we decided to head home.

We could only move at night and would be doing good to cover ten miles a night. It would take us at least twenty days to reach the border.

Since we didn't have enough food, we would have to live off the land or scrounge what we could. My bow came in handy for that.

As our food dwindled, our packs got lighter. We had halazone tablets to purify our water. I brought down several rabbits the first two days of the march. They helped the food supply.

We did everything we could to avoid people, but one evening, we were sighted. I had just shot a small deer, and we were field-dressing it. Steve noticed a man watching us butchering the deer from the woods.

We had choices. We could kill him; we could ignore him or do what we did. We signaled him over and, after taking a few cuts, gave him the rest.

He spoke no English; we spoke no Korean, but you could tell he was glad for the food. Harry pointed at each of us and then held his finger to his lips as though he wanted the man to be quiet.

He nodded his head enthusiastically. We went our way; he went his loaded down with half a deer. We never had anyone chase us from that incident, so communication must have occurred.

We continued like this for a week. More and more hills had to be detoured. Try that at night with no lights. We had to backtrack several times because of small box canyons or deep, fast-moving streams.

That is when we started leaving small blazes on trees and trail markers so we could backtrack as needed.

We did have a radio, but it was to be used sparingly, if at all. Once a week, Harry would call in and tell the Chinese military we were okay and still moving.

One night, we walked into a dead-end valley. It wasn't a straight trip to the end. It had several twists and turns, and we had to cross two streams.

It was getting near daylight, so we decided to camp there. For once, we got lucky. There was a rock overhang which we could sleep under. It was a shallow cave, but it would hide us.

The next day, we had a meeting. We were all tired and needed rest. We decided this was as good a place as any to spend a few days.

Our K-rations were long gone. We were now living off the land. It is a good thing these guys were well-trained. My Scouting experience was good but not close to their training.

They knew which plants we could eat. My bow was invaluable as I kept us in protein. Some days, it was only a small squirrel; once, it was another deer.

We feasted that night.

We holed up there for three days. After that, we were rested up enough to continue. A hard fact was that if we hunkered down, our diet would cause us to lose strength, and we would never make it.

As we had been avoiding human habitation, we only had a loose idea of where we were. The closer we got to the border, the more NK patrols there would be.

To get an idea of how far we needed to go, we headed a little north by west after backing out of the dead-end canyon.

This would take us near the coast of the Yellow Sea and villages; from there, we could figure out how far we had to go. Sometimes, you think you are smart, and then the world shows you how dumb you are.

We found a village. They had no signs! All we could do was to continue north, hoping to see a sign matching our map's writing.

We finally came to a town that had railroad tracks. Most importantly, it had a railroad station with a sign. We were able to determine we were only ten miles from the border.

I even briefly thought about riding the boxcars as far as we could until a slow train chugged into the station. It had a soldier sitting on top of each car.

We moved further inland and continued our journey. That night, we covered most of the ten miles. Harry took a chance, called in on the radio, and let them know we were approaching the border. It wouldn't do for us to walk all this way and get shot by the Chinese.

We holed up for what we hoped would be our last night on the road. I was looking forward to a hot shower and a shave. I had to stink something terrible.

After dark that night, we moved north. The border was easy to see when we reached it. Along their side of the border, the Chinese had a road. It had trucks with their lights on parked every fifty yards. It was kind of hard to miss.

I would like to tell you how we made a desperate run to the border with NK border guards shooting at us all the way. There wasn't a guard in sight. We strolled across the imaginary borderline and stood there waiting to be noticed.

It didn't take long. First, a Jeep came up to us. A captain in the Chinese army confirmed it was us. He then radioed to his command. From there, it was being handed off to ever higher-ranking officers. Along the way, we picked up soldiers to carry our gear.

Best of all, we were offered coffee.

Chapter 42

We were put in a van and taken to the local airport, where we flew to Beijing. We were taken to an army barracks on-site at the airport and allowed to shower and shave.

We were given new working uniforms, but they were on the small side. Only Harry Beal had one that fit. Once we were presentable, we were taken to the Forbidden City.

I still felt gritty and needed a haircut, but my appearance was much better than an hour ago. The team and I were taken to a private audience room where the empress waited.

She told us she was happy to see us make it out safely. They had been unable to find out why the soldiers had been moved next to the resort. They were still there and showed no sign of moving.

Daily overflights would continue because of Haoran and to learn what that unit was up to. The unit was near Pyongyang: were they in a position for a coup or to prevent one?

Our airplane ruse had worked. The NK had shot it down over water but had recovered the two bodies and the wooden box loaded with heroin. The official reports stated that it was two Chinese smugglers who had become disoriented and flew into NK airspace.

The report by the unit commander who had found the wreckage gave the amount of heroin recovered. It was listed as only half the actual amount.

The empress was pleased with this because they now could blackmail that commander at need in the future.

Since we had regular radio contact, there had been no great concern about our lives.

My largest concern at the moment was where I could get a real meal. Not something with chopsticks. Bacon, eggs over easy, toast, and hashed browns came to mind.

I mentioned this to Harry Beal, and he invited me to the American Embassy with the rest of his team. Since this would be my best chance at an American-style meal, I begged off from the empress and went with them.

She commented that they would be importing an American chef for the palace.

I asked her about the possibility of a McDonald's franchise. She didn't say no.

I had my meal at the embassy; it was wonderful. I finished up my plate and asked if I could have a second helping just like the first. The SEAL team ate just as much, so I didn't feel guilty.

After the meal, we went to the ambassador's office. All he knew was we had been on a black mission. He informed the guys that they were needed back in the States as soon as possible.

I realized I now had nothing that needed to be done immediately and had things to do in the States, so I volunteered to take them back to Little River. They had a choice: military transport or ride in luxury.

We would leave first thing in the morning.

They were staying at the embassy while I went back to the palace. I had to spend the evening there alone.

Harold had the latest scoop on why I wasn't invited to the formal dinner that was being held.

It seemed there were several young men there that could be considered suitors for May-ling's hand. It was thought that I would scare them away, being so big and all.

I didn't know how to take that. Wasn't I good enough? Not that I wanted to marry her. Well maybe. I found my thoughts to be very confused.

I used the time wisely and caught up on my sleep.

About mid-day the next day, we loaded up the 707 and took off on our journey back to the States. It was more fun than usual because a couple of the guys had not been on the plane before, and the others gave a tour.

Harry Beal opted out of the tour and spent his time with Marjorie, one of our long-time stewardesses. I think they were sweet on each other. They are both good people, and I wish them the best.

Somehow, Harold had rounded up the proper size uniforms for the SEALs. They each had a small bag containing all their badges, so we were sharp-looking when we got off the plane at Andrews.

I even wore my Coldstream Guards uniform, the working version, not the mess dress. I didn't argue with Harold about what to wear. It gave me a chance to wear my new Dragon parachute wings.

I would have to get back to England and go to Whitehall to obtain permission to put up the Lightbulb. I could see the reasoning behind the award, but it still seemed silly.

We were flown down to Norfolk in a small ten-seater. From there, a van went out to the base at Little River. I hadn't intended to go with them, but everyone from Harold to the SEALs acted as though it was what I had to do.

I didn't think about it a lot. I figured they wanted me to be part of a debriefing. They did, besides other things.

The debriefing was first. We had to go over the plan as it was developed before the insertion. Then, we found that our target zone was occupied and the steps we took to recover the jump possibility.

The American brass was interested in what we knew about the bodies left on the plane. As I told them, for all we knew, they came from Bodies-R-Us. My humor was not appreciated.

Then there was the jump itself. They wanted to know how the lights on the helmet worked out, as this was a new development. We all agreed that it worked well.

Next, we had to describe scouting out the immediate area around the resort and finding our target.

Then, the decision that the mission couldn't be carried out. We were questioned seven different ways, almost to the point of accusing us of cowardice.

At that point, I had had it.

"I'm not a member of your armed forces, and I don't need to take this abuse, Lieutenant."

It doesn't hurt to remind them who the senior officer is.

"Furthermore, these men risked their lives on this mission and deserve better treatment."

A Navy commander who had been listening smoothly stepped in.

"No insult was meant, Colonel; we have to make certain they made the correct decision."

"Well, I, Colonel Richard Jackson, Duke of Hong Kong, am telling you that the mission couldn't be accomplished. If you want to question me further, take it up with my direct superior and the mission sponsor."

The lieutenant fell right into my little trap.

"And who are they? We will need to talk to them."

"The queen of England and the empress of China."

The commander sharply told the lieutenant, "That's enough!"

The debriefing continued with us describing our trip out. The tension had gone down in the room when the lieutenant exited. He gave no excuse. He just left.

My best guess is he had been told to be the bad guy in the debrief but had exceeded the bad guy part. I noticed my SEALs were trying to keep straight faces, but you could tell they liked an officer getting his comeuppance.

When the commander was told about my bow, he was very interested. He wondered if they should carry one just like it on missions. Harry told him that a modified one would be handy.

"Why would it have to be modified?"

"None of us could draw the one hundred and fifty pounds required. Maybe a hundred, but not that one."

I modestly kept my eyes down.

It took five hours, but we finally were allowed to go. It was considered a shame that it didn't work out, but none of it was our fault, and we had done the best that could be done to carry out the mission.

We were wrapping up when the door opened. We were told, "Attention." We all rose to stand at attention.

In walked President John Kennedy. He almost barked, "At Ease."

He shook hands all around and asked everyone how they were doing. He saved me for last.

"Rick, you give me more headaches than I can count and do so much for our country. After hearing about the mission, I'm pleased to award these."

He pinned a set of US parachutist wings below my Chinese Dragon wings. They had a bronze star pinned over the parachute. He explained that the army was lobbying to make the star an official part of the wings. The troops had been using them since World War II, and it was time to make them legal.

The bronze star on the wings indicated the wearer had been on an assault combat jump. If jumping with an NK regiment occupying your jump zone wasn't a combat jump, nothing was. That was when I remembered that the US and NK were still officially at war.

I couldn't wait to apply for the Lightbulb.

Chapter 43

The guys and I had dinner together and reminisced about the mission. For some reason, the highlight appeared to be when I shot an arrow entirely through a deer. It was within fifty yards, and the arrow dropped it dead in its tracks.

They marveled at what it took to pull that bow. I got it then; talking about an officer to another officer, even from a different country, was not the thing to do. But by alluding to my strength in bending that bow, they could chuckle at the lieutenant's expense.

Knowing that, I said, "Lieutenant Allen was so interested in my bow, maybe I should send him a beginner's bow, say a twenty-five-pound pull?"

They roared with laughter. No breach of etiquette but humor anyway. On a more serious note, I was told I was welcome to team with them anytime.

I thanked them for the invitation but told them their lives were too exciting for me. This really got them going. They started asking me about some of my life's high-profile events.

Remembering something that Popeye had told me about sea stories, I started with, "No shit, this is what happened."

The next four hours of beer-drinking and tale-telling were the most fun I had had in a long time. I can't share my stories with many people because they come across as bragging. This group accepted them and had tales of their own, which made mine pale by comparison.

The next morning wasn't so much fun.

I ran, hangover and all. I had to stop and puke at the halfway point. I still would do that night all over again.

I had no real plans at this point, so I decided to go to England and report in. I hadn't done this in a while. I called my chief pilot and arranged to fly later tonight. I spent the rest of the day napping and eating lightly.

In the early evening, we took off for London. I slept a good part of the trip. When I woke up, by the time I showered, shaved, dressed, and had breakfast, we were getting into the landing pattern.

Since I didn't have an actual schedule, I wore a uniform, so I was ready for anything—no medals, just ribbons and, of course, my new wings.

I smiled at the thought and took the limo waiting for me. I think there is a limo fairy as I no longer have to ask for them. They just appear. I'm pretty certain the flight crew is doing it, but I don't want to ask. I prefer to think of a limo fairy.

My first destination was Whitehall. I didn't have an appointment, so I had to wait for my contact to be available. Sitting in a waiting room full of military officers in uniform was weird. It made me think of the admiralty waiting room in a Hornblower novel.

My turn came, and I was escorted to the brigadier's office. He was attached to the Imperial Staff, and I think his charges were odds and sods like me. None of us fit neatly into the command hierarchy and thus were viewed with suspicion.

I marched in, stood at attention, and saluted. That is what one does in the army. He waved back at me in a half-hearted salute. I had probably broken some rule about saluting indoors without a cap on. In my mind, it never hurt to salute a superior.

He didn't seem upset, so it was okay. He probably thought that I wasn't real army anyway.

"Colonel Jackson, how may I help you today?"

"Several things, sir: I need to know if I can wear these foreign badges?"

"I recognize the US parachute wings, and we recognize those. It is unusual to see a combat star, though. As for the others, what are they?"

"They are the new wings of the Chinese army parachute brigade."

"Didn't know they have one."

"It is being formed as we speak. I have the honor of being the first qualified."

"What is considered qualified?"

"Four daytime jumps and one at night."

"The same as us, so yes, I would think so. Why didn't you ask your direct commander?"

"I hesitate to put Her Majesty in a position of going against army regulations."

"Oh, yes, I forgot you're an aide de camp to Her Majesty."

"Yes, you can see how that could become awkward if she said yes and regulations said no."

"Thank you for helping us all to avoid a potential problem. Tell me more about the Chinese wings."

"They call them Dragon wings. This is the first pair issued."

"How did that happen?"

"It was for a combined mission between the US Navy and the Chinese Army. Very black. Her Majesty was made aware and gave her permission to the US president and Chinese empress."

"I don't think I want to know anymore. I suspect that directly affects the other set of wings."

"It does, sir."

"We need to get you a set of British ones."

"I'm afraid I'm only eligible for the Lightbulb."

"We can't have that; I will cut orders to have the Coldstream Guards second you to a SAS unit. Then you can wear the full set of wings."

"Then, if I may be so bold, I would like to point out that I'm also a qualified pilot on a multi-engine plane and am about to take a check ride on my 707."

"Then we need to see about getting you a set of RAF wings. Could you provide your logbooks for our examination?"

"Yes, sir, they are on board my plane, which is at Heathrow. I will have them delivered here."

Inside, I was jumping up and down with glee. The RAF hadn't treated me well, so I was glad to get their wings behind their back.

"Follow me."

We went down a hall, several flights of stairs, and then another long hall. All painted in that wonderful institutional green.

We barged into an office; the brigadier barged; I followed in his wake.

He knew the occupant because he called him by his first name.

"Billy, I've got a man for your roster. He's being seconded from the Coldstream Guards to the SAS so we can give him a full set of parachutist wings rather than that embarrassing Lightbulb thing."

Billy didn't seem thrilled about all this. Even after he heard who I was, he wasn't happy. He did ask about the strange pair of wings I was wearing. When I told him, he sat up.

"Then it's true. The Chinese are setting up a parachute regiment."

I saw no reason that it would be a secret, so I affirmed it.

"We will have to...wait, we already have!"

"What?"

"We have a tradition in the SAS that between all of our members, we wear a set of every wing in the world. Since you're being seconded, you tick that box."

"Glad to be of service."

"Any chance we could get some other blokes through their course?"

"I don't see why not; I'll ask the empress tonight when I call her."

He stopped for a moment, and you could see it click.

"You're the Duke of Hong Kong."

"I have that honor."

"This is better and better. It will put us one up on the SBS."

I kept my mouth shut, not wanting to get involved in any interservice rivalry.

"Where will you be staying, transient officers' barracks?"

The brigadier spoke up. "I suspect Buck House."

"I will be in my suite at the Plaza on the Strand."

"I'll have the shoulder flash and badges delivered there. Now, one more thing.

"The special forces community has a lot of backchannel talks. There is a rumor that a US SEAL team went into North Korea. Do you know anything about that?"

Again, I hadn't signed anything or been told I couldn't talk, so I briefed the SAS brigadier on the failed mission.

"I wouldn't call it a failed mission. No one has ever been able to get a team in and out of there. I originally thought you were a badge hunter. Any chance you would be available for missions?"

"Only if Her Majesty approves."

"Now, I read in the papers about that nonsense in Siberia. How much of that is true?"

It took the rest of the afternoon and two cups of coffee to retell that adventure. I was surprised that I had to go all through it. I thought my VC and other awards spoke to that. I guess not.

The day was getting away from us, and the day was now starting in China, so I asked if I could use the phone for an international call.

I was put through in short order to the empress's chief of staff. Speaking in Mandarin, I asked if we could get some British SAS operatives through their parachute course.

He thought it an excellent idea, as it would show the world their program and forces were real.

When I hung up, I gave the SAS officer contact information and told him they were approved to go through the course.

Eying my distinctive wings, he told me he planned to attend the course.

Chapter 44

I was at loose ends for a while. I didn't have anything on my schedule. That is unless Haoran turned up.

Just to have something to do, I drove to Pinewood Studios. I hadn't had any contact with them for some months now. We had parted on good terms, and it was a shame the movies I was to be in fell through.

They would reemerge at some later date, but I wouldn't be in them. This happened more often than the public knew. Things changed; it could be the actors, as in this case, or world events that would make releasing a movie on a currently sensitive subject impolitic.

Not that the studios were shy of sensitive subjects. It would be better to say they were shy of subjects that could hurt the box office.

Then there were movies like my surfing movie that had financial issues, such as grand theft in that one. That also occurred more often than reported. Usually, it would be fraud rather than theft.

It was a beautiful day to drive, one of England's rare sunny days in June. The temperature was mild, and I had the windows down. It was amazing how the simple things in life can bring great pleasure.

My good mood lasted all the way to Pinewood Studios.

Since I didn't have the proper stickers on my rented car, I had to go through the entire entry process. This took almost two hours before I was permitted to proceed.

You would think being a wealthy duke would make it easy. These people dealt with all types and weren't easily impressed.

I suspected the queen would be given a pass, but the question was, why on earth would she want to come here? Even then, she would have to wear her robes and crown to be recognized.

The studios were the most self-absorbed crowd I had ever come across. Even those I liked at Warner Brothers were of that ilk.

I was escorted to the office of the VP of Production. He is more powerful than his title indicates. He had the final say on production and what would be produced.

His office professionally reflected this. His wasn't over the top like some Hollywood offices I had been in. It was large but not gargantuan. He had a desk that was kept neat, and the "I love me" wall behind him was filled with legitimate awards and pictures.

In front of the desk were three comfortable chairs of the proper height. I got so tired of those guys with chairs that made you sit low so they could look down on you.

One thing I had going for me, at six foot five, even a low chair couldn't make me look short. One side of the office had a small conference table with six chairs.

The walls had posters of what I assumed were movies he had been involved with. They were all class acts.

Once inside his office, it was like I had never left.

What had I been doing lately?

When I shared that I made a cameo in *Escape from Siberia*, the VP of Production said that was nice but wanted to know what real work I had done.

"I did escape from Siberia."

"Yeah, yeah, but what movies?"

In their world, if it wasn't fake, it wasn't real.

"None; I have been taking care of my other business interests."

"Like what?"

"Launching a man to the moon."

"Which studio and when will it be released?"

"It isn't a movie; I have a company working on sending real live people to the moon."

"Do you have anyone working on a screenplay of the project?"

I began to get exasperated, then stopped. He had a point. Why wouldn't we have a documentary of the project? This would dovetail with my commitment to have British involvement in the process.

So far, they have had a few scientists working with us on the launch team. What General Booth was doing was deep in the background and would be a boring presentation.

"That is a good idea. I would like to assemble a production team to cover the whole project and release it as a documentary. We may even do it in several parts. We have to put someone into orbit around the earth, build a space station in orbit to support the trip to the moon, fly to the moon, and then establish a permanent manned base. This could be an ongoing project for some years."

"How will you get permission for the project and the funding?"

Is this guy for real? I held up my hand.

"Wealthy Duke of Hong Kong here. It's my company and my money. I can do what I want."

He got a little goggle-eyed at me.

"You're a real duke?"

"Yes."

"I thought it was just a publicity title, like Duke John Wayne. I wondered how you were getting away with infringing on his screen name."

"First of all, Duke is just a nickname that John uses. His screen name is John Wayne."

"Oh yeah, I remember now. He's Marion Morrison or something like that."

"You got it."

"Then, when I saw the queen awarding you the Victoria Cross on TV, it wasn't just a publicity stunt with some actress playing the queen?"

"That was real."

"I even made a note to find out who the actress is that played the queen. She was exceptionally good at it."

"I'll tell her that the next time I see her. I bet she would work for scale."

"Do you think so?"

What sort of dolt is this? He doesn't live in the same world as the rest of us, even if he has a nice office.

"Then you are telling me you can give the go-ahead on this and finance it?"

"Yes."

If I strangled him, I was certain no jury would ever convict me.

That was when he turned all business on me. I had entered his world, and he was darn good at it. He called a group to his conference table; he pulled together a team of accountants, lawyers, and screenwriters.

He had me describe the proposed project to the group. Fortunately for them, they were more clued in. At this point, mass murder was feasible.

I gave an overview of the moon project and then broke it down into its major components. There was a blackboard on wheels in the hallway, which was brought in.

The first order of business was to consider the number of film crews needed. After trying to divide it up like the production groups, we decided that wouldn't work.

We would need many teams to do it that way, and the teams would have significant downtime waiting for the next action phase of the project.

We finally decided on one film crew in England, one in the US, and two in China. There would also be a floater team on call if action picked up in one of the areas.

Then, a question came up that floored me.

"Who is controlling the entire mission?"

"Right now, I am."

"Just you?"

"The Yanks have a great bloody team in Houston they call Mission Control. Are you doing all of that?"

"I'm not certain what all they are controlling in Houston; let me check some things out and get back to you."

What I was doing was trying to buy some time. This entire project was gathering speed, and I wasn't prepared for it. I needed to talk to the expert in logistics, General Booth.

I asked them to appoint their own "mission controller" for the film teams and come up with some pricing while I did my homework. As a sign of good faith, I wrote a cheque for one hundred thousand pounds to get the ball rolling.

Future costs would be deducted from that. At least I knew the accountants would be on my side.

I hightailed it back to London. This time, it was not a leisurely drive. I had a mess to clean up.

By the time I got back, it was late in the day, so I called General Booth at Whitehall and caught him just as he was leaving for the day. I made an appointment for tomorrow morning.

He started to ask what about, then started laughing, "You've figured out that you have bits and pieces moving but not an organization in place to control things."

I had to admit that was the truth. I wasn't about to tell him that it was a movie production guy who set me on the right track. I was embarrassed enough.

"Come round in the morning, and we will sort it out."

I decided I needed to do something different, so I asked the hotel concierge to get me theater tickets, something light if you please.

He came up with a good seat at the Comedy Theater. It had a revue playing, *An Evening of British Rubbish*. It had been playing since January to good reviews. I particularly liked the segments,

"Penny Farthing", "Tiger Rag", "Dolly Gray", and, best of all, the skit, "Inventors Act".

Chapter 45

I was so anxious to see General Booth in the morning I was early for my appointment, a full hour. They let him know I was there. Luckily for me, this was the time of day he read the morning briefing papers over coffee.

He invited me into his office. I had been there before, so I expected the austere appearance. To look at it, you would think it was a spare office used for temporary visitors.

No "I love me" awards or pictures. The walls were painted institutional green. The flooring was old linoleum that looked like it had been there since the World War, the first one.

An overflowing ashtray was the only extra item on his desk. The in and out baskets were both empty. One chair in front of the desk was low and looked uncomfortable. I remembered it with distaste from my last visit.

Each to his own, I guess.

When the escort dropped me off at his door, the general grunted as I entered the room.

"Can't even let a man have his coffee in peace. Well, follow me."

He led me to another office, his real one. It was carpeted with a deep blue plush, the walls paneled a light oak.

Shelves with books took up the wall behind him. A few awards were posted, but they were on the other side of the room, and I couldn't read them.

His office was two offices joined together; the other office half contained a conference room table with eight padded chairs around it. A projector was on a table at one end and a screen at the other.

A copier was placed by the door, so you couldn't see it when you walked in. There were three file cabinets with combination locks.

There was even a kitchenette for tea and coffee and a small refrigerator for cold drinks. I mentally bet the door to one side led to a restroom.

This was the office I wanted when I grew up.

The general spoke up, "This is my real office. The other is for fools who want to waste my time. I didn't know who you were when you first came here."

I didn't know if I had just been complimented or insulted.

"Am I right in thinking that you are here because you have realized that you have set things in motion and are about to lose control?"

"Yes, sir."

"At least you woke up before it was too late."

He went over to one of his file cabinets and, after fiddling with the combination, pulled out a file. From that, he extracted an organizational chart.

"I knew this would be needed quickly, but even I'm surprised at how fast we got to this point. May I explain how I think this should be set up?"

"Please do."

I know a lifeline when I see it.

"At the top, as you can see, is Jackson Enterprises. It has overall ownership but no actual involvement in running the Space Division.

"Space Division is divided into three parts: Science, Launch, and Administration.

"Science will be responsible for identifying, obtaining, or developing all materials used in the flight program.

"The launch group will be responsible for all launches, recovery, and any mission above the earth's atmosphere.

"The administration will be responsible for human resources and infrastructure, including facilities, accounting, and purchasing.

Where needed, they will purchase whole companies to satisfy our needs.

"I suggest Science be located here in the United Kingdom as it will help our economy and, especially, slow or stop the loss of our best minds.

"Administration in the United States because their companies will provide most of the products we need to purchase, and most of the workforce.

"It has already been decided that China will have the launch facility. I suggest that their mandate be expanded so that they are still responsible if there is a need for a launch facility outside of China. This will head off any turf disputes."

Thinking out loud, I responded, "That all makes sense to me, but there is one thing I would like to include."

"That being?"

"Any companies we need to purchase, we own less than fifty percent. The rest should be offered to the public in which they are located. This is to avoid any future claims of Jackson Enterprises being a monopoly.

"JE should not be the sole source of items needed for space flight. I don't want to be accused of preventing others from trying."

"But you will still have a lot of control over those companies."

"I said I didn't want to be accused of being a monopoly, nothing about being one. I trust myself to exploit the initial exploration of space for the betterment of the world, but not everyone else."

"You realize every dictator of the past would have made the same claim."

"True, but by not owning everything, others can constrain me if I go too far wrong."

The general nodded, but you could tell he wasn't convinced. That worked for me; I'm not even sure I'm convinced.

He changed the subject.

"Our investigation group found the Soviets had developed the Proton rocket, which could be used to put items into high orbit. Unlike the American proposal for sea landings, they also have a capsule that could go into low orbit and land on the ground."

"You mean we could have a person orbit the earth right now?"

"Yes, do you want to fund a mission?"

"Not only yes, but hell yes."

I think Mum would forgive that outburst; she has a pretty rough tongue herself.

"Then we need to bring the rocket, capsule, and astronaut or cosmonaut together at Jiuquan."

"I would rather call them astronauts; do we have any?"

"We have the chance at getting the best one in the world."

"Who?"

"Jerrie Cobb; she and others have been let go by NASA because they aren't combat trained."

"Women aren't allowed in combat training. That sounds iffy to me."

"She has scored better in everything than John Glenn, Alan Shepard, and others. They didn't want the competition, so they got Lyndon Johnson to hold a congressional hearing where they scuttled the FLATs program. That is First Lady Astronauts Training. There were 13 of them that qualified, so they are called the Mercury 13. Only seven men made it, thus the Mercury 7. Tell me which group is better?"

"Can we hire them all?"

"Why?"

"Because I don't like Lyndon Johnson, and we want the best. By the time this program gets going, every one of them will have been in space. Think of it as my blow for women's rights."

"Then you better get your administration group up and running so you have an HR group to hire them."

"Oh lord, there will have to be contracts; those require lawyers. Why me?"

"Since they will soon come under the launch group, have the Chinese hire them on a short-term contract basis."

"That's brilliant!"

"I have been given permission, or rather, directly ordered, to put the Science group in place. I suggest you ask the Chinese to do the same with the Launch group. I don't know what to do about Administration in America. The last thing you want to be involved in America is NASA."

"You are right about that; they have a lot of good people, but they are now infested with bureaucrats, and it will only get worse. By limiting themselves to orbit and then trips to the moon without a permanent base, they have stifled their future. It's the perfect breeding ground for an inefficient, power-hungry bureaucracy."

"Now tell me how you really feel about it."

That made us both laugh.

"My corporate headquarters has gotten used to creating new organizations overnight. I will call them and dump it in their lap later today."

"One more thing. We could use some more money to get things going here."

"How much?"

"Ten million pounds if you can spare it."

I pulled out my checkbook.

"Who should I make it out to?"

For the first time, I saw General Booth flustered.

"Uh, we have to set up the organization first."

"How about I set up a drawing account at my bank in your name?"

"That works. You know, I thought I knew what rich was. I didn't even begin to dream."

I returned to my hotel in time to have lunch brought to my room. These days, my notoriety is so great I wouldn't be left alone for a meal if I tried to eat in the hotel restaurant.

After that, I called Jim Williamson. I would've felt sorry for him if I didn't pay him so much.

"Jim, I need some help."

From the groan on the other end, he knew it wouldn't be easy.

"I need an Administration group set up for the new Space Division."

I thought I would keep it low-key until he realized what I was asking.

"You mean with lawyers, accountants, and HR people?"

"That, and an engineering group for infrastructure worldwide and a purchasing group. Same deal as the IC Chip setup: partial ownership of any company we need for rocket parts."

"Okay, I thought you would want something big."

"Huh?"

"Rick, we know you. As soon as you said Space Division, we started identifying all those resources except for the facilities group. That one wasn't foreseen."

"This is why I pay you the big bucks."

Chapter 46

It is wonderful to have people working for you who watch and plan ahead. I realized that it was as much to their benefit as mine, but it was still a good thing.

General Booth sent me a hand-carried message by military courier two days later. The Chinese had built three Proton rockets and space capsules already.

This seemed strange. They had only obtained the licenses from the Russians two months ago. They would barely have had time to translate all the plans and drawings, much less build anything.

It seems Chinese spies had been very efficient and stole all the plans over a year ago—something to remember about my intellectual property.

I called the empress's chief of staff to get a status check on what was going on. He told me they were preparing the Jiuquan Satellite Launch Center in the Gobi Desert to launch a person into Earth orbit.

The empress had been told about the Mercury 13 lady astronauts being trained, then rejected by NASA. Offers of employment in the Chinese space program had been made. When the ladies arrived in China, they would find they were working for Jackson Enterprises Space Division Launch Group. Their pay would be almost ten times what NASA paid. That would be over seven hundred and fifty thousand dollars a year.

Within two days, all had replied to the offer, and nine of the thirteen had been accepted. I was glad that Jerrie Cobb was at the top of the list.

I had thought that someone mentioned that Lop Nor was to be the launch site. When I asked, I was politely told that it was being used for other purposes. With that level of secrecy, it must be their nuclear program.

The Space Ladies, as I thought of them, were to leave from Houston in the US three days from now. Since all the action was now moving to China, I decided to go there also, via Houston. I would give my latest employees a lift.

That may have been a mistake.

After spending a day on the phone taking care of business and stopping by my London office to sign the paperwork, I boarded the 707 for Houston.

I had taken a load of technical material that General Booth had gathered on the rocket and capsule. I wanted to study it and also share it with the Space Ladies.

I got some studying done, a few hours of flight time, and a night's sleep, and we were landing at Houston International Airport. It seemed like a quick trip.

Nine ladies were waiting at the private aviation terminal, all about five to ten years older than me. Word had got out that something was up because reporters were waiting.

Being the coward that I am, I stayed on board while the plane was serviced, and the ladies boarded.

They had been told a 707 would pick them up, just not which one. As they came aboard, I quickly realized I was facing nine females who wanted answers!

"Ladies, if you bear with me for a minute, I will explain what is going on."

I had the feeling if I waited longer than a minute, there would be a lynching, mine.

"First of all, do you have your signed contracts?"

A chorus of yeses followed.

"Okay, you realize that all of you are guaranteed the money for the next five years. Were you given evidence that the money has been put in escrow in your name?"

That one had a few of them talking to each other.

"Now I understand your desire to go into space, and you are willing to work in the Chinese space program to do it, especially after getting screwed over by NASA."

Lots of yes, mutterings, and downright swearing at that.

"Okay, some of you may know that I'm the Duke of Hong Kong and considered one of the richest people on the planet."

According to Forbes, I was the richest now by far.

"My company, Jackson Enterprises, has a space division with a launch division run by the Chinese. There is a science division run by the British, and the administration is run directly by Jackson Enterprises Space Division in America.

"The Chinese and British governments are active participants in this project. You may consider NASA a competitor to some degree. I say some degree because their announced plans are some missions to the moon and back, and that's it.

"Our mission is to have a permanent space station in orbit and a base on the moon. The base on the moon will be a staging area to explore the rest of the solar system.

"At this time, you ladies are the only ones trained to be astronauts who are available and will be performing the first flights. Others will be trained later, but you will be the first. This is by the order of the empress of China, Queen Elizabeth, and my mother."

If they thought I was kidding about Mum, they were wrong.

"Oh, by the way, we will use the Russian Proton rocket and capsule under license. We will have several test launches. I understand the first one is being placed on the gantry as we speak.

"Any questions?"

I thought my little talk would take the wind out of their sails. Silly me, they had questions, hundreds of questions. They were still asking them while we refueled in Anchorage.

After that, they gave me a break while we ate dinner. I had stayed up front with them the entire flight. A question about the rest of the aircraft gave me a rest from answering questions.

I asked our stewardesses to give tours of the entire aircraft. While they were on their tours, the chief pilot came back to see me. He had a newspaper in hand.

"Rick, I think you need to see this, the UP wire is prompt with their stories if nothing else."

On the second page of the *Anchorage Daily News* was an article with pictures. It seems the Duke of Hong Kong now has a harem made up of rejected astronauts. Someone in Houston doesn't like me.

I wonder if he is the vice president of the United States. If so, the feelings are mutual. After I had that thought, I chastised myself. I didn't know who it was, and I was letting my biases color my conclusions over what was a non-event.

The world would know the truth soon enough. I did tell the pilot not to let the ladies see it. We would have a riot on our hands.

When the ladies came back from their tours, they told me they would draw straws for my bed.

I didn't touch that line. I went up front and got a few more flight hours in.

The press was waiting in Tokyo, but we didn't get off the plane, so the ladies didn't learn about what was being printed. By the time we got to Jiuquan, it would be old news, and if I were lucky, there would be no English-language papers there.

We landed in Beijing to great fanfare. There was a parade to take us to the Forbidden City. There, the ladies were taken to a set of suites where they could rest and clean up. It was a long trip, and they had only started in Houston. I started in London.

Unlike them, I was chivied along in cleaning up and getting dressed. At least Harold, the coward who hid in his cubby hole the entire trip, advised me to dress casually.

I was taken to the empress's private apartment. It was different from her official apartment. That was for show; this was for living; I mean kick back and relax. I had to smile to see she was a fan of those Scottish Highland romances. Poor girl, rich, handsome, powerful Scotsman. If he lived four hundred years ago, even better.

The empress and I talked a little about the Space program. She was concerned that while we competed with NASA, that it would be considered in competition with the United States, and she didn't want that.

I told her that, unfortunately, the press and some government officials would spin it as competition.

She thought that they wouldn't take that attitude since Jackson Enterprises was paying for the bulk of the project and even having the administration conducted in America.

Why, even the astronauts would be Americans.

I then reminded her that NASA had a vested interest in being the only group in orbit. Alan Shepard, John Glenn, and the rest considered it their private domain. They felt threatened by the women who qualified as pilots equal to them and who scored better on the space requirements.

"What will they say about you?"

"I probably will end up being branded a traitor."

Chapter 47

The empress almost shrieked, "A traitor! You have done so much for your country. How could they do that?"

"Easily. It's not what I have done in the past. It's the fact that I'm not working for their special interest group."

"What group is this?"

"It will all revolve around NASA. NASA isn't the villain. It is those who live off NASA who will oppose me."

"How does that work?"

"NASA has to let many contracts, and the new zip codes track every part they buy. To gain congressional support for their programs, they let every congressman know how many jobs they are supporting in each congressional district.

"If they purchase ten screws from a small supplier who has twenty employees, they will report twenty jobs were created in that district.

"The congressman will turn around and tell the providing company they had put a good word in for them with NASA and please contribute to my re-election campaign. When you realize how many different purchases NASA has to make, it adds up. They are a powerful lobby in Congress for their project funding.

"They have gotten so large they could change their mission to something like controlling the weather, and Congress would fund them."

"Unlike private companies, the government can create a monopoly. No one else in America can build and launch rockets to explore space. Congress is all in favor of this because it keeps its election funds flowing. NASA can be a bureaucracy without the pressures of competition.

"Private companies support NASA because they are getting business from them. It is a closed-loop system. Until the loop is broken, progress will be at a governmental pace rather than private industry.

"Now, all these bad things said, when a government puts its mind to it, it can accomplish things faster than private industry. A better way to say it is when government gets out of private industry's way, things can happen. You saw what American industry accomplished in World War II when the government got out of the way."

I told the empress this: an oversimplified view of how special interest groups in America can have disproportionate power.

There were no villains in the group, even Congress. There will always be a bad apple or two, but most were trying to take care of their constituents by directing where government funds were spent to provide jobs.

Since I was trying to do something outside of this system, I would be branded as the bad guy. That was better than waiting around for fifty years or so, watching NASA accomplish nothing until the public woke up.

Even NASA accomplishing nothing isn't their fault. They would lose funding when it was realized there wouldn't be an instant payback for going to the moon. They then would languish for years as Congress found other special interest groups to fund their reelection campaigns.

Maybe I am getting cynical.

The empress asked, "Is there any way we can counter this?"

I started to tell her no; then I remembered the many sessions I had spent with publicity people.

"We need to spin this. We can't be perceived to compete with NASA. We need a different mission statement. Theirs is to be the first to land a man on the moon.

"Ours will be something like creating a moon base for scientific exploration. That is a different project, and we won't advertise. On second thought, we shouldn't use the word competition at all."

"Why don't you turn it over to a publicity team and let them handle it?"

"Excellent thought, Your Imperial Majesty. I get too wrapped up in the details."

The empress later met with the Space Ladies. That seemed to be their title going forward. She was gracious with each of them, inquiring about where they were from and some of their background.

While she conversed with them, she had refreshments served, so it was more like a lady's tea. May-ling was there, and she would occasionally smirk at me as I had to listen to this female talkfest. If they'd had quilts to work on, my American grandmother would have been right at home.

A critical question arose: who would be the first woman to orbit the Earth? A highly dangerous honor. No pun intended on the high part. Whoever was first would always be remembered. It would be dangerous because the rocket system and capsule had never been used in real conditions.

The Soviets had sent test flights up using the rocket. They had even had a capsule on one that came down safely. Still, no human had ever been up in one.

The empress asked the question. The ladies looked at each other briefly, and then one said, Jerri Cobb. The others agreed rapidly.

When asked why Jerri, they replied that Jerri was the one that had held them together in the dark days of the Congressional hearings and their forced separation from NASA. She was the one that kept their hopes alive.

After a while, I managed to slip out the door. I suspect it was noticed, but I wasn't needed for all the girl talk. When I left, they were starting on the shortcomings of men, with the empress leading the way.

The next day, we flew to Jiuquan and its primitive barracks. After we toured them, I had to apologize to the women. They told me that they had been in worse, a lot worse.

Besides, the view offset everything. What a view we had in the Gobi Desert!

Jerri pointed behind me. When I turned, I understood. About five miles away, a Proton rocket stood tall at the gantry with the pod on top.

This wasn't the one Jerri would ride into orbit but a test vehicle. We needed to know if we had built the rocket and pod correctly.

The Russians had provided technicians, drawings, and manuals. We still needed confirmation that it would work.

After a trip to the mess hall, we all decided we needed an American cook if we were going to survive this experience. The local Mongols hired as cooking staff had no idea of Western cuisine. Rice was okay, but there were limits, and they thought they were doing us a favor with yak milk for our coffee.

This had to be one of my highest priorities, or I would have a strike on my hands. I know I wasn't in charge of this base. However, the people who were had set it up like this. Now, to make changes without anyone losing face.

While the ladies went to a shed set up for orientation and training, I headed for the base's administration office.

The base commander graciously admitted me to his office. This welcome concerned me. He thought he was doing the foreign devil a great favor by speaking to him.

Now, how could this go wrong?

I thanked him for seeing me and that I would report to the empress how cooperative he was being. Hey, if you have a big gun, use it!

I noticed that his "I love me" wall was filled with some serious awards, so he was competent. He just didn't realize my place in his scheme of things.

"I'm very satisfied with how my money is spent here."

"Your money?"

"You haven't been informed where the funding is coming from? It is a consortium of Great Britain, China, and my company in the United States. Great Britain and China are contributing space, scientists, and general support, in kind, if you will. My company is supplying the funds."

"I wasn't made aware of this."

My Mandarin was getting good enough that I could pick up on nuances. He hadn't been told.

"This fault is mine. I must ensure that you and your people are given a complete briefing. This would best be done by you meeting with the empress and her staff, followed by you briefing your staff.

"I realized this morning I have committed another error. I had not requested that American food prepared by American cooks be available for the astronauts.

"They are used to an American diet, and it wouldn't do to have one sick in space from strange foods."

The commander asked, "Can you get us different foods and cooks?"

"Yes, I can arrange that if you approve."

"Approve! Do you know those cooks use yak milk in their coffee? I wanted to fire them all, but a contract was made by higher-ups in Beijing. The rice is okay, but it would be better with fish heads. Then the yak milk? Everyone knows goat milk is better."

To each their own.

"I think we will need three menus: American, Chinese, and Mongolian Chinese."

"I think you are right."

I felt like I had done a good day's work, and my food problem straightened out with no loss of face.

Chapter 48

When you looked over the Jiuquan launch site, there were five gantries for rocket launches. Three were complete, and two more were finishing up. There were plans for another five.

Unlike the US rocket program, which was scheduling specialized focused launches with plenty of time between them, we were looking at a commercial schedule. It was estimated that there would have to be at least two launches a week to implement a permanent base on the moon.

Many of these would be unmanned, sending building materials for a space station and infrastructure on the moon.

The rockets themselves would be built on-site in the enormous factory that was being put up. It would rival anything Boeing or Lockheed Martin had.

To do this, a city had to be built. Workers needed housing, groceries, doctors, dentists, a hospital, a police station, a library, schools, pharmacies, dry cleaners, and many other businesses.

All this in the Gobi Desert. The weakness would be water. The Chinese had started an eight-hundred-mile-long pipeline to bring water to the site. In the meantime, a fleet of trucks was hauling water twenty-four hours a day.

Railroad tracks were being laid. Concrete poured for a superhighway.

The city alone would cost over five hundred million dollars. The person who said easy come, easy go didn't know the half of it. I couldn't have supported this effort if I hadn't invested my business earnings. As it was, we would have to start watching expenditures like never before.

Once things got rolling, all the businesses I created to build rocket parts would start supporting the operation. I had hoped for some funds from the IC Chip project. The cargo container business was still raking in cash, but not enough by itself.

To top it all off, I had a proposal sent to me by my publicity group. It read well and achieved our objectives. The only downside was that I had to present it to our astronauts.

I had learned that you needed to face the dragon while it was still small, so I gathered them together.

"Ladies, good news and bad news. Our publicity department has a way of presenting our efforts in such a way that they don't appear to compete with NASA.

"That's the good news. The bad news is that they are going to refer to you as 'Homemakers in Space.'"

I held my breathing, waiting. I didn't have to hold it for long; cries of dismay and even some laughter broke out. At least nothing was thrown at me.

"Let me explain their thinking. NASA aims to put men on the moon, a bold, adventurous mission—the stuff real men do.

"As Homemakers in Space, you will be building a support space station which those bold men might or might not use; we certainly will. Then, you will build a habitat on the moon. Again, to support any bold, adventurous men that may go there.

"The only thing we won't point out is that we intend to have you there waiting for them when they arrive!

"I know the words are demeaning to what you will achieve, that many jokes will be made about it. But when all is said and done, you will have led the way."

I then explained why we had to do it this way. If we went head-on in a space race, we would lose—vilified and unemployable at the best, outcasts at the worst, not only us but our families.

They saw the logic but didn't pretend to like it. I made a counterproposal to them, not only to do it but also to own it. Do publicity tours of how you are going to make outer space livable. Just remember, you wanted a chance to go into space; this is it.

That last settled things down. Somehow, I didn't see I would get Jerri Cobb to play Susie Homemaker.

The next day was a big day for us. We had our first test launch scheduled. The integration steps had taken place. The rocket stages and payload, in this case, an empty capsule filled with sandbags equal to crew weight, had been joined in the tall assembly building.

While being assembled, everyone on base and at all remote sites was allowed to sign one of several scrolls with their name, which were put in the capsule. Even the queen and the empress signed.

The rocket had been rolled out to the launch pad. It took over a day for the crawler to move it in place.

The fueling had started the night before. These things drink hydrazine as if it were water. The pre-launch checks had started.

We were using something new. We had software we called the automatic ground launch sequencer. It took the final phases of the countdown through its steps. This was as opposed to the many pages of paper checklists used before.

This was a direct product of the efforts of our new computer division. Since this was the first effort, we ran it and the paper checklists simultaneously.

The higher echelon of the launch team and our astronauts were in a bunker built for dignitaries to watch the first launch. General Booth even came over from England.

It got real when the orbiter access arm backed away from the rocket.

At T-5 minutes the auxiliary power units were powered up, remotely this time as we had no pilot on board.

It was announced over the speaker system in the bunker that the solid rocket safety devices were armed. The rocket could be separated from the capsule downrange if there were problems, and then the rocket would be destroyed.

The main engine gimbal profile test was successful. Next, the oxygen vent arm was retracted. The orbiter transferred from ground to internal power at T-50 seconds.

The ground launch sequencer signaled that all boards were green, and the mission was a go.

The rainbirds were powered up, gushing water onto the pad to prevent the enormous sound emitted from blasting out and doing damage.

At T-10 seconds, the hydrogen burn-off system was ignited to burn up excess CH2 vented from the engines.

The main engine start at T-6.6 seconds went off.

Then the darn rocket just stood there. It seemed like forever but in 6.6 seconds, we had lift-off.

We were over a mile away and could feel the rumbling in our chests.

Everyone was yelling and cheering. The astronauts were hugging each other and crying.

Mission control, onsite at Jiuquan rather than some site picked to provide local jobs, kept us apprised of progress. They announced the speed and distance. As each of the three stages separated successfully, there were cheers. When the final separation occurred, we were all wrung out.

The capsule circled the Earth five times in seven hours; then, its onboard engines knocked it out of orbit.

It came down exactly where it was supposed to—only fifty miles from Jiuquan. We didn't want it too close if things went wrong. Exactly, in this case, was five miles from the big X some optimist had laid out in the desert. With this setup, there would be some wind drift.

NOTAMs had been sent out to the world that there would be a rocket launch. The name of the launch was Homemaker One.

Congratulations poured in from all over the world, even from NASA. I could picture the smirks on their faces when the Mercury 7 thanked the ladies for realizing their place was at home.

Two more launches occurred in the next week. The second was another test. On the third, Jerri Cobb became the first woman to reach outer space.

The ladies were getting into the Homemakers in Space. They insisted on the press release calling Jerri the Homemaker Astronaut. They even had it on the mission patch.

We had films of the first three rocket launches. The first was a little rough, but from the second one on, we had professional crews from Pinewood Studios in place.

Our publicity people were out front of the story explaining that female astronauts were being used to build "homes" in space, first in orbit and then on the moon.

I will never forget the look on Jerri Cobb's face when she was told she had to wear makeup while being filmed in the cleanroom atop the gantry. After the pictures were taken, she washed it off. I do think the pearls were over the top.

After the three successful launches and returns, I had to go to London. The main reason was that I had my official duty day as a Knight of the Garter. We put on our silly hats and went to dinner and church.

Harold gave me a stern lecture when I called it a silly hat. I bowed my head in shame as he did it, but I still thought they looked silly.

Then, there were two days of working sessions with General Booth. Things had sped up since the launch. I was surprised by the number of requests to take science packages into space.

My next planned stop was back in the US to check how the Administration group was coming along.

I also had a telegram from President Kennedy congratulating me on the launch and asking that I stop by the White House as soon as possible. I planned to do that on my way to California.

I set things in motion to return to the US next week.

Chapter 49

Returning to my hotel, I changed into my jeans, polo shirt, and blue sports coat. I then went to Treacher's for fish and chips.

It was almost summer here in England, so I went for a stroll down the Thames embankment. It was a beautiful moonlit night, and I passed many couples out for a romantic walk.

I didn't feel sorry for myself, but I wished I could have a relationship that didn't go south on me. Seeing which way my thoughts were heading, I turned and headed back to the hotel.

In the morning, there were several packages for me at the front desk. I had them sent up. One contained my flight logs. The other had RAF flight wings, SAS pattern parachutist wings, and a flying dagger shoulder patch for my right shoulder, indicating I was with the SAS.

Even with my medals and ribbons, I looked like what I was, an aide de camp on staff. Now, I looked like a badass. I had been there and done that.

Harold was beside himself; his favorite job was updating my uniforms. I had been sent one set of the new patches and badges. He needed to acquire twenty-some additional sets to update all my uniforms.

I don't know how he did it. I suspect there is a secret valet handshake that gets these things done. Later, I asked him and was sorry I asked. He would take the paperwork accompanying each item to the nearest military base and buy them at their post-exchange. In this case, the nearest was located in the Tower of London.

I called Mr. Norman, who invited me to a short meeting at the palace. It turned out to be not so short. I was led to a conference room where there were men in suits that I had never met before. We weren't introduced.

They cut right to the chase. Since I had been in North Korea, did I think it would be possible to assassinate Kim il Jung and Kim Jong-Il?

"I don't know. I didn't get that near either of them. They didn't appear on the patio that we had under surveillance. I would have no idea where to begin to look."

"If we could pinpoint them, could you do it?"

"We are done here. I'm not an assassin."

"Your Grace, I beg to differ. What were you going to do in North Korea?"

"Let me reword that: I'm not your assassin. I will do the bidding of Her Majesty the Queen or Empress Ping of China and take action against those that threaten me and mine."

"Does that include us?"

"Should it?"

The doors to the room slammed open. An irate queen stormed into the room.

"You all are under arrest for treason against the Crown."

Mr. Norman took me aside.

"I will explain all later."

This would be good. In the meantime, the four men in suits were handcuffed by the soldiers and taken away. They were handled roughly and weren't heading to a tea party.

Elizabeth only nodded to me as she left the room; she looked madder than a wet hen.

After they left, Mr. Norman explained.

"These men are the leaders of a group of hardliners in MI6. They want to take out the leadership of North Korea. They don't care if they set off another shooting war.

"Even worse, their real goal is to return India to the British Empire. This would be a disaster if war broke out between us. They realized that much, so they planned to start a war between India and

Pakistan so that after they fought to a standstill, they could go in and take it over.

"They have been abusing their privilege of using meeting rooms at the palace to intimidate people and make them think the Crown supports them. We needed to hear them commit treason before moving on them."

The next day, I read of a terrible crash on the A1. Four civil servants on their way to a meeting had veered off the road and run into a concrete abutment, killing all.

England is England, gentle deaths instead of public beheadings—the same results.

The following morning, I ran in Hyde Park along Rotten Row. I had just turned to head back to Trafalgar Square when a police car pulled up beside me.

A bobby leaned out of the still-moving car.

"Your Grace, there is an urgent message for you at the palace. We are to take you directly there."

"Whose orders?"

After being summoned to the palace the other day, it wasn't an automatic journey.

"Her Majesty's."

At that, they pulled to a stop, and I jumped in. With flashing lights and sirens blaring, we blasted by Harrods and sped to the palace.

When I got there, I was immediately escorted to Mr. Norman's office. He didn't waste any time.

"Rick, there has been another attempt on May-ling's life. She is injured but will be okay. You need to get to China as quickly as possible."

"I will tell them to get the 707 ready."

"We have something quicker."

I was flown by helicopter to Mildenhall, where a strange-looking aircraft waited. The 707 would follow along, but I would fly in the prototype aircraft. It had USAF markings.

There was leakage all around the aircraft, but no one seemed to mind that oil and fuel were on the apron.

I dressed in a special suit which was more complex than your standard flight suit. We were in the air in half an hour. There was the pilot and me. Once we were in the air, we circled as they refueled us. This thing was so fuel-hungry that it almost drained the tanks taking off.

The pilot had little to say to me the whole flight. You would think he was a spook or something.

I wondered how this thing would get me to China quicker than my 707, which could cruise at over five hundred miles an hour. I found out when I read the gauges on the panel in front of me.

Miles per hour weren't shown. Mach numbers were registered. We leveled out at 70,000 feet doing Mach 3.2. Twenty-two hundred miles an hour!

The view was incredible. I was used to seeing the horizon, but this was a clear view of the earth's curvature. The sky above wasn't the blue I was used to; it was the black of space.

The control panel had an identification tag. I was in an SR71 Blackbird from Lockheed Martin. I wondered if I could get one. Later, I could find no record that I had ever been in one, much less that it existed.

What took over twenty hours, we did in five. We landed at a Chinese Air Force base outside of Beijing. Armed troops immediately surrounded the plane.

The pilot lifted a plastic cover as we were exiting the plane. He flipped a red switch.

"We had better move it," he yelled.

Since he was running full speed away from the plane, I joined him; better to question later. The aircraft burst into flames. He had told me in flight that the airframe was titanium. I knew it would burn. It did.

The Chinese troops backed off from the burning aircraft, which would melt down into a puddle.

"Kid, I hope this is worth it. That is fifteen million dollars destroyed."

"If needed, I will pay for it."

That got his attention. It didn't last long as I was gathered up and taken to the Forbidden City.

I appeared in front of the empress of China, still wearing my running clothes from London.

"Thank you for coming so quickly, Rick. We need you to take May-ling to safety once more. The last attack was another rocket attack, and she ended up with a broken arm. You have successfully kept her safe, so I'm asking you to do it again."

"I will, but can you tell me the latest intelligence out of North Korea?"

"There is a lot of fighting in the DMZ right now. Kim il Jung is trying to stir up enough trouble that he can demand more concessions from the West. It is also thought he is trying to distract elements of his army which want to seize power."

"What about that regiment that was posted near the resort?"

"It has been moved to the DMZ. That is why we think he is trying to avoid a coup."

"I would like to talk to May-ling, if possible."

"Certainly. Follow me."

She led me to the bomb shelter. May-ling was there in a hospital bed. The room was purpose-built as part of a dispensary.

She was very pale, and her left arm was in a cast. She had a weak smile for me when I came into the room.

"Always you come rushing to me when I need you," she said.

"How could I not, Your Imperial Highness?"

"Where are we going this time?"

"We aren't. I'm going for a walk."

Chapter 50

It was time to end this. I spent the next two days preparing for a walking trip to North Korea. Nothing fancy this time, no airplanes. Nothing to alert the North Koreans that I was on my way.

I had thought about using a glider part of the way in, but they would be hunting for me if it were discovered.

We had left trail blazes and markers to avoid backtracking into box canyons. This had added at least a week to our journey. If I started at the Chinese border, I would have two hundred miles to walk.

It would take ten days to get there at twenty miles a day. With a marked trail, I was going for seven days.

The one chance I was willing to take was to have a pallet dropped into that deep box canyon with the cave. As I thought about it, I realized I could jump into the canyon with the pallet. That way, I could hide the food, water, first aid kit, and a radio in the cave.

That would save me forty miles of walking. It would be a HALO jump: High Altitude, Low Opening. I would need an altimeter to tell me when to open my chute.

I went out to the airbase and talked to the parachute instructor I had worked with. He agreed that it was doable.

While I was there, I saw the six 22 SAS troopers who had been sent to earn their Dragon wings. The brigadier was one of them. I think the two small rubies used as the Dragon's eyes were what attracted him and the others.

They were the classiest jump wings out there. I mentioned that to the instructor. He got a big laugh out of that.

"Yours have rubies. All the others will be painted red. The empress wanted something special for you as you are the first to earn it."

266

I decided not to say anything to the 22 SAS people; let them cross that bridge on their own.

I had to describe my plan to the empress and May-ling for their approval—no doubt who ran this country.

After that, I had to explain it in great technical detail to the army commanders. They had many good questions, but it looked like I had covered all the bases.

The only item I couldn't guarantee was that Haoran would come out onto that patio or that the North Koreans could decide to park another regiment there while I was walking in.

They could help with that. The South Koreans were being notified that China would no longer support North Korea. This should keep the North busy on their southern border.

The empress had directed this. She had no intention of replacing the Soviets as their financial backer. The Russians certainly weren't in a position to do it. She wanted China to be accepted in the larger world community.

At the same time, she let North and South Korea know this, and she also let the US and Cuba know that she wouldn't support the Castro regime.

While all this was happening, I packed my backpack and checked my bow and arrows to see if they were okay. No warpage or delamination, feathers intact. Spare waxed strings, armguard in good shape. I was ready to go.

It was a good night for the drop. The winds aloft were not against me. Even though the location wasn't lit, we had the coordinates. Once I was close to the ground, I should be able to see the moonlight reflected in the streams that bisected the canyon.

Counting on the reflection was a long shot, but the terrain features were distinct, so I should recognize them. I would be following my supplies down, so even if I missed the canyon with the good hiding spot, I would only have to find another.

The only thing left was to cross my fingers and hope it worked. I had my high-altitude oxygen bottle strapped to my chest and the mask adjusted tightly against my face.

At thirty thousand feet, I would be unconscious in a minute without it. I would be freefalling for about three minutes, so just because my chute should open automatically at one thousand feet, it wouldn't do to be unconscious at the time.

The jumpmaster and I both saw that I was hooked up correctly and that my gear was secure and tight. Was I nervous? You bet. Was I going to do it? Yes.

When the jump light came on, I was positioned in front of the open door. The jumpmaster pushed the small pallet out in front of me, then I followed.

It was strange jumping out in the black of the night. You couldn't even see the ground. I jumped using the arch position to give a stable flight pattern. I was able to hold it until I was jerked upwards.

The parasail opening was a complete surprise to me. Time seemed to flow slowly while I was freefalling. That, or it flew by. It was hard to judge.

I had lost sight of my pallet of supplies on the way down, but when my chute opened and slowed me down, I saw the light on top of my pallets exactly where it was supposed to be.

I had to follow the pallet down, as I couldn't steer it. I saw the reflection from two streams, so it looked like I was in the correct canyon. The maps didn't show any other canyons with two streams, several with one or none, but no others with two.

The pallet hit the ground and bounced. This gave me a good indicator of where the ground was, so I was able to prepare myself for my landing. I wish I had a motion picture of it as I landed on my feet and stayed on them as I ran forward.

I caught, then turned and pulled the cords on the chute until it collapsed, then rolled it up. It was an hour until daybreak, and I could confirm that I was where I wanted to be.

That was a long, cold hour. Even with my high-altitude gear on, it was cold. If this was summer in North Korea, I didn't want to be here in the winter.

I later realized that my core temperature had dropped from the high altitude. Once that warmed up, everything was fine.

At daybreak, I started north to see where I was. The north canyon wall was only a mile from my location. You couldn't see it because of the trees.

Looking at all the trees around me, I wondered how I hadn't landed in one. Even though the clearing was about five acres, it wouldn't have taken much to be dangling with a broken leg forty feet in the air.

We had thought we had taken all risks into account. The Chinese army was new at this. We should have passed this plan by the experts we had training with us. 22 SAS. Live and learn. At least live this time.

It took me until mid-afternoon to lug everything into the small cave in the north wall. There was no indication of any visitors since I was last here.

I set up the radio and squelched it twice at noon to let my control know that I was down safely. I waited and they didn't come on the air, so there was no change at the resort area.

I ate a cold ham sandwich, which I had brought along. It was very cold still from being in my backpack when I jumped. It was still tasty. I then unrolled my sleeping bag and kipped out until after dark.

When I woke, it was dark. Using the headlamp I wore on my balaclava hat, I strapped on my backpack and bow package and started my one-hundred-and-sixty-mile walk.

I made twenty-one miles according to my pedometer that night, which was good because this was the rough country portion of the trip.

Using one of the dependable fir trees, I camped for the day. Again, I slept all day and walked all night. The blazes we had left prevented me from wandering from the trail. The ones cut close to the tree's base were easier to find than the ones at head height. I thought it would have been the reverse. I didn't count on the fact you would be looking down mostly to keep your footing, only looking up occasionally to see if it was clear ahead.

Somebody in the daytime would miss the low blazes. The SEALs knew what they were doing.

The trail markers I had left from my Boy Scout training were not of much use. Small, stacked rocks and sticks pointing left on animal trails don't last long. What the animals didn't disturb, the rain washed away.

I wondered if I should write an article for *Boy's Life*.

Chapter 51

I arrived at our previous hiding place outside the resort seven days after starting the journey. That was an average of twenty-two miles per day. It was not as good as I had hoped for, but it was better than the estimates made before I set out.

There was no evidence that anyone had been near the hiding place, so I set up there for the day. I would have to scout the place at night before switching to days.

The nights were to explore the area to see if it was safe for me and the days to see if Haoran was still there and coming out on the patio.

After nightfall and a final cup of coffee brewed over my small kerosene stove, I moved out. I was sparing with the stove as the kerosene would have to last me until I returned to my stored supplies.

Running out of the ability to brew coffee was a non-starter. The fire was not enough to create smoke, but it was important to me.

First, I noted that the large flat field next to the river didn't have any bivouacked troops. That would have upset my plan to no end. However, I wouldn't have let it stop me.

Next, I made a large circle around the entire resort area to see if everything had remained the same. It would have been a messy getaway for me if the troops had moved to the other side of the resort so they could still chase me down.

I felt comfortable escaping through the woods. Lord knows I have had enough experience at it. Still, with several thousand soldiers on your trail, it could get difficult, if not impossible.

Thinking of that reminded me of a script that Warner Brothers had passed. It was titled *Mission Impossible*. They turned it down but thought it might do well on TV. I wondered if it would ever air.

My scouting of the area made me think it would be safe to continue my mission. Next was to see if Haoran was still there and spending time on the patio.

It took me two days to get my sleep turned around, so I felt comfortable watching the patio from the blind I had made about two hundred yards out.

It was better than the duck blinds used at home. While they could fool ducks, they wouldn't fool the human eye.

I used my training from the gillies in Scotland to build a low blind. It consisted of a tarp. I covered the tarp in the same vegetation that grew at that spot.

The night before, I had scooped out enough dirt so I could lie under the tarp without creating a rise in the terrain.

Since Haoran only came out in the afternoon, I didn't have to worry about the morning sun, which would have reflected off the binoculars I carried.

I spent two days getting my sleep turned around so I could be awake all day. I had to crawl into position before the first light and remain there all day without falling asleep.

I could just see myself falling asleep, rolling over, and pulling the tarp off me. I had a plastic bottle to pee in. I would then dump the pee in a cathole.

It would be awkward but better than peeing my pants. I hoped that my bowel movement schedule wouldn't change, or it could get messy.

I spent two days under the tarp before Haoran made an appearance.

Each night, I came back to the hide and worked on making a large fighting hole. To draw and fire the longbow, I had to stand with enough room to do so.

I would dig the dirt up and then spread it around so it wouldn't be noticed. The hole was four feet deep and six feet around. That was a lot of dirt to spread. I appreciated the thought that had gone into the entrenching tool.

The tarp was large enough to cover the hole. By the afternoon that Haoran showed up, I was thinking about improvements I could make to my hide, like some sort of brace I could lean on so my back wouldn't get so tired.

When Haoran came out, I saw him without using the binoculars. I looked through them to confirm it was him.

I carefully strung my bow, then selected three arrows and pushed them slightly into the ground so I could get at them quickly.

I gently pulled the tarp aside without standing up completely. Then I nocked an arrow. At two hundred yards, it should be an easy shot for me. With three hundred pounds of force, it was almost a flat trajectory.

You know it when your arrow is flying true. This one was. I still nocked a second one. I was beginning to bend my bow the second time when the first hit.

It was center mass. There was no doubt I had shot him through his black heart. I still loosed the second arrow. The first had pinned him to the chair he was sitting in. The second took him between his eyes.

That shot was a bit of luck. I was aiming for his chest once again, but the body sagged. I then calmly put the remaining arrow in my quiver and ran and stooped over back to the woods.

I wanted to make certain they knew who did this. A message had to be sent. The arrows were in my colors with my coat of arms on them. North Korea and then the secret world of intelligence had to get the message that you didn't mess with me and mine.

East Germany, the Soviet Union, and now North Korea had gotten the message, and I hoped not to have to send it again.

Back at my hide under the fir tree, I picked up my backpack, which was loaded and ready to go, and started my walk back to the border. I was a good two miles away when I heard a siren going off. I think they had discovered Haoran.

There was no sense in trying to run; I kept a steady pace for the rest of the afternoon and well into the night. From previous experience, I knew a cordon would be thrown out at the furthest distance they thought I could make by the time they had it in place.

My goal was to be farther along and keep ahead, as they would widen it as time passed. One advantage I had was that I was in the deep woods and had a marked trail. They didn't. They would put checkpoints at every crossroad and intersection.

The country up to the border was so rough I would only have to cross two roads during my entire hike.

I made over thirty miles before daybreak the next day. I had to sleep by this time, so I found a sizeable drooping fir and made myself at home.

Late in the afternoon, I started again. A light rain had started, so I put on my poncho and kept going. This was good for me as troops hated rain when on boring duty. Standing at a crossroads in the rain counted as boring duty. I hope they spent more time trying to stay dry than paying attention.

The rain slowed me down, and then I had to watch a road to make sure it was safe to cross. I only made twenty miles that day.

Halfway back to my box canyon supply point, I was tiring—another eighty miles to go. I slowed my pace down. If I made twenty miles a day from this point, I would be okay. I didn't want to use up all my energy reserves and be staggering around. That is when I would be spotted.

I came to the second road almost on top of the intersection. There were two troops there, sound asleep! I sidetracked far enough down the road to be out of sight and crossed.

It was my last night before the box canyon. I was up early the next morning and on my way.

When I arrived at the canyon, it was almost like coming home. It represented safety to me. That didn't stop me from scouting the area before approaching the cave. It was clear.

The first thing I did was heat the water for my first cup of coffee in two days. It was only instant, but it was heavenly. I remembered the first time I tried it in Bellefontaine and hating it. That seemed like a lifetime ago.

Next on my agenda was to clean up for the first time in several weeks. I went so far as to go down to the ice-cold stream and wash. It didn't take long, but it was needed desperately. When you smell your own stink, that is too much.

I didn't even try to shave with that cold water. After putting on clean clothes, I felt like a new person.

I then fired up the radio and reported.

"The evil prince is down, coming home."

Chapter 52

The danger increased the closer I got to the border, but I still felt like the worst was over. I had dealt with Haoran so that threat was gone. I doubted if he had fanatics working for him.

All indications were that he had to pay for everything. With the money flow cut off, those attempts would stop. Others would arise with time, but today wasn't the day to worry about them.

I had the best night's sleep in ages, even in a damp cave on hard rock.

In the morning, after taking care of the morning details and the last of my instant coffee, I was ready for my last leg.

I followed the blazes we had left the first time in. This had me slanting to the Yellow Sea coastline and a road. It was a two-lane highway and lightly traveled. The government, the elite, or high-ranking officials owned most vehicles in North Korea. Those were usually the same.

Walking close to but parallel to the road to avoid surprises, my caution was justified. There was a group set up off the side of the road.

The group consisted of about fifty North Korean troops. They were having tea around a large campfire. Their weapons were all stacked. Each stack contained five rifles leaning together to support each other. They looked like a frame for a teepee.

There was a large car parked beside the road. It was a monster. I had to look at it twice to realize it was a Bugatti. I didn't know what type of automobile it was, but I think it was called a Royale. It was long and designed to be driven by a chauffeur. It is an impressive vehicle.

That is when I noticed the passenger being driven. I recognized Kim Jong-Il as the number two man in NK and son of the current ruler. What was he doing out here?

As those thoughts were going through my mind, five officers with submachine guns opened fire on all the troops. They died quickly, trying to get to their stacked weapons. Several tried to run into the woods, but the clearing was too large for them to make it to the tree line.

This betrayal was astonishing. What happened next was more so. A higher-ranking officer ordered the other officers to make sure all the troops were dead.

I stood there frozen in my concealed position, watching this disaster unfold. Once all the troops were confirmed dead by the officers shooting them in the head, their leader told them to reload their weapons.

When they ejected the magazines to insert full ones, their leader raised his weapon and killed all five of them—a double betrayal.

I wasn't even surprised when Kim shot that officer in the back. Then he calmly went over and headshot all the officers to ensure they were down.

Kim then called his driver over to help him move bodies off the road. After that was done, what I thought would now happen did. He murdered the driver.

Not even Hollywood would present something this crazy.

While the shooting was going on, I assembled my bow. I had no intention of using it, as I was grossly outnumbered, but now I wasn't. As Kim turned to get into the driver's seat, I shot him in the back. I had to do it fast. I didn't want to get blood on the seat of my new car.

I dragged Kim's body to the side of the road and examined the vehicle. I now saw why all the killings had occurred. The car flooring was stacked with gold. There had to be several tons of it.

Things must be going wrong for the government, and he was fleeing.

It was now only six miles to the border. If I remember right, there was only one NK checkpoint. It could hardly be called that. Three or four troops and a swivel post acting as a gate.

My memory was correct as I drove right through their gate. The soldiers were sitting beside the road drinking something from a bottle when I roared through. By the time they stood up, I was past and heading to China.

When I got to the Chinese border, I stopped at the real frontier gate, which would wreck a tank. There, I showed my Chinese Diplomatic passport. They were expecting me to cross somewhere along here, so I wasn't held up.

They wanted me to stop and talk at their command post, but I told them I was on an urgent errand to Beijing. This was true. They were kind enough to fill the Type 41 Bugatti Royale's gas tank for me from Jerry cans.

I drove to the airport in Beijing. It was one hundred miles, but the car flew along. I was in love with this thing. It handled like a slug, but I attributed that to the weight in gold.

My 707 was parked there, so after admittance to the airport, I drove up to it and told them to load the car and its contents into the hold. They were to fly it immediately to Hong Kong and deliver it in person to Jackson House Asia, directly to Boris Badenov. He would know what to do with the car and contents. There would be a handsome bonus for all involved.

There were wide eyes when I showed them the bonus they would receive. Each would get an ingot. The ingots were what the banks called good delivery bars and weighed about twenty-seven pounds each.

I then asked for a car to take me to the Forbidden City. As soon as I arrived, I was summoned before the empress.

To say she was a happy empress would be an understatement. She wanted to know all the details. She knew Haoran was dead. Her spies had seen the body. This was our first time together since my little walk into North Korea.

May-ling was there. I asked if I could sign her cast. I found out this was a Western tradition, but she let me autograph it. How did I know this was to start a new trend?

We talked about how life after Haoran was. It was great; she could go shopping with only her regular guards instead of a mechanized division. At first, I thought she was kidding.

During this conversation, I learned that with the withdrawal of Chinese support, the South Koreans and the US had pulled out all stops and had invaded. The vaunted defenses in the DMZ were bypassed, or the NK troops were routed.

Troops were in Phyongwon already. Kim il-Jung had been killed in the fighting. I informed her of his son's death and the betrayals that had gone down. She wanted to know what happened to the car.

I informed her that it was the spoils of war and was on its way to Hong Kong. I made no mention of gold.

She appeared so disappointed over the car I knew what her Christmas gift would be. Did she celebrate Christmas? I bet she would this year.

The empress and Ann were covered. Now, what would I get May-ling? Then there were the British royals. Maybe I should rethink this whole Christmas gift thing, at least on such a lavish basis.

Ann would get her tiara, but I would find another excuse.

I excused myself to get cleaned up and don fresh clothes. I had to reck. When I was finished, I returned to the imperial family quarters.

There, May-ling was waiting with the others. When I entered the room, she ran up and hugged me. Not a light hug, a full body wrapped around mine hug.

"My hero, my knight in shining armor."

That wasn't true, I was wearing blue jeans and a polo shirt. I understood her sentiment, though.

"I'm glad to be of service, Your Imperial Highness."

My statement must have come across wrong, as she let go and backed away.

"Duke Richard, we shall never forget how you have helped China in her time of need. My husband and I will always look favorably upon you when I'm married."

That lowered the temperature in the room by many degrees. Her mother and grandmother both frowned at her statement. Knowing how May-ling viewed our relationship, I didn't understand why they were upset.

I excused myself shortly after that, pleading tiredness from my expedition. I returned to my room and thought about the fact that I had committed two cold-blooded murders within the last week.

What bothered me was that it didn't bother me. Both of those guys were the epitome of human monsters and had to go. Why should I feel guilty about it?

I called home to Jackson House and had a call with Mum and Dad. I told them what had gone on recently. They were aware of Haoran's demise but not Kim's. They agreed that the triple betrayal would be over the top for any work of fiction.

I told them in our family-coded speech about my spoils of war. Dad wanted the car. Mum wanted the total weight. I told her about seventy-two of my little sister. She went about fifty-five pounds the last time I had seen her.

Mum was impressed.

North and South Korea would now be reunited. The UN was claiming credit for this. As far as I knew, there hadn't been one blue helmet in any of the battles.

The empress was quiet on the whole issue. I had to wonder if she would take both Koreas, but it was probably more trouble than it was worth.

This soldier of fortune stuff seemed profitable. Maybe I should change my line of work.

Jackson, Rick Jackson, Soldier of Fortune.

Finished for now

Back Matter

To be continued in Book 14 Whats Under Down Under?[1]
https://www.enelsonauthor.com/

For information on hiring Janet E. Rupert to edit your fiction project, email:
janeteditorrupert@gmail.com

---

1. https://www.amazon.com/Richard-Jackson-Saga-Whats-Under-ebook/dp/B09HZJPF2L

Other books by Ed Nelson **The Richard Jackson Saga**

Book 1 The Beginning
Book 2 Schooldays
Book 3 Hollywood
Book 4 In the Movies
Book 5 Star to Deckhand
Book 6 Surfing Dude
Book 7 Third Time is a Charm
Book 8 Oxford University
Book 9 Cold War
Book 10 Taking Care of Business
Book 11 Interesting Times
Book 12 Escape from Siberia
Book 13 Regicide
Book 14 What's Under, Down Under?
Book 15 The Lunar Kingdom
Book 16 First Steps
In the Richard Jackson World
Mary, Mary
Stand-Alone Story
Ever and Always
Cast in Time Series
Book 1: Baron
Book 2: Baron of the Middle Counties
Book 3: Count
Book 4: Earl
Book 5: Earl of the Marches

Did you love *Regicide*? Then you should read *What's Under? Down Under* by Ed Nelson!

Coming-of-age stories don't have to be all teenage angs; they can be fun-filled adventures that become more serious with age. With humor, we follow a young man's coming of age in the late 1950s. Starting in the summer before his freshman year, it follows him through high school and beyond. He finds wealth as an inventor and fame in Hollywood as he searches for a girlfriend. Wealth and fame prove far easier than girls. The 14th book, What's Under? Down Under, has Rick exploring both Australia and space. Danger, fame and fortune, and adventure seem to be his lot in life. A girlfriend, not so much. His actions have caused a change in history as we know it. His decision to start a cattle station in Australia has far-reaching consequences. Computer breakthroughs continue. The space division gets ready to journey to the moon. This tongue-in-cheek saga is all true, give or take a lie or two.